# The burst of gunfire caught Bolan unawares

He guided his vehicle into the trees, killing the lights and the engine. Tracers lanced through the air, and over the hammering of automatic weapons he could hear a racing motor.

The Executioner went EVA, sprinting across the lane toward the winking taillights of the Mercedes. As Bolan narrowed the gap he heard blazing stutterguns. The men in the Mercedes were returning fire. He was halfway to the side road when a huge fireball mushroomed in the near distance.

The warrior stood a few feet from the edge of the road, taking in the scene at a glance. The German car was a total wreck. On the ground lay four twisted bodies, and there was no doubt who they were—Dolph Murray, his two lieutenants and their driver.

The man the Executioner had tracked to Europe had just been blown away.

What the hell was going on?

# Accolades for
# America's greatest hero
# Mack Bolan

# DON PENDLETON's
# MACK BOLAN

# *DEADFALL*

®

## A GOLD EAGLE BOOK FROM
# WORLDWIDE ®

TORONTO • NEW YORK • LONDON
AMSTERDAM • PARIS • SYDNEY • HAMBURG
STOCKHOLM • ATHENS • TOKYO • MILAN
MADRID • WARSAW • BUDAPEST • AUCKLAND

First edition February 1993

ISBN 0-373-61430-6

Special thanks and acknowledgment to
Charlie McDade for his contribution to this work.

DEADFALL

Printed in U.S.A.

If a man does not know to what port he is steering, no wind is favorable.
—Seneca, 4 B.C.–A.D. 65

Pursue one great decisive aim with force and determination.
—Karl von Clausewitz:
*Principles of War,* 1812

The enemy is my objective and victory is my final goal. These are the first principles of war. And make no mistake, this is war.
—Mack Bolan

# PROLOGUE

Jason Marley leaned back in the seat, letting his head drift toward the window. He was sitting where he liked, ahead of the wing, and the patchwork quilt of the German countryside spread below him. He had never enjoyed flying, and suspected it had held him back in his career. It had taken him longer than it should have to get where he wanted to be.

Fortunately the hypnosis had paid off, or was it the medication? Whatever the reason, he flew now when he had to. He still had white knuckles in the car on the way to the airport, but once the flight got off smoothly, he was able to relax, if not exactly enjoy it.

He marveled that something as big and heavy as an airplane could stay in the air. If he were religious, he would have called it a miracle. But Marley was anything but religious. And in his line of work, you had trouble enough believing in yourself, let alone in someone or something you couldn't see.

Now, as DCI—director of the Central Intelligence Agency—that unwillingness to accept the unseen was going to serve him well. Intelligence, after all, was the science of making the unseen seeable, the unknown knowable. He had a huge budget and an

army of cynics and skeptics at his disposal. He
planned to make maximum use of both, and try to
get the budget increased if possible.

Going over the figures for the coming year, he had
been impressed that his predecessor had managed to
justify so much money, especially since there was so
little to show for it. The idiots on the Hill were
swarming like ants, picking at the Agency as if it were
the carcass of a dead chicken. They wanted to strip
it to bare bones so they could go home and talk to
their constituents about fiscal responsibility.

But Marley knew better than that. He understood,    the congressional jokers didn't, that the
cold war wasn't really over; it was just entering a new
phase. The other side was fragmented, true enough,
but that only made the CIA more valuable. In ret-
rospect it had been fairly easy to watch the Soviet
monolith. But the symphony of national liberation
groups, ethnic minorities, political parties and religious factions was going to sound like chaos to anyone without a score.

It was fortunate, Marley thought, that the President understood that fact better than anyone else,
excepting, of course, Jason Marley himself But
Marley was as hardheaded an observer of his own
character as he was of the rest of the world, and he
didn't flinch from his own failings. One of them was
that he couldn't take the time, because he didn't have
the patience or the requisite respect to make Con-
gress see the world the way he saw it. If he couldn't

do that, he couldn't get the money he needed. It was that simple. Unwilling to play the stroking games, blowing smoke up every ass on Capitol Hill, meant he had to have someone who could do it for him.

That was where Harold Carmichael came in. Harold was the ultimate politician. He could smooth the wrinkles on an elephant's hide with one hand and untie the Gordian knot with the other, all the while carrying on a conversation about Mozart with some senator's wife, compliment the hag on her new hairdo and score a couple of points with her philandering spouse. And he loved it, every last fib and white lie. It was his highest achievement and the closest thing he had to a religion.

Standing up to stretch his long legs, Marley looked toward the rear of the comfortable salon. If he hadn't known he was in the belly of an L1011, he might have thought he was in a posh hotel. The floor was steady under his feet, and there was absolutely no sensation of movement. Carmichael was in the rear of the plane with two longtime Eastern Europe specialists. That had been Marley's beat six months before, and he knew it like the back of his hand. Filling in the dotted lines, crossing the *t*s and dotting the *i*s for the new chief of the Eastern Europe section, was more than a courtesy. He wasn't about to let things fall apart now. He wanted Richard Aspring to get it down cold. Hands on, that was the way. That's how he had done it, and that's how he wanted Aspring to continue it.

Marley looked at his watch and sat down. He still had ten minutes before the in-flight briefing, something he looked forward to because it helped keep his mind off the thirty thousand feet between the L1011 and the continent.

A moment later Carmichael appeared, followed by a steward. "All set, Jason?" he asked as he took a seat.

"Yes, but where are Jennings and Harkness?"

"They'll be out in a minute. Anything wrong? You seem on edge."

"You know damn well what's wrong, Harold. We're facing the most important challenge the Agency has seen since the Church Committee hearings."

"I wouldn't worry about it. The President is on our side. So is anyone in the NSC who counts. And we both know only three of them matter. The President is favorably disposed to the Agency. If we can't handle the Hill, we shouldn't have our jobs. It couldn't be any simpler than that."

Marley was about to respond when he saw James Harkness out of the corner of his eye. He turned to watch the man cross the salon, smoothing his jacket.

Harkness smiled stiffly as he took a seat across from Marley. The DCI returned the smile, not quite as stiffly, and said, "Is Jennings coming or isn't he?"

"He's not feeling well, I'm afraid."

"I don't give a damn about that. Go get him."

"I can't do that, Jason."

"The hell you can't. I'll get him myself if you won't."

The cabin steward cleared his throat, and Marley looked at him in annoyance. "What is—?"

Marley's jaw hung open, and the rest of the sentence was swallowed with a loud gulp. He found himself staring into the very black and very large round hole on the end of a sound suppressor. The steward smiled broadly. "Mr. Marley," he said, "I want you to do exactly as I say."

Marley finally regained his composure. "What the hell do you think you're doing?"

"Oh, he knows very well, Jason," Harkness said.

"What's going on here?"

"You're the director of Central Intelligence, Jason. Can't you guess?"

"Harkness, if this is your idea of a joke, I assure you I—"

Harkness cut him off with the wave of a hand. "It's no joke. Now you just do what I tell you, and everything will be fine."

"You can't possibly expect to get away with this. You can't get off this plane. You can't—"

"I can do whatever the hell I want, Jason." He reached inside his jacket and pulled out a small Heckler & Koch automatic.

Marley couldn't help wondering if that was why Harkness had been smoothing out his jacket as he entered the cabin. Ever aware of the sartorial proprieties, he must have been annoyed at the possibility of a bulge in an otherwise neatly tailored coat.

"What are you planning to do with us?" Carmichael croaked.

Harkness smiled. "It's only Jason I need, Harold."

"What about me?"

Harkness shook his head sadly, then pointed the gun in Carmichael's direction. "Sorry, Harold." He squeezed the trigger once, then a second time.

Marley jerked his head with each report. He glanced at Carmichael, who slumped in his chair. Two small red holes had punctured his forehead. There was surprisingly little blood.

"It's a .22, Jason. The bullets rattle around inside the skull, but they don't come out. Very important on an airplane, you see. It wouldn't do to puncture the fuselage."

"You bastard! That was cold-blooded murder."

"Yes, it was. But it was necessary, Jason. I trust it won't be necessary to repeat it. I would hate to go to all this trouble for nothing." He nodded toward the steward, who reached into his immaculate white jacket and withdrew a syringe. Removing the plastic safety sheath on the needle, he held the hypodermic aloft and pressed the plunger until a small squirt of yellowish fluid arced out.

"You see?" Harkness said. "Every precaution, Jason. It wouldn't do to risk an embolism. We need you alive. And very much want to see to it that you stay that way. Please, don't make that difficult. Because we will kill you if we have to. Do you understand?'' He nodded again, and the steward approached with the needle.

He reached out for Marley's left arm, jerked it toward him and pulled the sleeve back until he'd exposed the center of the forearm. Marley flinched as the needle went in. ''What the hell is that stuff?''

''Never mind. It's quite safe. In proper dosage, of course. But Ronny knows what he's doing. Sleep well.''

The plane started to bank to the left, and Marley felt himself slipping over some unnamed precipice. He tried to hold on, and in his mind had the image of himself on a high cliff, his arms flailing in a swimming motion as he tried to regain his balance. But his arms wouldn't work, and he tipped slowly over. Then he was falling. It felt good, and he wondered why he didn't feel the wind whipping past his face.

He watched the steward move toward the front of the plane and open the door to the narrow passage leading to the cockpit. Then he was out.

FIVE MINUTES LATER the flight controller in the tower at Tempelhof sat up sharply as one of the two dozen green dots on his radar screen began to change course abruptly. He adjusted his headset mike and tried to raise the L1011, but there was no response.

He looked over his shoulder for his boss and waggled his fingers wildly when he finally got a look. When he turned back, the blip was gone. He stared at the screen, Gerhard Werner hovering nervously over his shoulder. He tried again to raise the plane, and again got no answer.

He looked up at Werner. "What do I do?"

"Call him again."

But the blip had vanished.

"This is very bad," Werner muttered, shaking his head. "Very bad...."

"What do I do, damn it?"

"I'll handle it."

The flight controller wasn't so sure.

# CHAPTER ONE

Mack Bolan had been watching the hunting lodge for the past three nights. The conclave was a gathering of the leading lights of the extreme right—neo-Nazis, neofascists, American white supremacists and even a few members of the old Arrow and Cross.

The faces were sometimes familiar, sometimes not. But there was no mistaking the symbols. He could see the flags arrayed on the wall of the main room of the lodge, a huge Nazi swastika emblem at the center of the display. Whoever these guys were, they weren't backward about celebrating themselves in the safety of their own kind.

Rumors had been circulating for nearly two years about a united right organization, some sort of umbrella group of malcontents and long-suffering extremists, mostly from Europe, but with participation from places as far-flung as the U.S. and Australia. Bolan had followed three members of the Aryan Nation all the way from Idaho. Here in Bavaria, in the very same forest that had proved so fertile a soil for both Wagner's distorted archetypes and Hitler's legions, a new cancer seemed to be growing.

They had been preaching to one another for two days now, each speech bringing the same fanatic applause, standing ovation after standing ovation. He couldn't hear the words, but there was no mistaking the oratorical model of the speakers. The spastic gestures, the frenzied gesturing and the emphatic pounding of fist on podium all had a single precursor.

Bolan's particular quarry looked a little overwhelmed by it all. They got to their feet and cheered all right, but they spent most of the time looking at one another, trying to bolster their spirits through eye contact. Dolph Murray, the nominal head of the American contingent, was the exception. His dossier laid it all out. A philosophy major at Chicago, he had done graduate work at two German universities, and somewhere along the line he had gotten hooked on German political history.

Now he was trying to import it to America. He had seized control of a splinter group of the Aryan Nation and now claimed the founders had misunderstood their idol. He was trying to unify the American far right, and this conference of his European counterparts would go a long way toward establishing his bona fides on the furthest edges of the lunatic fringe.

The two men with him, Carl Heller and Mitchell Pierce, were small-fry, Murray's dewy-eyed lieutenants who, between them, didn't have a high school diploma. They were under Murray's sway, and that made him even more dangerous. Heller was wanted in three states, for murder in two and bank robbery in the third. Pierce was less draped in glory, having stumbled on Murray's teaching during a stint in a Colorado prison for armed robbery.

Murray himself was squeaky clean, as far as felonies and misdemeanors were concerned. He had never even had a speeding ticket. But at least a half-dozen murders were out there with the Murray signature on them. One had gotten him more than a little attention, since it had happened on the air in a radio station with Murray himself in attendance. Schuyler Hinton, a liberal talk-show host in Galveston, had shown the dubious judgment of inviting Murray to share his nightly microphone for a call-in debate.

Two men in ski masks had barged in and taken out Hinton with a spray of 9 mm bullets. Other than a scratch from flying glass, Murray was unharmed. He claimed it was because he had dived under the heavy wooden table at which he and Hinton were seated. Some others, with a slightly jaundiced eye perhaps, suspected that Hinton had been the target all along and that Murray had simply arranged the hit for maximum airplay.

The killers would know, of course. But they weren't talking. They turned up a month later in a ditch, their bodies riddled with slugs from their own weapons. That didn't do much to quiet the speculation.

True or not, Bolan still didn t know But the more paint he scratched off the gleaming surface of Dolph Murray, the more rust he found underneath. Murray was anything but what he claimed to be. That much was clear. What wasn't clear was what he actually was.

He had made enemies of the Klan, the Aryan Brotherhood and two dozen other groups, all in the name of his own brand of rightism. Now he was hobnobbing with the keepers of the flame in the very heart of the motherlode. But Bolan didn't know why.

There were disadvantages to flying solo, and this was just one example. It would have been nice to have laser ears, to have a janitor put a bug in the heart of the Nazi eagle on the wall, to have video cameras in the lodge. That's how the boys with access to money played it. They could afford the toys. But this time out, all Bolan had was guts and guns.

Looking at his watch, he guessed the night's session should be winding down. The warrior wanted to get closer, but security was tight. Armed men in pairs circled the lodge, and solo sentries with guard dogs were posted at several key positions. Getting close would be almost impossible, and once there, the risk of discovery would be overwhelming. There was no gain, so he resisted the urge, champing at the bit but keeping a tight rein nevertheless.

He would have to concentrate on Dolph Murray. Anything he was able to pick up beyond that would be gravy. Turning the glasses back on the speaker's podium, he was relieved to see the presiding luminary, Carlo Giancallo, leaning into the microphone. Giancallo was the leading light of Italian neofascism and seemed to be serving as master of ceremonies for the conference.

Bolan started to back away, then turned and sprinted for the hidden car. There was only one road in to the lodge, so he'd have no trouble picking up Murray and his lieutenants as they left.

The outdoor lights suddenly blazed, and Bolan could see his shadow on the ground as he wove through the trees back toward his rented Audi. Loud voices bantering in broken English, and half a dozen European tongues swirled through the trees.

The car was where he had left it. The warrior approached the Audi slowly, first making a full circle at fifty or sixty yards to make certain no one was hiding in the woods. When he was satisfied, he moved quickly toward the vehicle. Already he could hear the rumble of engines as the first of the conferees began to leave. There was one more day to go. He had learned that much by sticking close to Murray in Munich. Snatches of overheard conversation gave him part of the puzzle. It wasn't enough to know exactly what was going on, but enough to know the conference schedule and who some of those in attendance were.

Bolan cranked up the Audi and rolled closer to the road. He could see the first headlights spearing through the green tunnel, little bits and pieces of light reaching him through the trees as the cars pulled away one by one. Tailing wasn't easy on the deserted road. He had to be ready to move as soon as Murray's Mercedes went by.

The car turned left, and Bolan waited until it reached the first turn before swinging out onto the road. He drove without lights for the first hundred yards, letting the Mercedes get a little farther ahead of him. Glancing in the rearview mirror to make sure no one was on his tail, he clicked on his headlights and picked up speed. There was a network of country lanes ahead, but Murray was almost certain to head straight for his hotel.

They had covered half a mile when the Mercedes suddenly accelerated. Bolan stepped on the gas to keep up with the car, surprised to see it veer left onto a narrow road. As he got closer, he saw why. A dark green van had pulled across the road.

Bolan slowed, not sure what was going on. The first burst of gunfire took him unawares. He skidded into the trees, killing lights and engine. Tracers flashed through the trees, and over the hammering of automatic weapons he could hear a racing engine.

The van lurched to life, its headlights blazing as it turned and lumbered toward the side road. The driver angled the vehicle, blocking the road.

Bolan went EVA, sprinting across the lane and racing toward the winking red taillights of the

Mercedes. The car started to back away from the main road again, but stopped after fifty feet.

As the Executioner narrowed the gap, he could hear more gunfire, as if the men in the Mercedes were returning fire. He was halfway to the side road when a huge ball of fire mushroomed in the narrow road. There was one long burst of gunfire that seemed to last forever.

It stopped suddenly. Men shouted to one another in English, but Bolan couldn't tell what was being said. He could see the burning hulk of the Mercedes now, its doors yawning open. Shadowy figures raced away from the wreck, but there was no more gunfire. The warrior saw four men, possibly five, sprint toward the van.

Bolan stood a few feet from the edge of the road. The Mercedes was a total wreck. Its insides still blazed, and the leaves on either side of the road were seared and blackened by the heat. On the ground he could see four bodies, and there was no doubt in his mind who they were. Murray, his two lieutenants and their chauffeur had been chopped to pieces.

In the orange light of the gasoline fire, he could see the pools of blood seeping into the dirt road. They glistened wetly, the fire dancing on the slick surfaces almost as if the blood itself were burning.

He moved closer, trying to get a look at the van, but it carried no license plates and was free of markings.

As he reached the edge of the trees, doors slammed and the van's engine roared. The vehicle backed away as Bolan stepped into the open. The driver hesitated, and the warrior realized that they had seen him. He backed into the trees. At the same moment, a vehicle with a screaming siren raced up the road.

A police car stopped, its red-and-blue lights flashing, and four local police scrambled out. The next car from the conference lodge appeared up the road, and Bolan watched as it slowed, drifted to a halt beside the police car, then sped up and disappeared.

The van lumbered back toward the burning Mercedes, and five men dressed in black fatigues spilled out of the back and fanned out into the trees.

They were looking for Bolan.

## CHAPTER TWO

Bolan melted into the woods. He could see the vehicles from the lodge slowing as they passed the police car. As he got farther away from the wreckage of the Mercedes, he could hear the five men stumbling through the forest after him.

Two of them produced flashlights, and the blades of illumination cut swaths through the trees and undergrowth as the assassins swept the lights back and forth across their trails. The other three had tougher going. The woods grew deeper the farther the warrior traveled from the road. There was no moon, and the sky was barely visible through the interlaced branches.

Bolan angled back toward the lodge, intending to slip across the road and pick up his car.

Why Murray? He had asked himself the question over and over, but no answer asserted itself. And who were these guys?

One of the lights was coming closer. Bolan ducked into some brush, and the scent of flowers swirled around him. Lush ferns hid him from the probing beam, which was still far enough away that its light was all but dissipated by the time it fell on the fronds.

A horn sounded, and the beam swept away He could still see the burning wreck, but the flames had fallen off now, and at this distance he could no longer smell the stench of burning plastic and rubber. The other beam withdrew, too, and Bolan realized the search was being called off.

He was inclined to slip back toward the burning car, but it was tempting fate, and he hadn't lived as long as he had by taking unnecessary risks. A moment later he heard the rumble of the van's engine, saw its headlights come on. It rolled closer to the ruined Mercedes. He couldn't see the van itself, but heard the squawk of hinges as its doors opened once more. The doors banged shut again, and the van backed toward the road.

It had been a while since the last car rolled down from the lodge, and Bolan wondered if all the attendees had left the area. The police car kicked in its siren, and the sudden earsplitting howl led the van off through the trees. Soon the siren faded away to a faint wail, then died altogether

Bolan was alone in the woods. It could be a setup, but his gut told him no. He started back toward the side road again, guided by the orange glow from the dying fire. When he reached the tree line at the edge of the road, he stopped to listen and wait.

After ten minutes he hadn't heard a sound except the hissing of the wreckage. The flames were out now, and as the metal cooled, it cracked and pinged, filling the dark road with a collection of eerie sounds.

In spite of the police being on the scene, the bodies lay where they had fallen, limbs twisted in the final agony, hands scratching at the dirt, faces contorted. Riddled with bullets, the four men had never stood a chance. It had been an execution of the most cold-blooded kind. Bolan surveyed the scene from the edge of the trees, still half expecting to see the van come roaring back around the corner with its lethal passengers.

In the near darkness the warrior couldn't tell one body from another. Stepping out of the trees, he moved toward the nearest corpse, stood looking down at the remains of Carl Heller for a moment, then moved to the next corpse. This body was lying on its side, the head turned and one cheek ground into the dirt. It was Dolph Murray. In one hand he held a Browning automatic. The other groped toward a small canvas bag that the man obviously had been carrying when he fled from the car. It must have meant something to him.

Bolan reached for the bag, then slipped back into the trees before opening it cautiously.

There wasn't much inside—a couple of envelopes, a small, flat notebook held closed with a rubber band, and a second handgun, this one a 22-caliber automatic.

He zipped the bag shut, then, still clutching it, crossed the road and walked around to the other side of the car where the other two men lay There was nothing else of interest on the ground, and anything that remained in the vehicle was totally destroyed.

Bolan returned to the trees, and as he started back through the woods he heard a car engine laboring from the direction of the main road. Headlights flashed as the vehicle swept around a curve, then winked out. The engine died suddenly, and he heard the slam of a car door.

Bolan took cover in the brush and waited. He heard no other noise for several minutes and was about to give up when a shadow moved on the opposite side of the road. It stopped, and the warrior leaned forward. He could just make out the shape of a man in dark clothing.

There was another long wait before the man finally detached himself from the trees and headed toward the car in a crouch. Bolan watched while the man moved into the road and knelt beside the first body. He searched through the dead man's clothes, apparently looking for something in particular. Not finding it on the first corpse, he crept to the next, searched it just as thoroughly, then the remaining two. He seemed confused and disappointed.

The man muttered something to himself in German, then backed into the trees on Bolan's side of the road. Crouching in the brush, he watched the wreckage, as if expecting someone else to appear on the scene. Bolan still hadn't seen his face.

The man straightened abruptly and started back the way he'd come. Bolan slipped toward the edge of the road and watched him darting in and out of the woods as he tried to make time without exposing himself too readily. The Executioner fell in behind him, curious now who the visitor might be and more curious about what he'd been looking for.

The warrior half expected the man to turn right and head back to his car, but instead he went left, up the road that would take him to the hunting lodge.

Bolan wondered if Murray was supposed to have been carrying something that the man ahead of him was anxious to get his hands on. Then he realized that the stuff in the canvas bag had been the object of the mysterious search. At the narrow lane leading to the lodge, the man slowed, crossed the road in a crouch and disappeared. Bolan jogged across and sprinted up the opposite side. He reached the mouth of the lane two minutes later, but the man was nowhere to be seen.

The warrior made the last turn and found himself staring at the lodge. Lights glowed in its basement windows, but the two upper stories were dark. It was a massive building, its foundation of raw stone and concrete supporting a sprawling structure of logs and raw timber. Bolan scanned the front of the building, but there was no sign of his quarry.

Keeping to the trees, he skirted the driveway and got around the left end of the building. He still hadn't picked up the trail of the man he'd been following and was beginning to wonder whether he had gotten ahead of himself. As he slipped through a tall hedge and into a cloistered garden, he could see into the basement. Some of the staff was still at work, cleaning the kitchen and preparing food, most likely for the next day's meeting.

Bolan crept close to the building and knelt to peer into the basement. Two men and three women scurried around, obviously finishing up for the night. Then the staff filed out, the last person in line flipping the light switch. The basement went black, and Bolan waited, listening intently. He heard the front door slam, and the jangle of keys was all but drowned out by banter as the workers walked to their cars.

Almost in unison, three engines sprang to life. That would account for the three cars parked out front. The building was now dark. He listened until the cars rumbled down the lane and the sound of their engines was swallowed by the forest and the night.

Bolan backed away from the building and continued his recon. He heard a rustle in the shrubbery around the corner and stopped in his tracks.

Something clicked, and the Executioner crept toward the end of the lodge in time to see someone slide through a basement window. He moved toward the open window, waiting for the basement lights to go on, but all he could see was a dim glow, perhaps a small flashlight. Crawling on his belly up to the window, Bolan peered down into the darkness just as the shape of a man disappeared through a doorway. A glow-edged shadow lay on the floor, growing smaller and smaller as the man moved away from the doorway, then disappeared altogether

Now all he had to do was wait. The window was still open, which meant the guy had to come back this way, if not to make his exit, then at least to close the window and cover his tracks.

Bolan reached into his jacket and slipped the Beretta 93-R from shoulder leather. He snicked off the safety and stared at the window. He was prepared to wait all night, if that's what it took. Whoever was in that basement knew something about Dolph Murray, something he wanted to know. And he'd be damned if he wouldn't find it out.

For all Bolan knew, the guy in the lodge had engineered Murray's assassination. But even if he hadn't been involved in the murder, he knew something, enough to be looking for specifics, and was willing to take more than a few chances to get his hands on it.

Ignoring the impulse to enter the lodge, Bolan held his ground. Let the guy find it, he thought. Let him find it, then take him.

## CHAPTER THREE

Jason Marley was in a fog. His head throbbed, and he clapped his hands over his temples, afraid his skull was about to burst. His vision was all but useless. When he opened his eyes, everything was out of focus, as if he were looking the wrong way through binoculars.

His physical condition seemed to be just as bad. His arms were weak, and his legs would barely move. He tried to sit up, but the effort was too much for him. Even raising his head a few inches was torture. He lay there listening to his shallow breathing, wondering if he had died.

Marley tried to sit up again, and this time managed to raise his head a little. But someone he couldn't see shoved a spear of white-hot iron down his spine. He waved a hand over his head, trying to grab it, but there was nothing there. The effort exhausted him, and he let his head fall back on the cot. Slowly the fire in his backbone went out, and he realized he had been hallucinating an explanation for the stabbing pain.

He held a palm in front of his mouth and blew  He could feel the breath on his hand, and that reassured him  Where in hell was he?

Over and over the question raced around the inside of his skull, like one of those daredevil motorcyclists riding inside a wire sphere, faster and faster to keep from falling off the sides, the ceiling. But there was no answer. He couldn't even imagine one.

He had been on the plane. He knew that. But not where he was going or who had accompanied him. But this wasn't the plane.

Then he heard something. It was far away, and came to him out of the misty darkness, a scraping sound. It was faint but it was real. He tried to call out, but managed only a whispered croak.

The world suddenly exploded with sound and brilliant light. A great boom, like thunder trapped in a huge barrel, echoed all around him. Even through his tightly shut eyelids, the fire swirled all around him. He tried to open his eyes, but the light was too intense, the pain too sharp.

The thunder died away slowly, but the light stayed. He was in a stone room in the heart of the sun, and someone had opened a door to the outside. That's what it was. Or what it was like. He felt something on his face now, and a shadow covered his eyes for a moment, easing the pain from the brilliant light.

"Close the door, Ronny."

The booming sound came back, and the light died as if the thunderclap had blown out the sun. It was dark, and it felt better.

"Tough old bird," the same voice said. The words sounded as if they were spoken in slow motion. The voice was deep, its edges raspy with aspirated air. He was hearing things differently.

Someone touched him again. His arm was lifted, not roughly, but not carefully, either. Then far away at the end of the arm somewhere came a stabbing pain. His body turned itself inside out, and he lost consciousness, struggling to swim against the tide of numbness sweeping over him. The voice said something else, but the words were so slow and deep he couldn't decipher them. And the darkness was total once more.

"All right, Ronny, you can leave us alone."

Marley opened his eyes. The haze was gone. There was light, not harsh and not much. But he could see now. The circles of flame were gone. The walls swam into focus slowly.

"Well, Jason," the voice said, "how do you feel?"

That voice. Harkness. James Harkness. He remembered it all now—the plane, Harold, shot in the head, the hypodermic.

He tried to sit up, but his strength was too far gone. His muscles still wouldn't work.

"I wouldn't try that if I were you," Harkness warned. There was a gentle humor in the voice, not mocking really, but not genuinely concerned, either.

## THE GOLD EAGLE READER SERVICE™: HERE'S HOW IT WORKS

Accepting free books puts you under no obligation to buy anything. You may keep the books and gift and return the shipping statement marked "cancel." If you do not cancel, about a month later we will send you four additional novels, and bill you just $13.80*—that's a saving of over 10% off the cover price of all four books! And there's no extra charge for shipping! You may cancel at any time, but if you choose to continue, then every other month we'll send you four more books, which you may either purchase at the discount price . . . or return at our expense and cancel your subscription.

Of course not. Why should it be? Harkness had put two bullets in Harold Carmichael's head.

He rolled his head to one side and opened his eyes again, finding himself staring into the sardonic smile that made Harkness look slightly out of kilter, his face twisted a bit, like that of someone recovering from a mild stroke.

"How do you feel?" Harkness asked.

"You bastard!"

"Good. You're feeling okay, then, I gather."

"Where am I?"

"Now, Jason, be realistic. I can't tell you that. You should realize that. You do, don't you?"

"Murdering bastard!"

"It's a cruel world, Jason. You, of all people, should realize that."

"You won't get away with this. You understand that, don't you?"

"You don't think so?"

Marley ignored the mocking question, closing his eyes again. He wanted to drift away, but the blood pounding through his veins was too insistent for that. His heart was racing now, its beat echoing in his ears. He could feel it in his chest, like a fist trying to pound its way right through the rib cage.

Harkness walked to a corner of the room. Marley tried to ignore him, but was too curious. He rolled his head to one side and let his eyes open just a slit. He watched while Harkness popped a tape into a video recorder  He was aware now of a small camera, mounted on a tripod off to one side. When Harkness was finished tinkering with the machine, he came back, careful not to get in front of the camera

"There is so much you have to tell me, Jason. I think we might as well begin."

"I'm not telling you anything, you treacherous bastard."

"Too much profanity, Jason. This is being recorded. You don't want to sound like a boor for posterity, do you?"

Marley clenched his fists. He raised his right hand and tried to shake the fist vehemently in Harkness's direction, but he was too weak

"Shall we begin, Jason? I should warn you that there are other methods besides civilized inquisition to get what I want, what I need. I'd prefer not to resort to them. For old times' sake, you understand. But I will if you make me. This is far too important to let old friendships get in the way."

"Go to hell."

Harkness smiled. "But, Jason, old boy, haven't you noticed? This *is* hell. You should be familiar with it, old friend. You and I worked on the blueprints. We are Satan's architects." The smile vanished so quickly and completely it might have been the product of an electric current suddenly cut.

Marley tried again to rise, but Harkness shook his head. "No, Jason. Don't get up. There is so much more you have to tell me."

## CHAPTER FOUR

Bolan watched the upper stories of the lodge. From time to time he'd see the muted gleam of the flashlight in a window. The guy was moving from room to room. It was beginning to look as if he was making some kind of careful search rather than having entered to retrieve one specific thing. Either that or he knew what he was looking for but not where to find it. Bolan had been unable to get a good look at the man's face and didn't know whether he'd been present at the conference earlier.

It was several minutes before the flashlight's glow seeped back into the kitchen of the lodge. Bolan heard footsteps, as if the man inside no longer cared whether he made noise. He must have been through every room and convinced himself the place was deserted

The Executioner moved back to the basement window and dropped to one knee. He pressed himself back against the wall, about three feet away from the small opening. The man would have to come through lying on his stomach and hauling himself out with both hands. Even if he had a weapon, Bolan would have the advantage.

The light stabbed through the small window and splashed on the trees beyond the garden for a moment, then winked out. Moments later hands snaked through the opening, the palms turned toward the edges of the window frame. Then a head appeared.

When the man's shoulders appeared, Bolan leaned forward. Sticking the muzzle of the Beretta in the guy's left ear, he whispered, "Don't move, pal."

The man froze, started to turn his head toward Bolan, but stopped when the muzzle screwed a little more tightly into his ear

"What do you want?"

"What are you doing here?"

"I, uh, forgot something. I came back to get it."

"You usually break into a place like this when you leave something behind?"

"There was nobody here. I didn't think it—"

"Let's change the subject, shall we?"

"Can I get the hell out of this window? My arms are getting ready to rip out of their sockets."

"We can wait a bit for that I have a few more questions."

"Look, I'm fresh out of answers. My memory goes bad when my arms fall off You want to know anything, you better let me come all the way through."

Bolan twisted the gun a little, the front sight digging into the fleshy part of the ear. The man tried to twist his head away, but the gun followed him relentlessly

"All right, all right!"

"Start talking."

"I'm a journalist."

"For whom?"

"Reuters."

"Pull yourself forward a couple of feet until I can get at your wallet."

The man started to haul himself through the window, trying to keep the gun from reaming out his ear in the process. Bolan didn't let up the pressure, and he knew he couldn't afford to be careless. This guy had sand, not something he associated with journalists, as a rule. They were usually guys who took cheap shots from long range, then ran like hell when somebody shot back. But this guy was something else. He had a 9 mm slug six inches from the center of his brain, and he didn't seem to be scared.

"Far enough," the warrior growled. "ID's in the wallet?"

"Yeah."

Bolan jerked the wallet free. He flipped through it, but couldn't see well enough to read anything. "Shine the flashlight on the wallet while I look. And be careful how you move. If you've got a gun, you better tell me now."

"Why would a journalist need a gun?"

Bolan pressed the Beretta a little closer.

"Ouch! In a sling, under my right arm." Bolan slid one hand under the man's light jacket, felt the heavy bulge of a holstered pistol. He pulled the jacket open and withdrew the weapon. It was an H&K P-95 automatic, serious iron. Unless Reuters had started stockpiling weapons, it was an odd choice for a writer to be packing. He tucked the pistol into his own pocket and leaned away slightly while the guy reached for his flashlight.

With the light on, he quickly found a press card. It looked real enough. According to the card, the guy's name was Michael James Bradley Bolan flipped through the rest of the wallet, finding a New York State driver's license in the same name. There was a picture on the license. It matched that the press card, but both were kind of fuzzy. There was also a couple of credit cards, including an American Express card.

"How long you had American Express?"

"What?"

"How long?"

"I don't know, since '80, '81, something like that."

The card said 1981 He closed the wallet and set it on the ground next to Bradley's head.

"I'm going to let you up all the way. But if you make a sudden move, your next appearance in the papers will be the obituary column. You understand?"

Bradley started to nod, but the gun was still prodding him in the ear, and he mumbled an unhappy "Yes." Bolan backed off a bit and waited for the "newsman" to haul himself all the way through the window. The guy got up and brushed off his clothes. He stuck a finger in his left ear, then brought it close to his eyes, rubbed it with the tip of his thumb. "Son of a bitch, I'm bleeding."

"You'll get over it. Sit down and put your hands behind your head."

Bradley complied, and Bolan dropped into a squat four feet away. "Tell me what you were looking for. Now."

"I was covering the big meeting here, the witches' coven or whatever the hell you want to call it."

"What do you call it?"

"I call it a harvest of all the right-wing nuts in the Western world, that's what I call it."

"What did you expect to find inside?"

"I don't know—something, anything I could use for a story."

"You're lying."

"So I'm lying. Who the hell are you? What right do you have to ask me anything? You security or something?"

"If I were security for the men in this lodge tonight, you'd already be dead."

"Already? I suppose that means I'm going to be dead anyway. Is that it?"

"No."

"Then what?"

"Did you come straight from Munich?"

"Yes."

"Was that your twin looking at Murray's car?"

"How did you    ?" Bradley swallowed the rest of the question.

Bolan heaved a sigh. "My friend, you listen to me. I'm going to say this once, and only once. Then I'm through talking, understood?"

Bradley nodded.

"If you're a reporter, then I'm Connie Chung. My guess is you're an intelligence agent of some kind. CIA, ONI, DIA, whatever. You came here to spy on our elegant fascist friends. You either knew something was going to happen to Dolph Murray and took a look to make sure, or you heard about it somehow, maybe from the men responsible. Hell, maybe you were in the van, I don't know  But you know a hell of a lot more than you're telling me, and I'm running out of patience very quickly "

"So shoot me."

"No, I'm going to do something better  I'm going to run you into Munich and turn you over to the CIA. If that's who you work for, you'll have some hard questions to answer  If you work for one of the other agencies, you'll be the laughingstock of the U.S. Intelligence community  Stand up."

Bradley swiveled his head and peered into Bolan's face. "Wait a minute. Let's not be hasty "

"I don't have time to waste fooling around with you."

"I don't have time to waste, either '

This time it was evident Bradley was telling the truth. Bolan waved the Beretta, indicating Bradley should continue.

"Who are you?"

"Not important."

"The hell it isn't. You're not security, are you, for these goons?"

The warrior shook his head.

"But you won't tell me who you are or what you're doing here, will you?"

Bolan didn't respond. Bradley sighed. It was evident he was trying to decide whether to trust the big man. He had no reason to. But he had no reason not to.

Finally Bradley made his choice. "All right. I came here to pick up a tape."

"And did you?"

"No. It was gone. The machine was still in place, but the tape was missing."

"How did you know about Murray?"

"We were supposed to meet after the conference broke up. When he didn't show, I came looking for him."

"A meet?"

Bradley nodded. "Yeah, a meet."

"An interview  Murray bought your Reuters fairy tale?"

"No."

"What then?"

"He was one of ours."

"An agent? Keep talking."

"There's no time."

"Why not?"

"Because there's supposed to be some sort of terrorist strike in Munich tomorrow. But I don't know what or where. That's what Murray was supposed to tell me."

## CHAPTER FIVE

"You're sure you have no idea where the attack was to take place?" Bolan asked. He and Bradley had moved to a small room inside the lodge.

"None. I'm sure Murray didn't know himself. He was trying to find out."

"So why was he hit? Was his cover blown somehow?"

"Impossible."

"Nothing's impossible. You should know that."

"Yeah. But I'm sure. I've handled him for five years. We've always been careful. Dead drops so complicated you'd need to be a psychic to find them. There was never any direct contact between us, not by phone, not even by radio. Hell, I've never actually been close enough to the man to touch him. This was going to be the first time we broke that rule. And that was because there wasn't enough time to go the usual route."

"Well, I'll give him one thing. His cover sure as hell was convincing."

"That was Dolph's idea. He said he had to play it to the hilt. The guys he was in with, they'd have gutted him like a trout and pinned him to a barn door if they even had a hint he might be an agent. Hell, remember they have killed people right in the public eye. They're not afraid of anything. They're stone crazy, for sure. Dolph knew a mistake would put his neck in a noose and there'd be no shortage of volunteers to kick the chair out from under him. A true believer—that's what he had to look like. And the fanatics on this side of the lake are even worse. Paranoid about security. But they have the contacts and money to burn. That's why this was an important step. Something's shakin', something real big, but…" He shrugged. "So he wanted to look like the genuine article. Had to."

"He managed that, all right."

"What he managed," Bradley said, "was to get his ass in a sling. You saw the body. He looked like ground beef."

"Forget about it. We got more important things to do."

"Forget about it? You think I can forget something like that? Hell, I been with the Company for ten years. I never saw anything like that before, ever."

"If we don't figure out where they plan to hit, you'll see it again. On the front page of all the papers."

"Let's look at the bag again. Maybe there's something in there that can give us a clue."

Bolan shoved the stuff across the table to Bradley, then leaned back and watched the younger man pull the zipper open with a look of distaste. "I feel like I'm opening the man's grave."

Bradley picked up the notebook and scanned each page, hoping something would jump out at him, wave a red flag. He looked up for a second. "You're sure there was no tape?"

"I'm sure."

Bradley nodded, then turned back to the notebook.

"Airports, airlines, anything like that in the notebook?" Bolan asked.

"Hard to tell. I mean, this looks more like some kind of working diary than anything else. Except for one thing. There're no dates."

"Find something that refers to the conference. Maybe we can date it from there."

"I'm looking, damn it. If you think you can do better, be my guest."

He flipped the notebook across the table. It was stifling in the small room, and both men were sweating. Their tempers were getting shorter as the minutes ticked away "You're sure Murray said tomorrow?"

Bradley nodded.

Bolan worked through the pages quickly. There were more than forty of them, each filled with Murray's tiny, cramped penmanship. Fortunately it was clear and readable. But it was more stream of consciousness than anything else.

"He wrote in this thing every day"

Yeah, he did He told me that He also kept a bigger, more detailed book, but he kept that one in a safe place, and he wrote it in code. He used this carry-around notebook just to remind himself of the things he wanted to include in the master journal.''

"When was the last time you heard from him?"

"Three days ago. Why?"

"Because at that point he didn't know what the target of the attack would be. If we can figure out where the entry is for that day, we know the answer has to be between that point and the end of the written pages. Assuming he wrote it down."

"I never thought of that."

Bolan started at the last entry and began thumbing his way back. "Wait a minute, here's something...Badalamente. That would be Giovanni. He arrived three days ago, at the start of the conference. He was the last one to show up. Playboy of the Western world with two blondes crammed into his Cadillac convertible. This entry must be for that day."

"You sure?"

"No, but it's a decent working hypothesis."

"Okay, then." He handed Bolan a pencil "Mark it off, and we'll go from there.'"

Bolan tracked the text line by line with his fingers. The more closely he looked at it, the denser and more impenetrable it became. It was maddening to see the words, understand them and not know what they really meant to their author

Here s something, maybe. Bolan pointed to a set of numbers. "That look like anything to you?" He shoved the book across to Bradley, keeping his thumb on the line.

"Not really. It could be anything from a credit-card number to a—"

"Looks to me like it could be a flight number, maybe a gate number with it. And a time."

"What airport?"

"If we can find the airline, we can check the rest."

"Let me try something." Bradley walked to the phone and made a quick dial. "Get ready to give me those numbers.

"Janice, Mike. Listen. I need a favor. No, not that kind. Listen, this is critical. I'm going to give you some numbers. What I need you to do is plug them into the computer, travel skeds. See if you can get me a match.... Yeah, I know, but this is really important. I know, I know. Okay, great. Here they come."

Bolan listened while the numbers were read off, then Bradley said, "No, I'll hold, okay? Yes, I need it now. It can't wait till morning. No, I can't tell you what it's about. You'll just have to trust me that it's life and death. Literally, yes...."

THEY MADE IT with ten minutes to spare. It was a guess, but it had to be right. The odds against the three numbers matching anything else were astronomical. The Munich airport was smaller than the Tempelhof, but it still handled heavy air traffic.

They couldn't get into the terminal with their weapons, so they had to take the long way around. Bradley's car rocked to a halt beside a chain link fence by the end of one of the runways. They had no way of knowing which runway the incoming flight would use, but there was no other way to go.

Bradley had alerted the U.S. consulate, which passed the word to the German government, and terminal security was wound up tighter than a cheap watch. That left Bolan and Bradley to cover the outfield. If the attack was to be an assault on the terminal, they would be of no help, but if it was an attack on the plane itself, they might be able to do something.

Across the open field beyond the runways, Bolan spotted something that made his blood run cold. He flashed a glance at the sky, looking for incoming Lufthansa planes. The flight was a Boeing 737, and he was watching for its profile. So far, there was nothing in sight. He pointed across the open space.

"There."

"There what? A maintenance van. So what?"

"No, not maintenance. That looks just like the van the hit team used when they took Murray out."

"You sure?"

Bolan nodded. "Come on." He raced back to Bradley's car and got behind the wheel.

Bradley tumbled into the passenger seat beside him. The car was already in reverse as the CIA man shouted, "What the hell are you going to do?

They're inside the fence. We're outside. We got to climb over.''

"No time." Bolan trod on the gas, and the sudden acceleration slammed Bradley's door shut. The car was racing head-on at the chain link. Already Bolan could see the rear doors of the van opening.

They hit the fence at nearly sixty. The impact crumpled the front fenders, but the fence gave way at the bottom, its sharp lower tines raking up over the hood and across the roof as the old Buick slid beneath it.

Four men had jumped from the rear of the van. One of them pointed to the sky, and Bradley stuck his head out the window. "The plane's here. Damn!"

The car rocked and rolled over the uneven ground, still picking up speed. The right fender flapped loose, and the left screamed against the front tire, but Bolan never wavered. One of the terrorists had spotted them. The other three were busy hauling something out of the back of the van.

"They've got a missile," Bolan shouted.

He pushed the car as hard as he could. They were closing fast, and two members of the attack unit opened up with automatic rifles. The windshield shattered as bullets peppered the front of the car. It was just a matter of time before the engine block went. The vehicle was already leaking coolant, and Bolan had a hard time seeing through the clouds of steam.

Bradley was returning fire from the passenger window, and he sent the attack team scurrying for cover The man with the missile stood his ground He dropped to one knee and took dead aim on the car

"Looks like a Stinger. Get out of here." Bolan opened his own door and gave Bradley a shove to the right before ducking out. He hit hard and lay still as the Buick pushed on, hearing the telltale whoosh of the missile as it rushed across the field toward the car.

The commotion had caught the attention of security, and sirens blared as three jeeps sped up the nearest runway.

The missile found its mark, and the Buick disintegrated, the cloud of swirling metal fragments obscured by a ball of bright yellow for a second, then spinning out of a cloud of black smoke.

The van lurched to life as Bolan tried to get to his feet. He started toward the van, but it was already under way. Behind him he could hear Bradley calling to him, but he raced after the van, his legs churning but losing ground with every step. The back doors of the van were open, and the security jeeps lurched into the grass and sped after it.

There was a second whoosh, and the lead jeep was consumed by a spectacular explosion. The remaining two vehicles plowed into the wreckage. Their gas tanks erupted on impact as Bolan hit the deck.

When the smoke cleared, the van was far across the field. More cars raced up the runways, and Bolan sprinted back toward the gathering crowd. Bradley was already talking to one of the security men.

"I need a car," the warrior growled "Now!"

## CHAPTER SIX

Bolan tracked the van through the winding mountain roads, coiling up through the deep Bavarian forest toward Czechoslovakia. High up, the blocky van looked like a child's toy as it lumbered around the hairpin turns, slowly climbing higher and higher into the mountains. He had gotten in behind it right after the attack in the airport. Rather than go head-to-head, he'd decided to hang back, follow the van and see what happened.

He'd followed the van for nearly three hours now. He wondered about the extra man. There had been five the night Dolph Murray was killed. Now there were six. He wasn't sure if the first five were part of this team. He hoped so, not liking the thought that whoever was orchestrating the terror had an unlimited supply of soldiers, plugged in like modular parts in a complex electronic machine.

Eleven looked too much like a huge organization. And where did Mike Bradley fit in? The guy seemed straight, but that was his business. Lying was more than a science with the Mike Bradleys of the world; it was high art, polished, sophisticated and nearly perfect They changed lives like other people changed clothes, and they had an explanation for everything. That made Mack Bolan uneasy.

The van lumbered toward a distant intersection. Bolan waited for the telltale brake lights, but they stayed dark. The van rumbled past, and Bolan sprinted back to his car. Gunning the engine, he spun his wheels in the gravel, found traction and backed into a tight K-turn. He tossed more crushed stone out and over the precipice as he roared back into the road and floored it.

There were no speed limits here, except for those imposed by common sense and the willingness to see just how close to the edge you had the courage to come. Bolan wasn't short on courage, and he pushed the Audi to forty-five, then fifty miles per hour. The van was doing little more than half that, and he could close the gap in ten or fifteen minutes.

Nearing the bottom of the mountain, he braked into a hairpin, downshifted and kicked the gas. The Audi responded with a throaty roar, and he could feel the rumble of its engine through the floorboards. Five minutes later he was heading into the long straightaway and pushed the engine to its limit. Halfway up, the road started to snake again, and he had to back off. They were four thousand feet up and still climbing.

The twists and turns in the road wouldn't let him see the van until he was right on top of it, something he wanted to avoid at all cost. The crest of the low mountain was about three hundred yards, and he backed off on the gas again He           the last turn at a little over twenty, in time to see the van's brake lights wink on, off and then stay on as the square back tipped forward and the van started down the far side.

Bolan drifted down to a coast, the Audi barely gaining ground at all now. He was so intent on the van that an approaching vehicle had barely registered. A blaring horn jerked his eyes to the rearview mirror A Volvo was coming up fast. It veered to the side and narrowly missed him as it raced past. Leaping ahead, the vehicle suddenly skidded sideways. Bolan hit the brakes, expecting the driver to right the car and pull over.

But he was wrong.

Three men spilled out of the Volvo and took cover behind the front and rear fenders. Bolan jerked the Audi into reverse. The tires spun on the pavement, screeching. Slowly the Audi started to move back as clouds of burned rubber swirled up and around it.

Bolan ducked low as the first shot slammed through his windshield and showered fragments of glass over the dash and the steering wheel. He had the accelerator floored and tried to keep the Audi on the road. He felt the right wheels slipping off the pavement into the soft shoulder, and the car swerved as he tapped the brakes, trying to steer without looking. Three more shots drilled through the windshield, punching holes the size of golf balls in the safety glass.

For a second he thought about spinning the car and making a run for it, but he couldn't bring himself to fold his hand that easily. Locking the brakes, he let the Audi lurch to a halt and banged the passenger-side door open.

Crawling across the seat, he slid onto the shoulder and down into the tall weeds along the edge of the road, just as a burst of machine-gun fire took out the rest of the windshield. He felt the hunks of glass pelting his legs and ankles as he left the car.

Pulling his Desert Eagle, he clicked the safety off and started down into a shallow gully. The land leveled for a few yards, then sloped out and down at a steep angle. It wasn't the best position, but it beat charging straight up the road.

The SMG chewed at the Audi, rupturing both front tires and punching half a dozen holes in the radiator. The car lurched as the tires blew, coolant spewing through the ruptured grille. The hissing and sputtering as the coolant boiled off the engine block sent clouds of steam swirling up into the sky as Bolan started to work his way along the gully.

The hammering of the SMG stopped now, and he heard a shout as he ducked into some thick greenery clotting the narrow depression.

The slope above him concealed the car, and he tried to gauge the distance to the Volvo as he worked his way through the tangled growth. The first gunman appeared over the edge of the hill, and Bolan held his fire. He wanted to know where the others were before giving away his location.

The gunman turned back over his shoulder and shouted something in German, but it sounded as if German wasn't his native language. A moment later Bolan heard a rush of footsteps, and the remaining two gunmen appeared alongside the first. The second two looked like poster boys for some Aryan genetics manual—broad shoulders and blond hair, their rounded faces still flushed with youth.

The third man was taller, but nearly as muscular. His cheeks were drawn, almost sunken. A small black mustache matched the man's dark complexion. Italian, Spanish, maybe, Bolan thought. Definitely not native to the area, at any rate.

The three men seemed uncertain what to do, whether to press the assault and risk trying to flush Bolan from cover, or wait him out. They backed away until they were out of his sight.

A second later all three men spilled over the crest of the hill and started down the slope. They had spread out, and Bolan was pincered by a hulking blonde on either end. The gaunt-faced man with the mustache took the middle. The blonde to Bolan's right jerked his head around, as if he'd heard something, and the Executioner squeezed the trigger of the Desert Eagle. The enemy was hit dead center, the bullet slamming into his breastbone and breaking it with an audible crack  Incredibly he staggered down the hill a couple of steps, but then lost his balance and fell to one knee.

He waved his subgun as if to ward off a swarm of invisible insects. He was firing blind, but the bullets were just as deadly  Bolan hit the deck, listening to the hail of fire clip leaves and snap branches just above his head. The hammering stopped suddenly, and the warrior peered over the brush in time to see the gunner pitch forward onto his face.

Bolan's first shot had sent the other two hardmen scurrying back up the slope, and he didn't know where either was positioned. A voice called, "Heinz?"

But Heinz wasn't up to answering. The caller seemed to realize it, and a howl of rage ended abruptly in a choking scream. A second later the other blond man broke over the crest and barreled down the slope on the diagonal  Bolan rolled once, then brought up the big  44 automatic. Branches prevented him from aiming, and he pushed at the brush as the gunman closed on his cover

The gunner carried an automatic. It looked to Bolan like a 9 mm H&K, and he was firing the gun as fast as he could pull the trigger  Stupid, Bolan thought as the last shell ejected and the slide locked open  Angry, yes, and understandably so, but still stupid.

Without missing a step, the gunner dropped the empty clip and fished another out of his pocket. Bolan had him in his sights now, and aimed low  He wanted one of the attackers alive, if he could manage it. He squeezed, and the shot shattered the blonde's knee. The gun went flying as the man fell, then rolled onto his back, his hands clawing at his ruined leg.

The man with the mustache poked his head over the top of the crest for a second. He caught a glimpse of the wounded man and ducked back. Bolan scrambled up the slope, trying to muffle the sound of his charge. Mustache poked his head up again, and this time saw Bolan racing toward him. He ducked, then stuck his hand out over the crest and fired blindly.

Bolan veered to the left, and the shots sailed harmlessly by. He took the last yard in a single leaping step and broke up over the hump. Mustache was on his belly, and his eyes widened when he saw the big American. He brought his gun around and fired.

The shot went wild, and Bolan squeezed off one of his own as the gunman's barrel wavered toward him for another try. The slug hit home. The hardman's long frame lifted off the ground for a moment as a bright red flower seemed to blossom on his white shirt. The gun dropped from Mustache's lifeless fingers and slid down the slope a few inches until stopped by a rock embedded in the soft soil.

As the Executioner moved toward the wounded man, two quick shots whistled past his ear. He turned in time to see the second blonde sitting, one hand clasped over his shattered knee, the other gripping a reloaded automatic. Bolan snapped off a pair of shots, catching the gunner high on the chest and punching his body back to the ground, where it lay still.

Without checking, Bolan knew there would be no one to interrogate. He was still in the dark. And now he had a new question. How had these men found him?

He knelt beside Mustache and went through his pockets hurriedly. There was a wallet with a driver's license, issued by the State of New Jersey. There was some other paperwork, most of it useless. A quick search of the other two gunners turned up nothing at all. He retrieved the SMG and two clips, then climbed back to the road.

The van had a huge lead on him now, and maybe he wouldn't be able to catch up. He looked at the Audi, with its shattered windows and holed fenders. The borrowed vehicle could be traced to him, but it couldn't be helped. He'd call Mike Bradley and tell him what happened. Cleanup was for someone else to worry about.

He climbed into the Volvo, shoved the MAC-10 and its ammo under the seat and turned the key

# CHAPTER SEVEN

Bolan spent the next two hours searching for the van. There were few intersections and most led to dead ends. He was running out of possibilities as he turned off the main highway one more time. Unlike the others, this was a dirt road that showed the tire impressions of a heavy vehicle.

Parking the stolen Volvo in the trees, the warrior grabbed the captured MAC-10 and two clips and pocketed the ignition keys. The road ahead wound uphill through a forest of birch and pine.

Combat senses alert, he listened for the slightest sound. But the night was absolutely quiet. He moved closer to the trees, where tall, stiff grass whisked against his pants and crackled slightly under his feet. There had been one set of tire prints, as close as he could get to proof that a vehicle had gone up and not come down.

The air was chilly, almost cold. His breath clouded a moment before disappearing into the trees. But he felt a chill that had nothing to do with the weather.

Something was up there, and his gut told him it was the van.

A half mile later the road started to narrow There was still no sign of a building or the van. Twenty yards farther on, the warrior stopped and knelt, running his fingers over the ground in the darkness. The depressions were gone. If the van had come this way, he had already passed it.

Backtracking, he stopped fifty yards downhill. Still no sign. Another fifty yards, and he found the tracks again. Unwilling to risk a light, he felt along the damp earth until he found a place where the tracks veered to the left He crept ahead, following the curving impressions, and found himself flush up against a wall of trees.

Shifting the MAC, he moved to the right and slipped in among the damp greenery. And there was the van. A hollow space had been carved out of the woods, then covered over with severed brush and trees. It wouldn't last long, but it had fooled him. Once.

He crept close to the vehicle, placing each foot carefully and pausing to listen between steps. Total silence. As near as he could tell, the van was empty He reached the back of the vehicle and placed an ear against the door, but heard nothing. Moving quietly alongside, he reached the front and put a hand on the engine compartment. It was still warm

The warrior tried a door and, finding it unlocked, eased inside the vehicle. He removed a penlight from a pocket and searched through a pile of canvas bags, turning up some grenades and tucking three into his jacket pockets.

Playing the light around the walls, he saw several racks of automatic weapons, and magazines, fully loaded. But the prize was a slab of plastique and a box of electronic devices—radio detonators, two palm-size transmitters and two spring-action triggers designed for pressure detonation. He stuffed the explosive and the radio gear into an empty canvas bag and left the van.

Working his way back to the road, Bolan was about to step out into the open when he heard voices in careless conversation. Two men were coming downhill. He froze, his finger on the subgun's trigger, then backed through the trees until he could see the van.

"Son of a bitch gets awful grouchy," one of the men said.

"He's a pain in the ass, is what he is, if you ask me."

If those papers are so important," the first man said, "he shouldn't have left them in the goddamn truck."

"He doesn't care about that. We're his gofers. It's easy to sit up top and make everybody else jump."

'Maybe so, but I'm getting tired of this."

"You getting tired of the money, too?"

The first man laughed. "Hell, no. Besides, you re in this one, you're in for the long haul. Fact is, I think we got to watch our asses. I got a funny feeling we'll be yesterday's newspaper, soon as this op winds down.''

"No way"

"You think not? I think we already know too much. And if I think so, you can imagine what he thinks. You know how it goes. Use them and toss them away. Make sure there's no embarrassment walking around. We'll be about as useful as a Coney Island whitefish.''

"Maybe we ought to get in the van and get the hell out of here.''

"Could just be you're right. I've thought about it, believe me. But if we run, he'll have us killed for sure. You think what we did to that asshole Murray was something, you better forget about it. That was nothing.''

"Didn't go so well at the airport, though, did it?''

"That was different. Somebody got on to us. But he's taking care of that. Forget about it.''

"I'd like to forget about the whole damn thing.'' The speaker paused to light a cigarette. In the glare from a pocket lighter, Bolan could see their faces. One man was slim, with weasel-like features. The other had a big moon face and huge hands.

Americans, no doubt. The Texan accents were all that was necessary for that conclusion, and the brief glimpse of their faces confirmed it. Both men were dressed in dark fatigues that bore no insignia They were members of either a covert-action team or a private army.

"Hang on a minute, Ernie. I'll get those papers."

There was a rustling in the brush, and Bolan crouched, taking a step backward. He heard the van door slide open and bump against the rubber doorstop. The door slammed again almost immediately, and footsteps crunched back toward the road.

"Got them?"

"Yep. Finish that weed and we'll head on back. It's cold as a witch's tit out here."

The voices were drifting off. Bolan waited a moment longer, then moved to the edge of the trees. He could just make out the dark shapes of the two men as they trudged uphill. He slipped into the open, staying close to the trees, and followed, letting them hang at the limit of his vision.

The ground started to level out, and Bolan let them get a little farther ahead. They continued to banter, their voices drifting back to him in tatters, only a word here and there intelligible.

The voices died away abruptly as Bolan found himself nearing the crest of the hill. As he reached it, a block of light suddenly appeared below him. He saw the two men slip through a door, and the light disappeared. The warrior sprinted toward the memory of the light. A two-story building gradually assumed shape in the darkness. Its windows had to have had blackout curtains, because there was no trace of light anywhere.

Bolan circled the building and found only the front door and a smaller door, more like an escape hatch, in the rear. The windows were covered with sheet steel painted in jungle camouflage. The metal panels were bolted in with prison screws. The nuts were on the inside. There was no way in except through the front door or the hatch.

The explosives he'd taken from the van would get the door open, but he had no idea how many men were inside. If the men from the van were present, there were at least six, and possibly more. But there was no other way. Quickly he molded the block of plastique around the detonator. It was crude but ought to work. If the plastique went, the door would come off, and maybe half of the front of the building along with it.

The Executioner jammed the plastique against the base of the door, then looked for something to channel the blast. Several large logs lay off to one side. He couldn't lift them alone, and tried rolling several before he found one he could jostle toward the front of the building.

He pulled the aerial on the transmitter, raced to the trees and pressed the button, lowering his head just as the explosive went off. There was a stutter, then a roar as the plastique peeled the steel door back and stripped sheet steel from the front windows of the building.

Almost instantaneously the area was flooded with light. Bright arc lamps mounted in the trees smeared pure white light around the building, throwing shadows that crisscrossed where the paths of the lights intersected.

Shouts erupted from inside the building, and men started to spew out the front. They carried automatic weapons and sprayed unaimed bursts into the trees. They were well trained, and they worked like a well-oiled machine. Fanning out, they charged toward the tree line, ceasing fire at a shouted command.

Six of them. Bolan had the MAC-10, and he had the advantage of surprise, but that wouldn't last long. He had to hit them hard. And fast.

He took out a grenade, removed the pin, counted down and tossed the deadly orb into the trees, flushing one man. Bolan took him down with a short burst, then ducked back and sprinted twenty yards to the left as a hail of gunfire poured into the underbrush where he had been just a moment earlier.

The wing man was about twenty yards away, but he was well covered. Bolan had to get outside him and come in from the flank.

The warrior swung wide, edging toward the building at the same time. He was inside their perimeter now. The wing man got out of his crouch and started to back up, as if he'd sensed something. Bolan switched to his Beretta, single-shot mode. The slight pop was swallowed by the night, and the guy never knew what hit him. He fell to the ground and lay still.

Bolan moved on, seeking the other four men. Their fatigues blended well with the shadows cast by the floods. Charging into the open would get him killed, so he backed deeper into the trees along the side of the building, then dashed across a narrow clearing and slipped in behind the structure.

He could see the right half of the clearing in front of the house, but it was deserted. Swinging along the back, he was almost to the corner when two men turned it and stood there, frozen in surprise. Bolan swung the MAC-10 and laced a figure eight, and they went down. But not before one of them squeezed off a short burst from his AR-15.

Bolan sprinted to the corner and bent to snare the AR, then backtracked to the right end of the house. He heard a shout and saw the remaining two men charging toward the opening into the lane. He fired the AR, but they were too close to cover, and the .223 hellfire was too little too late.

Bolan tossed the empty weapon into the woods. Ducking into a crouch, he ran for the shattered front door, dived through and landed in a shoulder roll. A quick room-by-room search turned up no one.

A stairway led down to a dark basement. The warrior groped along the wall at the head of the stairs. Light flooded the cellar and a sudden burst nearly took his legs off. Chucking his second grenade down the stairs, Bolan crawled around the corner. There was a bright flash, then a peal of thunder. Smoke billowed up the stairwell.

The next time he tried the stairs, he had more success. The gunman lay crumpled in a corner, outlined by light coming from a small room just beyond him, its steel door half-open. Bolan approached the door cautiously, his subgun up and tracking.

But the room was deserted. A briefcase lay open on a desk, its contents partly covered with fallen plaster. There was a map on the wall, pinned to some cork. The warrior ripped it off, folding it with its pins in place. He jammed it into the briefcase and raced back up the stairs.

As he came out into the open, he could see headlights coming up the lane. Tucking the briefcase under his arm, he hotfooted it for the trees. He'd done enough work for the night.

## CHAPTER EIGHT

The area was roped off. Mike Bradley watched the choppers, three American Hueys, fanning out from the center of the area. They reminded him of buzzards, the way they swooped and circled, climbed, swooped and circled. And he knew they were looking for bodies.

Dan Mitchell was running the search-and-recovery operation. He was a brusque man, with a no-nonsense crew cut and shoulders a mile wide. He didn't have a shred of humor in his two-hundred-and-twenty-five-pound body. Ordinarily that got on Bradley's nerves. But not this time. This time there was nothing to laugh about.

Mitchell spotted him as he stepped over the yellow plastic tape that cordoned off the crash site. German police were controlling the crowds of the curious, but Bradley didn't see a soul beyond the tape who wasn't stamped Made In U.S.A.

Taking leave of a couple of uniforms, Mitchell walked toward him with that peculiar head-forward strut that reminded Bradley of a bull trapped in a human body. Mitchell didn't bother with a handshake.

"'Bout time you got here, Mike."

"I have a life, Dan. I also have a job. Sometimes I think there's no difference."

"Well, now you got a new job."

"What's that?"

"I can't tell you all of it here. But I can tell you that you better forget about a life until this is over."

Bradley glanced past Mitchell at the wreckage behind him. There were a couple of sections of the plane that looked almost undamaged, but they were small and they spewed technological guts all over the muddy ground. Wires, cables, twisted seats, everything charred black, spilled from the ruptured fuselage. There were no wings, and Bradley realized they must have broken loose while the plane was still in the air. The tail section seemed almost intact, but it was canted almost forty-five degrees, and it ended almost before it began.

"What the hell happened? This is no ordinary plane crash, Dan."

"No shit. When was the last time we got involved in an ordinary plane wreck?"

Bradley shrugged. "It's happened."

"Yeah, but how often?"

"So what's the Company angle?"

"Can't tell you right now."

"Then why am I here?"

"Because you're a warm body, and we need every one of those scarce little items we can get. I want you to walk around, get the feel of this thing. Look at every angle. Don't talk to the Air Force boys. Don't talk to anybody. What I want is your gut reaction on this thing. I know you flew in Nam, and I know you know a hell of a lot more about airplanes than I do. Instinct is what I'm looking for, pure and simple. You'll know why after the briefing.''

Bradley nodded. "You're the boss."

"That's correct, and the boss says talk to nobody. I don't care who. Got it?"

"Got it."

Mitchell reached out and clipped a plastic badge on Bradley, giving him clearance to be in the area, then clapped him on the shoulder. "You see anything that seems off, I want to hear about it pronto." Giving him a shove, Mitchell drifted toward two Air Force captains who were peering into the tail section.

Bradley walked toward the nose of the plane. The cabin fire wall had peeled back and lay almost flat. He started to climb up into the wreckage, but someone shouted at him. "Get the hell out of there, buddy."

Bradley turned to see who yelled and spotted two Air Force officers rushing toward him. One of them tripped over a piece of wreckage, landed on his knees and skidded a couple of feet. His companion looked back but never broke stride.

Bradley stayed where he was, with one foot on a blackened sheet of steel, the other still on the ground.

The Air Force captain reached out to grab him by the shoulder, but Bradley knocked his hand away.

"You ought to be more polite, Captain."

"Polite, my ass. You get—" He stopped when he saw the credentials dangling from Bradley's jacket. "Oh..."

"That'll do, Captain."

"Sorry, I thought—"

"Forget it."

The second officer, a major, limped up, shaking the mud from his uniform pants. "You better have a good explanation, buddy."

Bradley flicked the plastic with a fingernail. The major shook his head. "Shit, they let anybody in here, don't they? You know what the hell you're doing, Bradley?"

"Yeah. I just don't know what this is all about."

"Join the club. What we got is one L1011 busted up real bad, eleven bodies and three missing passengers. All they want us to do is tell them what happened—by tomorrow morning. And they're telling us shit."

Bradley surveyed the scene again. "Good luck."

The major shook his head. "It'll take more than luck. It'll take a fuckin' miracle."

Bradley turned back to the cabin, asking, "Whose plane was this, anyhow? It doesn't look like an ordinary L1011."

The major shook his head. "I'm not at liberty to discuss that. Sorry, Bradley. Your people will tell you if they want you to know."

"Funny thing about my people, Major. There ain't too much they want me to know."

The major laughed. "Sounds like the Air Force." He waved, pulled the captain by the sleeve and left Bradley alone to climb into the cabin. But the CIA man had changed his mind. He left the plane to drift across the ground, watching the work crews gathering and tagging evidence.

Next to every work crew was an officer with a sheet of grid paper, plotting the location of each find, referring to stakes driven into the ground and carrying tiny pennants that flapped audibly in the breeze. There was so much debris, spread over so wide an area, that there was no way anyone would have a definitive answer the next morning. Or the next month. The investigation would take months, the report months more. And there would still be dozens of unanswered questions.

That was the way it went. Always. So why was this time different? What was so special about this plane? Or was it the cargo? Or the passengers?

He wanted to see the site from up above. It would give him a better idea. He was no expert, but he had seen enough plane wrecks to know that the pattern of debris distribution could tell him a lot, not only about what had happened, but where and when. He went looking for Dan Mitchell.

One of the uniforms speaking with Mitchell turned sharply and moved away from the cops. "You finished looking around already?"

"I want to go up."

"Up where?"

"I want to see what the site looks like from the air. Can you get me on a chopper?"

Mitchell looked irritated. "I don't know. I mean, it's not really up to me. What do you have to do that for?"

"I don't *have* to, I want to. You brought me out here to look around. I want to look around. But you got to see things from up top. That's the best way to get the big picture."

"I don't know...."

"Then who does know? Who can I talk to?"

Seeing Bradley wasn't going to be put off easily, Mitchell waved a hand. "I'll see what I can do. Just let me finish up here."

"How long?"

"Maybe ten minutes."

Bradley was getting the funny idea that Mitchell didn't really want him to look around all that carefully. But why? Why call him all the way out here and then make him sit on his hands? It didn't make sense.

A half hour later Mitchell found him. He was standing with his hands in his pockets, watching the search helicopters, a couple of miles away now, flying low over some wooded lowland.

"They looking for something special?" Bradley asked.

"Just looking. By the book—that's the way they want to do it."

"I don't think so."

"We're not paid to think, Mike. We're paid to do what we're told. Meet me in my office at eleven-thirty."

"Tonight?"

"You got it."

"Can I bring a friend?"

"This isn't a party, Mike."

"Oh."

"You be there. And you keep your lip zipped tighter than a nun's pussy. You understand me?"

## CHAPTER NINE

James Harkness paced nervously. He kept looking at the door, stopping and listening, then resuming his agitated strut.

"Why don't you sit down, James?"

"Because I can't sit down. For Christ's sake, you ought to be capable of understanding something that simple, don't you think?"

"Ah, the famous Harkness sarcasm. I was wondering when it would rear its ugly head."

"You don't understand the pressure I'm under."

"Maybe you aren't the man for the job."

Harkness whirled. His lips were pulled back to bare his teeth. The other man thought it made Harkness look very much like a baboon. He smiled. "Touched a nerve, did I?"

"It's easy for you. You come and go. You give orders and walk away. I have to be there to see the mess. Then I have to clean it up."

"If you do your job properly, there will be no mess to clean up. Slow and steady wins the race. Haven't you ever heard that expression?"

"Yeah, I've heard it," Harkness barked. "But I was there. I put two bullets in Harold Carmichael's skull. That's messy work, by my definition."

"When will you be finished with your interrogation?"

"How the hell do I know? How the hell do you know when the man has nothing more to tell us?"

"How do you know when the lemon is out of juice? You keep squeezing until it's dry."

"He's an old man. He can't take much more. I don't want to kill him."

"Of course not. But we have to be certain. What we are planning is a very delicate matter. There is no margin for error, absolutely none. You know that as well as I do. We have to be sure."

"I'm doing everything I can, damn it!"

"Are you?"

"Yes." Harkness was suddenly subdued. He collapsed in a chair against the wall. He sat there, tapping the back of his skull against the wall. The dull thump of his head on the Sheetrock echoed in the small room. He ran his fingers through his hair, then shook his head. "Yes, I'm doing everything I can."

"Good. I'm counting on you, James. And I don't mind pointing out that I'm paying you very well for your services. For your alleged expertise."

"Alleged?"

The man opened his arms, palms up. "So far, yes, alleged."

"Look. He gave us Dolph Murray. That was a surprise to you. As far as I'm concerned, you've already gotten your money's worth."

"This isn't piece work, James. This is one single job, and I expect you to see it through to the end. I hope you're not thinking of asking me for more money."

Harkness said nothing. He bumped his head against the hollow partition twice more.

"Are you?"

"No. Don't worry about it. This is only partly about money."

"Oh, I wish I could believe that. The trouble with men like you, James, is that you are all alike. You are so boringly predictable. For all your supposed subtlety of thought, you are as transparent as a pane of glass. It's like looking at a watch with the back off, watching your mind work. I can see all the gears spinning, the little hesitations, the slow, steady advance of the hands. And it is just as predictable. Eleven o'clock always follows ten o'clock. Three o'clock follows two." He paused for a moment, then cleared his throat and added, "And so on."

"You smug son of a bitch. Are you challenging me to surprise you? Is that what you want? You want me to do something so unexpected it will knock your socks off?"

"Of course not."

"Then shut your fat mouth. Stop sticking your nose into my end of things. Don't mess where you don't belong."

"But I *do* belong, James. More than you think. More even than you belong yourself. That's what you don't seem to understand. And that's what you'd better learn."

"Don't threaten me."

"I never threaten, James. That's for school yard bullies. I simply make up my mind what I want done, and then I see that it gets done. You might try to be more like that yourself."

"I'm doing just fine, thank you."

Harkness stood again. He seemed suddenly revitalized, as if the rest had allowed him to tap into a new source of energy. He seemed more confident, more determined. He looked almost happy. The abrupt change in his demeanor went unremarked but not unobserved.

"You know that there is a great deal more we need to know. The summit is all but set. We don't have a great deal of time to root out the flies in our ointment, James. And that is just the beginning."

"Don't worry about it. It'll get done, but it takes time. I can't go in there and stick his balls in a vise and twist until he gives me a name. I need to crosscheck, double-check. I need to verify everything he tells me. We can't just go around blowing away anyone and everyone. It's counterproductive."

"A good word."

"It'll do." Harkness walked to the door. With his hand on the knob, he turned to look over his shoulder. "Unless you have any more insults you'd like to pass along, I better get back to work."

When nothing was said, he yanked the door open and jerked it closed, still keeping his hand on the outside knob to prevent it from slamming. Harkness walked down the long corridor, listening to the echo of his footsteps rapping on the concrete floor.

When Harkness reached the end of the corridor, he turned right and entered a small, dark room. He reached for the light, clicked it on, then stepped in and closed the door behind him. He flopped down behind his desk and reached for the phone. Pressing the intercom button, he waited for the harsh buzzing to die, then heard a click on the other end.

"Ronny?" he said. "What have you got for me?"

"Nothing new. Tough old bird."

"You better come over. We have to talk."

"Be right there."

After a moment there was a rap on his door, and he mumbled, "Come in."

Ronny Hisle opened the door and stepped in. "What's up?"

"They keep turning the screws. They want us to put more pressure on the old man."

"Christ, Jim. I don't know if that's a good idea. Didn't he have a heart attack a few years ago?"

"Yeah, he did. Three years ago."

"Maybe we got all there is to get."

"No. I know that's not true. Murray was a Johnny-come-lately. They've been running agents inside the right wing for forty-five years."

"Maybe, but even so, Marley can only tell us what he knows."

"But we pinched him at the right time. The whole reason for his trip was to get Aspring up to speed. Seems some folks are uneasy about having one Germany. His nibs sent the director out here to gather all the moss he could about who's making waves."

"Maybe we should look up our friends from the other side. They could tell us more, I'll bet."

"I've thought about it."

"What about Mann?"

"What about him?"

"He's got to know it all. Hell, he'd be the one to squeeze if we have to squeeze anybody."

"No way. The man keeps his own counsel. You know that. We try to push him, we'll be pushing daisies instead. You can bank on that."

"Maybe we should take him out."

"I've thought about that, too. Once this beach ball starts rolling, we can't bring it back. If he gets wind of it, and he almost certainly will, we could be in deep shit."

"What do you want to do?"

"I don't know. I don't want to push Marley too hard, but we have to get him to give us something. We need to keep the pressure off."

Hisle shrugged. He'd been through this so many times. It was always the same. The interrogation was one thing, the drugs were another. It was his specialty, but he wasn't sure just how much he trusted chemically induced information.

"I'll see what I can do, Jimmy. But you better figure out what to do about Klaus Mann."

"I'm thinking, I'm thinking. Just let me worry about Mann. In the meantime, get me another name. Get me one I can verify. That'll buy us some time. It'll keep the old man alive, anyhow."

"They'll ice him anyway, you know that."

"No, they won't."

Hisle snorted. "We'll see."

## CHAPTER TEN

Giuseppe Badalamente enjoyed the good life. Technically he was royalty, but royalty wasn't something that cut any ice in Italy anymore. That didn't stop him from surrounding himself with the trappings of his lineage, which he traced back to the sixteenth century. The family estate, which was nearly ten thousand acres in the hills south of Naples, made him one of the largest landowners in Italy. His position as chairman of the board of Italtec made him one of the wealthiest.

All that wasn't enough for Badalamente. But things would get better; he was sure of that. The conference had hinted at changes to come, and soon.

But there were things that had to be done first. Important things. Things that could only be entrusted to a man of his station. And that, after all, was what mattered most. Money was important, but station was something that money couldn't buy. He knew where he belonged. He also knew where others belonged. He could tell just by the way a man wore a hat, by the state of his fingernails, even by his choice of words, whether he was the right sort of person. Don Giuseppe's sort of person.

His son was another matter. Giovanni was spoiled.
He had too much money and not enough sense of
himself to know what to do with it. Giovanni didn't
understand that money didn't buy respect. Respect
was something that had to be earned. Even at the
conference, it had been obvious that the others didn't
respect Giovanni. The boy was arrogant, and he
was a troublemaker. What bothered Don Giuseppe,
though, wasn't the idea of trouble, but the kind. And
that's where he had his quarrel with Giovanni.

Now, sitting on the veranda, the wide sweep of the
blue-green Mediterranean dwindling away toward a
hint of Africa, he wondered what he was going to do
with the boy. How could he pull him back from the
edge? What could he tell him? Nothing. It was too
late for that. It made him feel sad, but it was a distant sadness, the way Africa was distant; there, but
almost not.

The sun was high. It was nearly noon, and Giovanni was already late. Don Giuseppe looked down
at his body, still hard, but not as hard as he thought
it should be. He was nearing seventy. He didn't have
that much time to pull Giovanni back from the
brink, assuming he had any at all, but that wasn't up
to him.

The boy was arrogant, and he was headstrong.
Don Giuseppe looked toward the sliding glass doors
that led onto the veranda. Rosa was there, her uniform crisp and stiff with starch. She was getting old,
too. She had been with the family long enough to

earn his grudging respect. He nodded, and she stepped out into the sunshine.

"Where is Giovanni? Is he up yet?"

"Not yet, Don Giuseppe."

"We were supposed to have breakfast at ten-thirty."

"I'll go call him, Don Giuseppe."

He nodded, then stood and walked to the edge of the veranda. He leaned both hands on the marble railing and looked down into the garden. Giovanni's Ferrari was parked half in the circular driveway and half on the neatly manicured lawn. The Cadillac was where it was supposed to be, but the top was down. Little pools of water still glittered on the back seat, remnants of last night's rain. He shook his head sadly.

Discipline. The boy had no discipline. That was what was missing. And he didn't know how to change that. For thirty-two years he had tried, and he was no closer now than when Giovanni was a boy. Hell, he was still a boy, and that was his problem. He liked to play at everything he did. He played with his cars, he played with his women, he played tennis for fun instead of to win.

Games. The fundamental problem was that Giovanni didn't seem to understand there were some things you played to win or you didn't play at all. Like politics. He had caused nothing but trouble at the conference. He had been asked to leave and had made a scene.

"It's a beautiful day, Papa."

Giuseppe turned sharply. He hadn't heard the footsteps behind him. His son was wearing swim trunks. So handsome. Too handsome, Don Giuseppe thought. A goddamn playboy, that's all he was, and that was because he was too handsome for his own good. He looked like his mother, God rest her soul. He took after her in almost everything. But Carmela had had discipline. She had known the rules, which lines to cross, which to respect. Giovanni knew those same lines, but unlike Carmela, he didn't give a damn. He acted as if they weren't there, or, worse yet, sometimes called attention to the act of crossing them. And flipped you a fig for your troubles.

"Sit down, Giovanni. You're late."

"I was tired, Papa."

"And drunk."

"Not really."

"Enough, though. I saw where you left the car."

Giovanni walked to the rail and looked down. He laughed and turned back to his father, an impish grin distorted somewhat because he was squinting into the sun. "It's only grass, Papa. Nothing will happen to it. Not like the time I parked in the garden."

"No," Don Giuseppe said, "not like the time you parked in the garden. Or the time you parked in the swimming pool. Or the time you—"

Giovanni laughed and raised both hands. "All right, Papa. I know I'm not the world's best driver. But I'm not the world's worst driver, either."

"And that you settle for, Giovanni? Is that all you care to do with your life, walk down the middle somewhere, settle for mediocrity?"

"It's easier that way, Papa."

"Then why do you go out of your way to look for trouble? That isn't easier, is it?"

"What, are you still grousing about the conference? It was a joke. I didn't know they would be so upset."

Don Giuseppe sighed and walked to the table. He sat in his chair, folded the newspaper he had been unable to read and tucked it under the chair. He nodded toward the second place setting. Giovanni walked toward the table. He started to say something, but when he saw the look on his father's face, he changed his mind and sat down meekly.

Rosa was in the doorway again, close enough to attend to Don Giuseppe, but far enough away that she wouldn't be an intrusion. Another sign of respect, of discipline. He nodded sharply, and Rosa disappeared. Leaning back in his chair, the old man sighed again.

"I must tell you, those are very serious men you have offended. They weren't happy with you. They weren't happy with me, either. And that was because of you. Sometimes I think your sole purpose in life is to make me uncomfortable."

"Oh, come on. They were windbags."

"They are serious men."

"You live in a greenhouse, Papa. You're protected from everything. You don't understand anything about the world except the little tiny piece you allow yourself to see. Life is more complicated than that. The world is so big. You should get out more."

"It doesn't have to be."

"But it does."

"You will not understand, will you, Giovanni? You have never wanted to understand."

Rosa appeared in the doorway again, a silver tray in hand. She looked for the nod, received it and approached the table. She set two coffee cups on their saucers and poured coffee for both men. From a small silver bowl on the table, she took one lump of sugar with a pair of silver tongs and dropped it into Don Giuseppe's cup.

She reached for another, but Giovanni covered the bowl with his hand. "I'll get my own, Rosa. Thank you." With his fingers he snatched up four lumps and dropped them into the cup, sloshing coffee over its sides and down into the saucer.

Rosa withdrew.

"Too much sugar, Giovanni."

"I have a sweet tooth."

"You have no discipline."

"Discipline is overrated, Papa."

"Things will be different soon. You were there. You know what is coming."

Giovanni smiled. "Yes, I know what is coming."

"No, I don't think you do."

"Don't be disappointed if your brave new world doesn't come anytime soon, Papa."

"It will, Giovanni. Nothing will prevent it. Nothing." He looked sadly at his son. "Nothing."

"Why so gloomy? It's a beautiful day. I'm going for a sail. Why don't you come along?"

"I have business."

"You promised. Besides, you always have business, Papa."

"It's what I do. Some other time, Giovanni."

Giovanni took a sip of his coffee. "No, what you do is plan other people's lives for them. That's just a little arrogant, don't you think?"

"Someone has to plan them."

"And you think it's your right, do you?"

"Not a right, no. A responsibility, Giovanni. Something you know nothing about."

Rosa was back again, with a second tray. She got the nod and came forward to set the tray on the table.

"Sailing, you say?" Don Giuseppe asked.

Giovanni nodded. He looked at the food, but wasn't hungry. "In fact, Papa, I think I'll go now. I don't feel like eating just yet."

Don Giuseppe nodded. As his son stood and walked into the house, he walked to the railing and looked down. A moment later Giovanni appeared, still dressed in his swim trunks, a shirt and canvas bag dangling from one hand. He climbed gracefully into the Ferrari, waved up at his father through the windshield and backed away, taking care to get the car off the grass as soon as possible.

A good boy, for all his crazy ways, Don Giuseppe thought. He watched the car as it headed down the driveway. Far below, Giovanni's little Sunfish bobbed on the water, a bright yellow speck. Don Giuseppe watched the car all the way to the dock. Sunlight flashed on a window as Giovanni got out.

The phone rang, and Don Giuseppe almost didn't hear it. On the third ring he was back at the table and picked it up, holding it absently to his ear.

"Hello?" He was still looking toward the small harbor, but the railing blocked his view. He turned to look at the olive trees to the right of the veranda. "Yes, he's just left. Sailing, yes."

He put the phone down and walked back to the railing. He saw the sail go up on the Sunfish. There was a stiff breeze, a hot wind sweeping across the water and kicking up small whitecaps. The boat was just a dot now on the blue-green water, and the sail looked like a tiny piece of paper caught in a wind.

And then a blinding flash obscured both boat and sail. It took a while for the sound, like the distant clap of huge hands, to reach him. And there was nothing but smoke.

"Too many games, Giovanni. No discipline." Don Giuseppe reached for his eyes as if to wipe away a tear. But there was no tear. His eyes were dry.

## CHAPTER ELEVEN

Munich was quiet. The streets were shiny with rain as Bolan rolled through the broad avenues, the Volvo cruising easily over the hissing pavement.

Mike Bradley had an apartment on the western edge of the city, and Bolan wanted to get there by nine o'clock. He was convinced the key to what was happening lay somewhere within the contents of the briefcase, maybe even laid out clearly on the map, if only he knew how to read it.

There was a small parking lot, bordered with neatly trimmed hedge, to one side of Bradley's building. He coasted the Volvo across the lot and rolled against the cast concrete bumpers, its tires bouncing back a few inches before he put on the brakes.

Bolan sat there a couple of minutes, looking up at the building. He wasn't entirely sure he trusted Bradley, but things had taken a dramatic turn during his four days in Europe. Not only had Dolph Murray—who was the reason he had come to Germany in the first place—been shot to death in front of his eyes, but now he knew Murray wasn't what he had appeared to be.

Or so Mike Bradley had told him. It wasn't that hard to believe. Stranger things had happened.

The Executioner got out of the car and leaned back in for the briefcase. It happened quickly. The window of the driver's door blew out, and he heard the shower of broken glass as it cascaded onto the hood and the dash. Bolan rammed into the front seat just as a second burst of silenced fire rattled through the Volvo, taking out both windows on the passenger side.

He reached for the MAC-10, dragged it out from under the seat and slipped the safety off as the car lurched to one side as both passenger-side tires blew.

The warrior backed out of the car, knowing it didn't offer him enough cover. Whatever the hell was being fired at him, the slugs would have no trouble punching through the car doors, even those of the heavy Volvo.

He'd have to leave the briefcase, he thought, sprinting toward the hedge. It was almost five feet high, and he launched himself in the air as he crossed the curb and stepped onto the broad grass border on the far side of a narrow walk.

He cleared the hedge but barreled heavily into a stack of empty trash cans on the far side. Getting to his feet, he raced along the back of the hedge until he reached the corner, then turned it in time to see two men racing for a small car parked across the street from the parking lot.

The door opened in the back, and both gunmen piled in as Bolan took aim with the subgun. He laced the side of the car, the slugs tearing through the bodywork as the vehicle lurched into gear.

Bolan fired another burst as the car fishtailed on the wet pavement and tried to hang a right. The MAC-10 ran dry as Bolan broke into a run. At the same moment the small car veered left and jumped a curb. It plowed through a news kiosk, scattering newspapers and magazines, then bounced off a brick wall, scattering sparks as it scraped down along the front of the building until it reached an archway jutting out over the building entrance. The car stopped, bounced back, then slammed again into the stone abutment.

Bolan was already across the street, and he could hear the whine of the engine as the driver's foot stayed pressed against the accelerator. The rear door flew open, and two men tumbled into the street.

The gunners scrambled to their feet and broke into a dead run. Bolan was on their tails, his Beretta ready, set for a triburst. The men raced down the street, their pounding feet echoing off building walls on either side.

They splattered through a rain puddle, breaking the reflection of a streetlamp into a thousand splinters, then swung left and into an alley. Bolan skidded to a halt. He ducked low and stuck his head out for a second, then jerked it back. A storm of lead clawed at the bricks waist high as one of the gunmen cut loose.

Bolan knew he couldn't get across the broad mouth without getting cut in two. He glanced up, but there was no way to climb the front of the building. It was a smooth-skinned modern affair with no fire escape.

He reached behind him, grabbed the lid of a garbage can and held it out for a split second. Once more a spatter of deadly hail blew down the alley. Several slugs ripped at the lid and tore it from his fingers. One of the gunmen, at least, was still there.

Bolan backed away from the alley and tried the front of the building. The main door was open, and he found the fire stairs with no trouble. Pounding up the steps two at a time, he took the eight flights to the roof, knowing that he risked losing the gunmen altogether. But it was the only way.

He unbolted the door to the roof and dashed out onto the gravel-covered asphalt. A low wall edged the building, and he sprinted across the roof, his feet crunching on the gravel. At the wall he moved toward the rear of the building, unwilling to lean over until he was behind the gunmen. He wasn't sure exactly where they had holed up, but the back of the alley seemed like a good bet.

At the corner Bolan peered down into the alley. Filled with blocks of light from several windows, it looked like a bizarre checkerboard, long and narrow, with bands of light and dark in a single tier. He couldn't see anyone in the shadows below.

A second alley, perpendicular to the first, cut behind the building, separating it from a lower structure, nearly fifteen feet away. With a skeptical eye Bolan judged the chasm. It was too far for a standing broad jump, but if he got a running start, he should be able to make it. It was a matter of timing.

He backed up and broke into a sprint. Getting one foot on top of the small wall, he launched himself out and down. The arc of his flight carried him well past the edge of the lower building, and he landed with a thud that echoed off the wall of the building he'd just left.

There was a shout in the alley below, and he bounced to his feet and back to the wall in time to see one of the gunmen racing back toward the street. The warrior squeezed off a 3-round burst and saw the runner stagger, then veer toward a stone wall and claw at it with his hands as he slid slowly to the ground.

Another burst from the silenced subgun clawed its way up from below, tearing chunks out of the old brick in front of Bolan. More footsteps pounded away as the second gunman raced to the corner. A moment later he barreled around the edge of the building and disappeared.

Remembering the briefcase, Bolan looked around hurriedly, needing some way down. He found the fire door, set in a low cupola, and jerked it open.

Pounding down the stairs, he could hear the thunder of his footsteps in the narrow stairwell above him. He hit the ground floor running and raced across the tiled lobby and into the street.

The gunman was nowhere to be seen. A block away the ruined car, on fire now, was surrounded by a circle of curious onlookers. In the distance he could hear the rise and fall of a wailing siren and the clang of a bell. He ran to the small knot of onlookers, pushed his way through and saw that the driver was gone.

Racing back to his car, he kept the Beretta in his pocket, his fingers curled around the grip. As he approached the shattered Volvo, a shadow moved against the hedge.

"Pollock, is that you?" a voice hissed. It had to be Bradley. He was the only person in Germany who knew Bolan by that cover name.

"Yeah."

"What the hell's going on?"

Bolan stepped in close, then tucked the Beretta up under Bradley's chin. "Maybe you better tell me."

"Hey—"

"I was just on my way to see you, Mike. Only somebody was waiting for me. Somebody who didn't want me to see you. Somebody who didn't want me to walk away from this." He jerked a hand toward the Volvo. "Now, suppose we take a little walk."

"Where?"

"I have something I want to show you."

"Sure. Just put that damn gun away. I don't blame you for being pissed off. I would be, too, if somebody tried to kill me, but I had nothing to do with it."

Bolan nodded and backed away a couple of steps. "There's something I have to get first."

"The briefcase?"

"How did you—?"

"I looked in the car. It was obvious what happened. I stuck it in the hedge."

"Get it."

Bradley nodded. He moved toward the hedge and reached down with one arm, his face toward Bolan and the other hand held high.

"Go easy."

The CIA man backed away from the hedge a step, then raised the briefcase over his head. With both hands held up, he stepped across the grass and down off the curb.

"All right, put your hands down. Stay two steps ahead of me and walk up the street toward the commotion. I'll have a gun on your back."

Bradley didn't seem frightened and, strangely, he didn't seem angry, either. "You're the boss."

Bolan tensed as the agent moved past, then fell in behind him. Bradley let the briefcase swing a bit, in a natural stride. The casual observer would never have guessed he was two yards away from instant death if he made a wrong move or a sudden stop.

The fire engine roared up the street and swept past them with its siren grinding down. The bell still clanged, and the din was deafening. The crowd backed away, letting the fire brigade get to work. They used foam from a small tank and smothered the burning wreck.

"Your handiwork?" Bradley asked, turning to toss the question over his shoulder.

Bolan didn't answer.

"I thought so."

They moved past the burning car, keeping to the far side of the street. When they reached the end of the block, Bolan told Bradley to cross the street.

On the far walk, Bolan said, "Left, into the alley."

Bradley hesitated. He looked back again, and the warrior could read the question in his features.

"No, I'm not going to kill you. Unless you leave me no choice."

Halfway down the alley, half in and half out of a block of light, the body of the gunman was slumped against the base of the wall. Bradley whistled. He stopped in his tracks, looked back to see if anyone was watching him, then knelt beside the still form. He rolled the man onto his back. This time he didn't whistle. "Good God! Tony Merchant!"

"Don't tell me."

Bradley nodded. "One of ours."

## CHAPTER TWELVE

Bolan sat in the back seat, the briefcase on the floor beside him. Bradley was in the front, driving with one eye on the road and one on Bolan in the back seat.

"Look, Pollock," Bradley said, "I know you're not too sure you can trust me right now, but you're going to have to make a choice. You want to cut loose, go out on your own, you go ahead, but don't expect me to stay out of your way. I can't walk away from this. There's something going on that I can't get a handle on, but I can tell you I don't like it one damn bit. I'm supposed to be at a briefing in a couple of hours. When I'm not there, there's going to be some trouble."

"Briefing on what?"

"Some plane went down up north in the middle of a barley field."

"What kind of plane?"

"An L1011. Don't ask me any more questions, because I can't answer them."

"Can't or won't?"

Bradley heaved a sigh. "Both, really, but the truth is, I don't really know anything, so I couldn't answer you even if I wanted to. I just know there's something off kilter somehow. They never called me in for a plane wreck before. But I know they must have a damn good reason. There must have been something or someone pretty important on that plane."

"Call in when we get where we're going."

"Right. You're going to let me make a phone call?"

"Look, Mike. Put yourself in my shoes. I show up at your place, and there's a hit team ready and waiting. What was I supposed to think?"

"Hell, I don't know. But you know, they could have been waiting for me to come out, too."

"Why would they be waiting for you?"

"I don't know. But you don't know why they were waiting for you, either, do you?"

"I guess I must have rattled somebody's cage."

"Yeah, maybe. But I think there's more to it than that. And I don't like what's been happening. First Murray gets wasted. Then the attack on the airport. You said you were sure those guys were U.S. issue. Then Badalamente goes down. That's two of our agents in two days. And tonight you take down Tony Merchant. He's after you for sure, and maybe for me, maybe for both of us. You see what I'm saying? You see a pattern, or what?"

"Not exactly a pattern, but there sure as hell is a strong set of connections to the CIA. I'll grant you that. But they're your people. You tell me what's going on."

"I wish to God I could. But I can't. I'm starting to worry about my own scalp, though. That's why I think I have to go under for a couple of days. I'll call Dan Mitchell, tell him what happened, and tell him I'll check in when I think the heat's off."

"Will he buy that?"

"Why not?"

"Suppose he's behind it? You'll be telling him what he wants to know."

"But we'll be ready. And if they make a move, then we'll have a pretty good idea he's in on it."

"Or that your communications are compromised."

"Hey, Pollock, it's not a perfect world. I can only do what I can do. And what I can do now is get us off the street someplace reasonably safe. The rest we got to do on our own. We're big boys, and I think we should be able to handle it."

Bolan was almost convinced. But not quite. He didn't say anything, and Bradley didn't push it. He paid attention to the road. Bolan could hear the hissing tires on the rain-slick pavement, and the lights of the city gradually thinned and finally disappeared as the car Bradley had rented to replace his ruined Buick drifted into the rich farmland to the east of Munich.

They were going to a safe house, one Bradley was certain would be secure, even if there was a leak. He wouldn't tell Bolan why, but swore that there was no way Tony Merchant's boss, whoever he might be, could know about it.

Out the window Bolan watched the night, then looked at the windshield, where he could see a reflection of Mike Bradley's face, tinted green by the dash lights.

He was trying to put the pieces together, but he didn't have enough of them to make a coherent picture. They drove for just under two hours, the country getting higher, the barley and wheat fields slowly giving way to forest. There was a brooding kind of beauty, even in the pitch blackness, but Bolan couldn't allow himself to be seduced by it. He stared through his window into the darkness, still watching Bradley but beginning to relax a little.

The kid was right, in a way. He hadn't done anything the least bit suspicious. But there was still a set of coincidences to be explained. He kept thinking back to the Volvo, the two blond giants, both obviously Germans, and the sunken-faced man with the mustache. He had been an American. Everywhere Bolan looked, there was an American connection, even when Bradley couldn't have been remotely involved.

Why?

They were pulling into a winding lane, the last leg of the trip, before Bolan realized that was the only question that really mattered. It was the centerpiece of an elaborate tableau. If he could answer it, he'd be well on his way to unraveling the whole tapestry. All he had to do was to keep picking at the stray strands, find the one thread that held it all together and give it a good, hard tug. But to do that, he had to stay alive. For that he just might need Mike Bradley.

The house was deserted and all but invisible in the darkness. Bradley got out of the car, Bolan right behind him. The big guy had the briefcase in one hand, his Beretta in the other.

Bradley stopped and leaned close. "You mind giving me my piece? I don't think there's anything to worry about, but if all hell breaks loose, I don't want to have to start throwing stones to stay alive."

Bolan set down the briefcase, reached into his jacket pocket and pulled Bradley's Browning free. He handed the automatic back, then tossed the clip. The agent snatched it out of the air and rammed it home. Taking the safety off, he worked the slide and nodded. "That feels a lot better."

"Lead the way," Bolan said. They made a circuit of the house to satisfy themselves the place was as deserted as it appeared to be.

Once inside, Bradley led the way to the basement stairs, stepped in and turned on the light. When Bolan stepped through, he pulled the door closed, nodding in appreciation when the heavy steel-plated door banged shut. He threw three heavy bolts, then dropped a steel bar in place.

"You going to call Mitchell?"

"I've thought about that and I've decided not to. Maybe we better take a look at your little package. The more I know, the better I'll feel."

"How tight are you wired in?" Bolan asked.

"That's my favorite question. Since Casey, we've been looking more and more like a nautilus. Every chamber has a bulkhead. I'm not sure how many chambers there are, and I don't know who knows what's in them all, if anybody does."

"Too many secrets. Good way to shoot yourself in the foot."

"Tony Merchant never shot anybody in the foot. Not even by accident. He was the number-one ice man. In the old days, before I came on board, there was a little thing called Executive Action. It was an assassination group, only heads of state. It was turned up by some commission investigators in the mid-seventies, supposed to have been disbanded. Now I'm not so sure."

"Why not?"

"Because Tony Merchant was the leader of the band. I didn't even know he was still on board."

"Maybe he's not. Maybe he was free-lancing."

"That's possible," Bradley admitted. "But somehow I don't think so. He was a true believer. He ate, breathed and slept Company manners. If he was after you or me, then somebody in-house sent him. That doesn't mean it was a policy decision, because there are as many private agendas as there are agents. At least, that's how it feels sometimes. Every once in a while, it would get to be too much, and I'd want to bail out. But there's no golden parachute for a peon like yours truly."

"Let's take a look at the papers," Bolan suggested.

He walked across the low-ceilinged room and set the case on a table. Popping the catches, he lifted the lid, leaned forward to blow more of the plaster dust out of the case and pulled the map out. He opened it carefully, hoping the pins stayed in place. All but two of them were still there, pressed flat, but with their points still embedded in the heavy paper.

The remaining two pins slipped to one side. Bolan leaned close to see if he could tell where the pins had been, but there were more than a dozen holes in the map, any two of which might have been the site of the stray pins.

Bradley leaned over Bolan's shoulder. "A map of the continent. Standard issue. You could buy this in any bookstore or travel store."

"The pins mean something," Bolan said. "I just don't know what."

"Let's start with what we know."

"Well, it looks to me like this pin—" Bolan indicated one of the green-headed map tacks "—is pretty close to where Dolph Murray got hit."

"It is. But what about the others?"

"Well, there's no pin at Munich airport, but there *is* a hole. One of the loose pins could have come from there."

"This one must be Giovanni Badalamente," Bradley said, his voice climbing half an octave with excitement. Another green pin stabbed into the boot of Italy, near Naples.

"Okay, that's three," Bolan said. "But these others don't mean anything to me. How about you?"

Bradley sat on a chair and stared at the map for a long time. He touched each pin with the tip of a finger, moving back and forth among them all, as if trying to decide which one to pluck.

"I can't be sure," he said finally. "But this one is awful close to where that L1011 went down."

"You sure?"

"Almost. But that's it. I draw a blank on the others."

"Okay, let's come at it from another angle."

"What other angle is there?"

"The pins are two different colors. The things we know happened are all the same color. Maybe it means something."

"Like what?"

"Maybe one color represents things that have already happened, the other things that will happen, that are planned to happen."

"No way to tell."

"Not without more data, no. And there's one more possibility. Whoever made this map could have been planning these things or he could have been tracking them. It could be a game plan or it could be just the opposite, tracking events and looking for a pattern. We won't know that until we get more information.''

"I think I know just the place to get it," Bradley said.

"Can you trust the source?"

"Do we have a choice?"

Bolan knew the kid was right. He didn't hesitate. "Set it up."

JASON MARLEY FELT the fog lift again. It moved slowly, swirling around him as if he were wreathed in it, prostrate on the prow of a rudderless ship. It didn't disorient him now. He knew to expect it, knew that James Harkness would be somewhere in the fog, waiting, that unbearable smirk on his face.

He could hear the voice long before he saw the man. It started as a slow-motion rumble from somewhere deep in the mists and slowly resolved into words, snatches at first, then whole sentences. And always Harkness used the same condescending tone, the way an overbearing adult lords it over a powerless child.

This time was no different.

"So, Jason, you're awake. How do you feel, hmm? A little rocky? A little disoriented, are we?"

"Go to hell."

"Oh, I suppose I will, Jason, I suppose I will. But that isn't for you to decide. Or me, either. That is for a higher authority than the director of the Central Intelligence Agency, or is there no higher authority for you? Is that it, Jason? Are you God? Are you the man who makes all the rules?''

Marley struggled to sit up, his slack muscles resisting the effort not with pain but with an incredible inertia, bone deep and insurmountable. It didn't hurt to make the struggle. There was no pain. But it hurt to fail. It hurt to want to do something you couldn't do because your body refused to let you. Marley found himself thinking of aging athletes, a halfback who is a step too slow, unable to hit the hole before it closes, a power hitter whose swing is just a hair behind the fastball. It made him sad for them, and for himself. It seemed strange to look at things from such a perspective, he thought, but maybe it was the only way to deal with his circumstances. Trivialize them to make them manageable.

He tried to glare at Harkness, to arrange his features into that foreboding mask his subordinates had learned to dread. But he couldn't pull it off. He felt the flesh sagging on his face like melting wax, refusing to accept any shape, pulled down by gravity.

Harkness arranged his long limbs carefully on the wooden chair, draping one heronlike leg over the other, then adjusting the razor crease in his pants. ''We have a lot to talk about, Jason. I hope you're up for a marathon session.''

Behind Harkness the specter of Ronny Hisle floated in and out of Marley's field of vision. The chemist, as Marley had started to think of him, was as impassive as a robot, his face flat and expressionless, his eyes two black pools of deep, dark water.

"Why should I tell you anything, Harkness?"

"Because you have no choice, Jason. None."

"What is this all about?"

"I'm afraid I can't tell you that. If I do, I'll have no choice but to...eliminate you when this is all over. I don't want to do that. Fellow feeling, old times' sake and all that."

"You don't have any choice now, Harkness. I know you well enough to know that you're just marching to the beat of another, much larger drummer. This isn't your brainchild, bastard though it may be. And whoever you're working for will not let me go. I don't think he'll let you go, either. He can't afford it."

"Not everyone thinks in such irrevocable terms, Jason. Not everyone sees the world in only two colors. Not everyone uses people like tissues, tosses them into the trash when he's finished. The man I take my orders from is above that sort of thing. People are resources, to be conserved, to be used cautiously, with respect and the understanding that they aren't easily replaced."

"You think I'll just walk out of here? Are you that obtuse?"

Harkness shrugged. He placed one thin finger alongside his patrician nose, just enough to tilt his head a little to the side. "But, Jason, when you walk out of here, you will return to your job. You will have been compromised, of course, but only a select few people will know that. You, of course, will not want to tell anyone, so you can keep your job. That will make you even more valuable to us. There's an elegance to the plan, you see.''

Marley snorted. Even to his own ears, it sounded feeble. He was putting on a brave face, but it fit rather badly and he knew it.

Harkness smiled distantly. ''You should know that everything you have given us so far has proved to be accurate. Things are going very nicely, actually. And we have you to thank for that.''

''What are you up to, Harkness? What mad scheme is this, that has so completely seduced you? You used to be a good agent, Harkness, one of the best. What happened?''

''You can ask that? You expect me to believe that you don't know?''

''Know what?''

''That you kept me down all these years. I should have your job, Jason. I'm the better man.'' He gestured expansively. ''I mean, look at us . . . which of us is in charge here, Jason, you or me?''

''You're not in charge of anything, Harkness. You're being played for a fool, you're being used and you're going to be thrown away like the tissue paper you mentioned. You can count on that.''

Marley tried to sit up to look Harkness square in the face, but his body refused to cooperate. He rolled his head back and forth, a slow-motion parody of frustration. Harkness sat there watching, a tiny hint of contempt creeping into the corners of his thin-lipped mouth.

"You're an old man, Jason, too old for the work. You can't cut it anymore. You should never have taken the job."

"What should I have done? Let you have it, let you run the Agency into the ground with your schemes and pipe dreams?"

"The world is changing, Jason. You're too rigid, too set in your ways. You can't see past this afternoon, and I'm looking into the next century. Your vision has failed you, Jason, failed the country."

Marley spit, but it was little more than drool trickling down his chin. "You're a disgrace, Harkness. If I could get up, I'd wring your goddamn neck for you."

Harkness smiled again. "Enough of personalities, Jason. You must tell me more about Trojan Horse." He turned to Ronny Hisle and nodded.

Marley saw the hypodermic and gnawed at his lower lip. He watched as Hisle approached him.

Gently, almost compassionately, he took Marley's arm and turned it, placed it on the cot and slid the needle in. Marley watched the plunger slide, the gradual disappearance of the pale amber fluid in the syringe and, finally, the needle being withdrawn.

A ball of cotton materialized, and Hisle pressed it on the puncture. He straightened, and Marley felt the weariness start to wash over him like cresting breakers as the drug coursed through his veins. Marley knew what was happening, but he was unable to resist and, after a few minutes, was no longer aware that he ought to resist.

Harkness pulled his chair closer. Marley could hear everything very clearly. The wooden legs of the chair scraped on the floor. The joints of the chair creaked, Harkness's knee cracked as he bent it. Even the hiss of his tweed sleeve against the pocket flap of his jacket came through loud and clear.

"You've been very helpful, Jason, truly. But we need more help. I know you want to help us, I know you *can* help us. Names, Jason, I need more names."

The voice was so persuasive, so soothing. There was no hint of a threat. Marley was only dimly aware that his senses were distorted by the drug, but his defenses were down. Harkness was no threat. Harkness could be trusted. But somewhere deep inside him, Marley could hear a tiny voice crying out in alarm, warning him to be careful, that something wasn't right.

He tried to listen to that voice, but it kept getting drowned out by the thundering voice of Harkness, front and center in his diminished consciousness. He tried to push the words aside to hear that small, frail thing, so far away, so fragile, like an insect, its voice tinny, raspy, like the legs of a cricket scraping against one another.

But it was too hard to hear. And then it was gone.

He was answering the questions. Slowly they would form in his mind. He could see each one as it dripped into his mind like a fluid. It crystallized there, hanging suspended in front of his intelligence like an object. He could walk up to it, feel it with his fingers, even walk around behind it, see it from every angle. He felt like a man in an art museum trying to make up his mind about a piece of sculpture.

But always he would know the truth of the thing, and he would walk away from it and tell Harkness exactly what he wanted to know. Then the next question would come, and the next, and the next.

Marley tried to hang on to some objectivity, to keep the questions in his mind so he could compare one to another, try to piece together a pattern. But each one slipped away as the next began to materialize. There was a pattern; he knew that. Even in his drugged haze he could sense that Harkness was looking for specific things, but he couldn't guess what or why.

It lasted an eternity. Then no more questions appeared, and he knew it was over for this time. He lay there suspended somewhere between awake and a dream. He floated. He could feel nothing under him. His body seemed to have no weight at all. He tried to feel the inside of his mouth with his tongue, but everything was dormant, every nerve seemed to have fallen asleep.

Then, as it always did, the darkness would come and would drift and drift and drift.

## CHAPTER THIRTEEN

Berlin at night seemed as if it was waiting for something to happen. Bolan had been here before, but the world was different then. And no city on the planet reflected that difference more precisely than Berlin. The Wall was gone. The artificial barriers had all been disassembled. It was still possible to see where the ugly wall had been. The ground bore scars, not permanent, but certainly long-lived, and the people bore them, too.

In the old days the city had worn a look of perpetual expectation. Something would happen, maybe soon, maybe not. And only the most optimistic souls permitted themselves to believe that whatever did happen would be something positive, something good.

The people were different now, too. The night people, who had drifted through the tension-filled streets with one furtive eye permanently fixed over a nervous shoulder, now had a more relaxed stride. There was a spring to their steps, and their faces no longer looked as if they had been carved from stone.

But the city still had its dark side, and Bolan was heading into its heart. As he rolled past the former site of the infamous Checkpoint Charlie, he could see the difference between East and West Berlin as clearly as if the Wall still stood. The East hadn't had the benefit of Bonn's affluence, its burgeoning economy, its industrial resurgence. It had fared better than other parts of the Eastern Bloc, but its Western cousin had left it far behind.

To the east, ruined buildings could still be seen. Bolan thought of pictures he'd seen of Dresden after the firebombing, of Berlin in late 1945. Parts of walls, the broken ends of their bricks now less angular with nearly fifty years of weather to smooth them out, still stood in some quarters. It looked as if someone had frozen the place in time as a reminder of just how brutal modern warfare could be.

That war was over, and the colder one that had taken its place was supposedly all but over. But Bolan knew better, knew that it wasn't so. A fifty-year-old mind-set couldn't be swept away with the wink of an optimistic eye. There were men in the East, and men in the West, who had been frozen in time even more surely than the ruined blocks of East Berlin.

Such men were out there even now, remembering how it used to be, how it had felt to wield power with a nod of the head, the snap of fingers. That kind of power wasn't given up easily.

Klaus Mann was almost a legend in the West. In the East he was almost a god. He had run an agency outside the official East German Intelligence apparatus, reporting directly to Moscow Center, for more than thirty years. He knew everything there was to know about the East. And a lot more about the West than anyone in London or at Langley wanted to believe. And Bolan needed to know just a little of it.

Mike Bradley had pulled a couple of mysterious strings to arrange the meeting, strings he claimed he couldn't and insisted he wouldn't discuss. The rest was up to Bolan. It hadn't been easy, and the most dangerous part of the trip lay ahead of him.

The eastern sector was dark, and a fine misty rain was falling. In spite of the few streetlights, Bolan found Zimmerstrasse with no trouble. A police patrol rolled past in a jeep, but they paid no attention to the warrior as he slowed and turned into the narrow Heydrichstrasse.

He was in the section of still-ruined buildings just inside the former border. There were some warehouses of recent vintage, but much of this part of East Berlin looked as it had in the aftermath of the war. A solitary streetlight burned far ahead of him as he coasted along with the engine just above idle. He was looking for a clothing warehouse with the sign Kleinmann in blue letters on a white background.

There was nothing ostentatious about commerce in this part of the city, and he nearly missed the sign. He caught a glimpse of it high on a featureless cinder-block wall, braked and backed the car to the beginning of the building. A long, dark alley ran the length of the structure, and he pulled in backward, ready to bolt at the first sign of trouble.

The alley fed into a loading area surrounded by a high fence. Tight coils of razor wire dropped over the top of the cyclone fence like some high-tech ivy. Bolan backed toward the fence and killed the lights, but he left the engine running. Just in case. He had a straight shot toward the street, assuming no one blocked the alley. He didn't like confined spaces, but the message had insisted he be in the shipping yard.

He got out of the car and walked along the fence, looking for another way into the yard. It would be impossible for trucks to negotiate the narrow alley, so there had to be another way in and out. When he found it, it made no difference. A huge gate, itself draped in the shining wire, was held shut by a thick-linked chain at top and bottom. Two massive padlocks held the chain in place, and the poles of the fence on either side of the gate, as well as the gate frame itself, were heavy-gauge stainless-steel pipe.

This was a cul de sac if he ever saw one. He decided not to return to the car. Keeping one ear attuned to the street beyond the fence, he climbed onto the loading dock and checked the single glass door leading to a shipping clerk's office. The door was locked, as he'd expected. So were all the corrugated freight doors. If he had to get into the building in a hurry, he'd have to break the glass on the office door and hope he could get through. He thought about doing it now, to save himself some time, but it might be wired.

At one end of the loading dock, a large truck stood with its tailgate lowered to the level of the dock. The rear of the truck was open, and Bolan ducked inside to wait. He hadn't heard a sound since the police car had passed, and there had been no traffic at all on either of the streets bracketing the warehouse.

He could hear a siren off in the distance, so far away it was impossible to tell whether it was coming toward him or heading away. In the mist and fog the sound was diffused, and direction was all but meaningless.

Then he saw the lights.

They picked out the hood and grille of his rented car as a vehicle turned into the alley and drifted quietly toward the shipping yard. The car rolled to a stop, and Bolan could see the shadows of two men in the front seat. The passenger got out and walked behind the Audi, peering inside, tilting his hat back to get closer to the dark glass. He turned and said something over his shoulder. The driver got out, and the two men stood talking quietly for a moment.

When they started back toward their own car, Bolan left the truck and stepped onto the loading dock. "You looking for me?"

Both men whirled and dug for weapons inside their coats. Ducking behind their car, they stared into the shadows, finally picking Bolan out as he walked toward them along the dock. When they were satisfied that he wasn't about to open fire, they straightened. The passenger took his hat and walked toward the opposite end of the dock. When Bolan was close enough, the passenger said, "Herr Pollock?"

Bolan nodded.

"You startled us." He glanced toward his hip, where Bolan saw the butt of a machine pistol sticking out from the flap of a suit coat.

Bolan took the explanation at face value. It was reasonable enough. "Are you Klaus Mann?" he asked.

"No. Herr Mann wants us to bring you to him."

"He doesn't trust me?"

"Not just you. He doesn't trust anyone. Even me, I think." The man laughed. Bolan noticed that it wasn't forced. The driver was hanging back, and the warrior kept an eye on him. The passenger noticed and shrugged. "Heinrich is not the most sociable of men, Herr Pollock. But he is good at his work, so we put up with him."

"I understand. Do I go with you?"

"That is the best way. The meeting will be in a public place. You can come with us and save some time. Do you know the eastern sector very well?"

"Well enough."

"You can find your way back to your auto, then?"

Bolan nodded.

"Very well. Come with us, then. Gasoline is expensive. No point in wasting it, I think."

The passenger stepped back to give Bolan room to jump from the dock, then led the way to the waiting car. The passenger then asked Bolan to put his hands on the roof of the car. He patted him down, leaving the Beretta and the Desert Eagle undisturbed.

The Executioner was surprised for a moment, then realized they were looking for a radio transmitter or a microphone. Beneath the civility there was a casual professionalism. These guys knew exactly what they were doing.

"I have a briefcase in my car. You'll want to look at it." He waited until they finished the body frisk, then walked to the Audi and got the briefcase. He opened it, and they poked through the contents for a few minutes. The driver swept a hand-held frequency scanner over the case, then up and down Bolan's body. Heinrich shook his head.

When the search had been completed, Heinrich climbed behind the wheel, and the passenger opened the front door and gestured for Bolan to slide in.

"Before we go, we have a couple of, what do you call them, ground rules, I think . . . ?"

"That's what we call them."

"At the rendezvous, before the meeting, in fact, before you get out of the car, I will have to have your weapons."

"No."

"Then there can be no meeting, Herr Pollock. Herr Mann has many enemies. He must be careful."

"I have enemies, too."

"We are not among them. If we wanted to shoot you, we would not go to the trouble to take you away from this place. What would be the point? Why leave you with your weapons now? We are not afraid of you, with them or without them. But we have a responsibility to Herr Mann. I must insist.''

There was a certain logic to the request that the warrior couldn't deny. ''All right. You hold the weapons. But I'll want them back as soon as we finish.''

''Of course.''

''What else?''

''You will have to wear a blindfold to approach Herr Mann's car. You will keep your hands below your shoulders. There will be guns trained on you at all times. If your hands approach the blindfold, whether you intend to remove it or not, you will be shot.''

''Understood.''

''Very well. Heinrich, it is time to go.''

The car backed down the alley at high speed. They sped through the narrow streets over the wet pavement as if it were a race track, the car responding easily and surely to its driver's demands. Fifteen minutes later the car slowed abruptly as they rolled into a broad square.

Bolan could see a Mercedes on the other side of the square, a bulky shadow in the fog. The passenger got out of the car and opened the warrior's door. ''Your weapons, please.''

Both guns were handed over without comment. The passenger pulled a thick silk kerchief from his pocket and moved in behind Bolan to put the blindfold in place. Before tying it, he pointed the Executioner across the square toward the Mercedes. "I'll give you a moment to get your bearings."

Bolan watched Heinrich get out and go to the rear of the car. Opening the trunk, he removed a leather case and quickly removed a sniper rifle with an infrared scope. The French FRF1 was state-of-the-art sniper gear. Bolan whistled softly. "You don't take any chances."

The passenger chuckled. "I am paid very well to be careful, Herr Pollock. And don't make the mistake of thinking Heinrich is the only one who will be watching you."

"I wouldn't think of it." Bolan looked again at the Mercedes. When he was reasonably sure he could negotiate the square, he picked up the briefcase and said, "Let's do it."

"If you start to lose your way, someone will come to guide you. It shouldn't be necessary."

Bolan nodded. The passenger tied the blindfold tightly and gave him a gentle push to start him across the rain-slick square. He could hear the mist sifting past his ears and the occasional splash as he stepped in a shallow puddle.

He tried to guard against the tendency to walk in a circle, visualizing the square in his mind's eye and aiming for the shadowy Mercedes.

He was more than halfway across when a bright flash pierced the blindfold and he felt searing heat on his face. The concussion slammed him backward before it registered. An explosion. He felt himself falling and started to reach for the blindfold when he slammed into the concrete and lost consciousness.

## CHAPTER FOURTEEN

Bolan struggled to break free. He was securely bound, both hand and foot, and something too sharp to be rope was cutting into his wrists. The room was dark, and he could hear nothing.

His head ached and he felt something sticky in his collar, almost certainly blood. He remembered the explosion, but he hadn't been able to see anything but a blinding flash, and that had been muted by the blindfold. But the thunderous roar and its subsequent echo told him something big had happened. Judging by the flash and the direction of the sound, it must have been right in front of him. But he didn't know whether the Mercedes had been hit, whether it had been a near miss, or whether something else had blown.

But whatever it was, he was on the hook. He heard a dull click, and a razor-thin band of light slashed across the floor about a dozen feet away. It was about three feet wide, almost certainly coming in under a door.

At this point his first concern was staying alive. His second was answering the swarm of questions buzzing inside his skull like angry bees. Who was holding him? Had Mann's people taken him because they thought he was responsible for the explosion, or had he been taken by someone else? He kept coming back to Mike Bradley, wondering whether he was in on it or whether this had been another of those curious coincidences for which German soil seemed so fertile.

He heard a dull booming sound, then a series of sharp clicks. Someone had closed a metal door, probably down a long corridor. That same someone was now walking rapidly toward him. He could tell just by the sound of the footsteps that the person was determined, and probably angry.

The warrior expected the door to swing open, but the footsteps veered off and gradually died away. Their last echo had faded when the same distant, echoing boom flooded the air and another set of feet tapped their way toward the door. But they, too, turned left and died away.

Bolan could hear voices now, distant but distinct. A woman and a man, and there was no doubt the woman was angry. They were speaking in German, but Bolan had no trouble understanding the conversation.

"How did this happen, Willi?"

"I don't know, Erika. I saw it but I still don't believe it."

"It is this Pollock's fault. He is the one who is responsible. Kill him."

"He had nothing to do with it, Erika. He couldn't have. I know. I was there. I saw it. Besides, we took every precaution. He was blindfolded when it happened. We searched him for a radio beacon both before and then again when we brought him here. He didn't know where we were going. He couldn't have had anything to do with it."

"Then it is your fault, Willi. You were followed."

"No."

"It must be."

"No. There was no time. It happened so quickly that whoever is responsible must have been in place even before we got there. There is no other possibility."

"But how could that be? Father was always careful, too careful, I used to tell him. You know that. I certainly do. How could anyone have known?"

"That's what I have been asking myself. There is only one explanation possible."

"And what is that?"

"Someone on the inside, someone here, must have betrayed your father."

"Impossible. There is no one who would do that. There is no one new. Everyone has been with us for years. It couldn't be."

"And yet it happened, Erika."

"Yes, it happened."

The voices died away, and another door banged, then came the tapping of high heels. Bolan saw two spikes of shadow dead center in the band of light. He steeled himself for the flood of light when the door was thrown open, but it didn't happen. The shadows stayed in place a moment, then moved away, the heels rapping the floor. Again the woman's voice. "Willi?"

More footsteps. Other shadows broke the band of light. This time a key ground in a heavy lock, and the door swung inward. The surge of light nearly blinded Bolan for a moment. Through slitted eyes he could see the shadowy forms of a man and a woman. When his eyes adjusted, he opened them slowly.

The passenger from earlier in the evening stood there, a quizzical expression on his face. "How's your head, Herr Pollock?"

"It's been better."

"Enough pleasantries," the woman snapped. He could see her clearly now. It was a revelation. Classic German beauty. The strong features and long blond hair framed the bluest eyes he'd seen. She wasn't happy, and she didn't care who knew.

The passenger nodded toward her. "Let me introduce Fräulein Erika Mann."

Neither the woman nor Bolan acknowledged the introduction.

She brushed the man aside. "I'll handle this, Willi. "Why did you want to meet with my father?"

"I needed information. I was told he was the one man who might have it."

"Told by whom?"

"I'm not at liberty to say."

She snorted. "You are not at liberty at all, in case you hadn't noticed."

"I noticed."

"Good. Then answer the question."

"I can't."

"You must."

"Fräulein Mann, you seem to know the nature of your father's business. You have to realize that I can't divulge the name of my source. It was all legitimate. My source made the arrangements, but I don't know how or whether they were intermediaries. Ask your father."

Her composure began to erode for a moment. He noticed the quiver of her lower lip, but it was short-lived. Almost before it registered it was gone.

"I am asking you," she snapped, her voice hard and cold as steel.

"Ask me another question."

"All right, then, tell me what happened."

"I don't know what happened. There was an explosion of some sort, but I didn't see it. I was blindfolded. The concussion punched me to the ground and I hit my head. I was here already when I regained consciousness."

"You are lying."

"No, I'm not. Ask Willi. He was there. He saw what happened. He saw a hell of a lot more than I did, as a matter of fact."

Erika Mann seemed to lose her determination all of a sudden. Her face collapsed, and she turned and ran from the room.

Willi ran after her, but she slammed a door, leaving him to knock and call to her through the panel. "Erika, open up."

The door opened and then closed. Bolan sat there wondering exactly what was going on. It now seemed clear that something had happened to Klaus Mann. What, he didn't know. But if the explosion that had knocked him down from halfway across the square had originated in Mann's car, there was almost no way the man could be alive.

Then he knew it for a certainty that Klaus Mann was dead. He had to be. That was the only thing that made sense, the only thing that explained Bolan's presence here in this bunker. He tried again to free his hands, but they were too tightly bound.

He heard the door again, and a moment later Willi appeared. He carried an ugly knife. He saw the look on Bolan's face and smiled. "Don't worry," he said. "It's just for the rope."

He slipped behind Bolan and slid the blade down between Bolan's wrists. The ropes parted, but the Executioner was unable to move his hands. A thick wire had been wrapped around his wrists and twisted almost to the point of cutting off circulation. There was a sharp click, and the wire parted. Bolan spread his hands, and Willi pulled the heavy wire free.

"What exactly did happen?"

Willi grunted. "I don't know, Herr Pollock. Not precisely. Something, an RPG I think, hit Herr Mann's car. There were no survivors."

"And you have no idea who is responsible?"

"I was hoping you could help. I know we have nothing to exchange now. But Herr Mann was willing to talk to you. I would like to know who killed him. I will take care of the rest."

"I don't know who killed him."

"I understand. But you will let me know if you learn anything that might be useful."

"If I can."

"Again, understood."

"How about you, Willi, do you have any ideas?"

"Too many. Herr Mann was an old man. He had lived a very long time in a very cruel business. He had more enemies than I could count."

Bolan knew how that felt. He had never met the man, but knew his reputation. It was easy to dismiss the attack as an occupational hazard, payback from any of a hundred possible sources. But the Executioner knew better. Mann's death was somehow connected to Murray's, to the conference and perhaps even more directly to Mann's willingness to speak with him.

He rubbed his wrists. "I'll need my weapons, Willi."

"Not here. I will return them when you pick up your car. I will drive you."

"Fräulein Mann agrees with this?"

"Yes. She is angry and she is hurt. But she is very much like her father. She sees things clearly and she thinks with her head, not with her heart. She wants revenge, of course, but not blindly. If you need our help, you will have it."

"Thanks. I just might."

"You will, Herr Pollock. You can be certain of that. You most definitely will."

"Why, Willi? What's going on?"

But the man just shook his head. He was as much in the dark as Bolan himself. "I wish I knew," he finally said. "You will tell Mr. Bradley, of course."

"Then you knew how I made the connection?"

Willi smiled. "I knew. But I also knew you wouldn't reveal it. Or at least, I hoped you wouldn't."

"Why?"

"I am a professional, Herr Pollock. I know another professional when I see him."

## CHAPTER FIFTEEN

As Bolan climbed into the car, Willi handed him the briefcase. "This is yours." The warrior nodded and clicked the latches open. He started to go through the papers, still dusty, and Willi said, "Everything is there."

Bolan finished checking. When he was satisfied all the documents were still in the case, he closed it. "Thank you," he said. Willi nodded and walked around the front of the car as Bolan placed the case in the back seat.

Willi said nothing on the way back to the warehouse. Bolan was content to ride in silence. They had traveled no more than a mile and a half when Bolan noticed the German watching the rearview mirror intently.

"Trouble?"

"Not sure. But maybe."

Bolan turned to look through the rear window. In the fog he could just make out the headlights of a car. It wasn't trying to close on them, but it wasn't falling back, either, as if the driver was afraid of losing sight of them in the swirling mist.

"How long?" Bolan asked.

"Since the beginning. At first I didn't think anything of it. You know how it is, you get behind somebody else in weather like this and you hang on. It's comforting to see a taillight ahead of you."

"So maybe that's all it is."

"I don't think so. I've been making detours, and they're sticking right with us. It's highly unlikely they would take the detour with us, unless..." He trod on the gas suddenly and swerved into the next side street, keeping it floored.

Willi had made a quantum leap in his technique, handling the car like a racing pro. He skidded to a halt, slammed the car into reverse and backed into an alley, killing the lights at the same time.

A moment later a car hurtled past at high speed. "You see?" Willi asked.

Bolan nodded. "Now what?"

"We wait. If we're right, he'll be back. Did you get a good look at the car?"

"Good enough. It was American made, an Oldsmobile. Not too common over here, I'd guess."

"Definitely not."

Far down the street, they heard the abrupt squeal of tires on the slippery pavement. "He's coming back," Willi said.

"What are you going to do?"

"Follow him, of course."

"Can you?"

"Not easily. The fog favors the hunted. But it's worth a try."

The silver Olds roared back, speeding past the alley. Willi counted to five, then raced out of the alley and fell in behind the other vehicle. They could see the taillights up ahead. The driver had slowed a little, obviously looking for them.

Willi kept his lights off and stayed far enough back that all he could see were two ruby holes in the fog.

The Olds hung a right, and Willi goosed it a bit to get to the corner. The lights were smaller now, as if the Olds had sped up. Willi gunned the engine, closing the gap quickly, but the lights vanished.

"He's trying the same thing," Willi said, coasting to a halt. It was dangerous to sit in the middle of the road with no lights, so he nudged the car to the curb, then up and onto the narrow pavement.

Five minutes ticked off, then ten.

"He's gone," Bolan said.

"Just wait. Maybe not."

After fifteen minutes the fog slowly turned pink. "Here he comes, Herr Pollock."

The tail end of the Olds loomed up like an iceberg at sea, the pink fog swirling around it, sometimes obscuring it altogether, sometimes lifting away like a piece of cloth, leaving the taillights flashing off the chrome bumper. Willi threw the car into reverse and started backing up. He backed around the corner and stayed close to the wall of the buildings. When he was far enough down the street to be hidden from the Olds, he let the car coast to a stop.

Bolan wasn't sure whether they had been seen. He asked for his weapons, and Willi nodded. "They're in a canvas bag under your seat."

The Executioner reached under the passenger seat, found the sack and pulled it free. Both guns were inside, wrapped in clean cloths. Bolan slipped the Beretta into its sling and checked to make sure the Desert Eagle was loaded. Stuffing two extra magazines for the Beretta into his jacket pocket, he rolled his window down.

A moment later the Olds backed into the intersection. It was still rolling tentatively, the driver tapping the brakes every couple of feet.

The Olds stopped and its lights went out. The big sedan was just a shadow in the fog now. Bolan heard the muffled click of a door latch. He waited for the telltale interior dome light, but it never came.

"They've seen us," he whispered.

"I don't think so."

"They're being too careful. At least one of them is out of the car."

Bolan reached up and removed the plastic lens over the dome light and twisted the bulb loose. "Anything else light up when the door opens?"

Willi shook his head. "No. What are you going to do?"

"I'm going out there to take a look."

"Be careful."

Bolan nodded. Slowly pulling the door handle, he managed to get it open without making a sound. He moved the door cautiously, guarding against a squeaky hinge, then slipped out of the car. He closed the door but didn't let the latch grab. He used the vehicle for cover and slipped across the street.

The Executioner waited patiently, knowing that if he was right, whoever had gotten out of the Olds would keep to the far side of the street to stay hidden until the last moment. Rolling to his left, Bolan stayed flat, his shoulder up against a brick wall. In the stillness he could hear two engines running and nothing else.

Then, fifteen feet away, he caught a glimpse of a shoe. It vanished immediately, then reappeared, a little closer. Then there were two. Someone was walking on tiptoe. Bolan made sure the Desert Eagle's safety was off and held the .44 up and ready.

The footfalls came closer. He heard a metallic clicking sound, but couldn't be sure what it was. He could see the shape of the man now. He was tall, but his face was obscured.

Bolan kept the Desert Eagle trained dead center. Then he realized what the clicking sound was. The guy was nervous, tapping the side of a ring against the side of the Uzi in his hands. His head swiveled back and forth, but he never looked down. He was too close for the Executioner to move now without being heard.

The man spoke. "I got it. Come on."

Bolan realized that the man was talking into a radio transmitter. He backed away a few steps, and the fog closed over him again. The warrior got to his feet and sprinted along the wall. When he was opposite Willi's car, he stretched out on the ground. He wasn't going to try anything until he knew what he was up against. At this point the odds were manageable, but that could change at any second.

A burst from a 9 mm stuttergun shattered the silence. The slugs went wide of Willi's car, slamming into the wall just ahead of it. Bolan could see the muzzle-flashes, and knew that only one gun was involved. He had no idea how many hardmen were part of the play.

The subgun barked again, and this time Bolan heard the dull ping of bullets ripping through metal. There was no return fire, and he had to wonder whether Willi had been hit. He sighted a foot or so behind the flash and squeezed off a shot.

Bolan heard a grunt as the gunman fell to the pavement. Another Uzi opened up, the 9 mm slugs chewing into the wall above Bolan's head. Chips of brick showered over him. He sighted on the muzzle-flash, shifted his aim a few inches and fired again.

"Christ almighty, where the hell is he?"

The curse was delivered in the unmistakable accent of Philadelphia. The gunners were Americans.

The Uzi ripped again, and Bolan squeezed off another shot. This time he heard a groan, and the Uzi stopped firing. But it didn't clatter to the ground. The warrior couldn't tell whether he'd nailed the second gunman.

Two men suddenly materialized out of the fog. He fired twice and saw one of them go down. The other turned and disappeared into the swirling mist as easily as he had appeared.

A car door slammed, then a single gunshot rang out.

The Executioner got to his feet and raced across the street. But the car was empty. It sat at an odd angle, as if both its left tires had blown. Gasoline pooled on the ground behind the rear fender, and he could hear the steady gushing of more fuel leaking from the vehicle.

"Herr Pollock?"

The voice was nearby, but he couldn't see Willi through the fog. "Here."

"Hurry."

Bolan moved toward the voice, and Willi assumed shape ten feet away. "We'll have to take their car," the German agent told him.

"Who were they?"

"Americans."

"I know that. But who were they affiliated with?"

"I don't know. But I'll find out. Believe me."

# CHAPTER SIXTEEN

Mike Bradley was getting restless. He had wanted to go with Bolan, but the big man said there were more important things that he could do, things that had to be done if they were going to get any closer to understanding who was ripping through the guts of an Agency operation Bradley said was called Trojan Horse.

His mind drifted to Dan Mitchell, and he felt a chill wash down his spine. Mitchell would be pissed, for sure. Just how pissed, he didn't want to think about. He watched the clock in the claustrophobic confines of the safe house. It would be an hour yet before he would make the call. That gave him sixty minutes to plan what he would say. Bolan's instructions had been unequivocal: get whatever you can, but tell him as little as possible, nothing if you can manage it.

But telling Dan Mitchell nothing under the circumstances was worse than waving a red flag at a psychotic bull. His job, if he still had it, would be hell for a long, long time. Mitchell had a memory like an elephant, and a temper as explosive as his memory was long. He wasn't going to be happy to hear from his subordinate, and even more unhappy when he heard that Bradley was going to be unavailable for a day or two.

Mitchell, of course, would demand that his agent come in, tell him face-to-face what was going on, which wouldn't be a pleasant experience. People said Mitchell's temper was like a blowtorch. Men who had come under its scorching assault claimed paint peeled off the walls and paper burst into flame on nearby desks. Bradley had never had the pleasure, but he knew more than one man who had. That man, no longer with the Company, had once told him, "If you get on his shit list, Mikey, run your own ass through a meat grinder. It won't hurt as much."

While he waited, Bradley tried to frame his presentation into some sort of cogent argument. But it sounded feeble to his own ears, and he knew Mitchell wasn't going to buy it no matter how carefully he structured his brief.

He turned then to trying to answer some of the questions Mitchell, and any other rational man for that matter, would ask. But there were no answers. He didn't know who had killed Murray and Badalamente. He had an idea why, but it was just a gut feeling, amusing as a logical toy but utterly without evidence to support it.

When it came to Pollock himself, Bradley realized that he knew virtually nothing about the man. He was impressive, for sure, clearly knew his stuff, and seemed to be as on the level as one could be in his line of work. And he realized with a wry amusement that he didn't even know for sure what that line of work might be.

But the attack on the airport had to be connected. If it was, there was a very strong suggestion of some coherent pattern, some germinating plot that had its roots in the extreme right fringe of European politics. The connection between the murder of Dolph Murray and the missile-wielding crew at Munich airport was undeniable. But where was it all leading?

Not having the answers to such questions put Bradley on extremely shaky ground. Mitchell was good at his job. Like all men good at that kind of work, he was the supreme skeptic. You didn't go to him with hunches. If you had suspicions, a few shreds of support were required. He could go with that, would give you the time to find a few more. But hunches were for detective novels with thin plots, Mitchell liked to say. This was real life, and you had better be prepared to face that fact. But Mitchell hadn't been at the airport, hadn't seen the shreds of bloody meat that used to be Dolph Murray. If their positions were reversed, Bradley wondered, would his attitude be any different? To Mitchell's credit, and Bradley's profound disappointment, the answer was no.

The clock was moving far too slowly for him. Forty-five minutes remained before he'd make the call to Mitchell. He felt like a nautilus in a shell with no exit. The room pressed in on him, and he got up and started to pace. He was beginning to get nervous. Suppose, he thought, Mitchell was in on it. Someone in the Company certainly was. The Munich station was a small one, the main CIA station being in Bonn. But the traitor could be in Berlin, Munich or Frankfurt. It could be anybody, a clerk or a secretary, some middle-level paper pusher, anybody at all. He'd better cover his ass, and that meant carrying some artillery.

Bradley went to the small arsenal in the basement of the safe house. There was a combination lock on the heavy steel door. He racked his brain for the combination, made a stab at it and twisted the dial. When the door swung open, he stepped inside and clicked on the small overhead light. He took a couple of the 9 mm clips for his Browning, teflon-coated ammo, just in case. But he wanted something with a little more punch, a little stopping power.

There was a pair of Browning A-5 shotguns cut down to pistol grips. He tried one, didn't like the heft of it and tried the other. It felt good, and he pocketed some 12-gauge shells, then loaded the 5-shot magazine.

He clicked off the light and shoved the door to the arsenal closed with a hip. Without looking, he reached back to twirl the dial.

Bradley looked at his watch. It was almost time to go. He took the stairs two at a time and made his way to the front door, which was secured with several bolts, only one of which was locked. He opened the door and stepped outside into the coolness of the night. Closing the door behind him, he stepped off the small porch and headed toward his car.

Turning the ignition key, he felt the satisfying tremble of the floorboards as the engine caught. He flicked on the headlights and headed toward the deserted road fifty yards from the house. Passing through the tree-lined lane, he glanced in the rearview almost instinctively. He saw nothing unusual.

On the quiet road the headlight beams were swallowed by the night. It was nearly eleven o'clock. The nearest public phone was in the tiny hamlet of Schoendienst. Bradley wasn't happy about using anything that close, but there had to be limits to how far he could stretch his paranoia. The town was nearly eight miles away. As long as he got on and off in short order, there'd be no time to pinpoint his location.

After two miles he was beginning to settle down. The headlights behind him didn't concern him much when he first spotted them in the rearview. But they were closing fast, and he leaned on the gas a little. The following car continued to gain on him. He was already doing forty miles per hour, a little too fast for comfort on the winding road, but the headlights kept getting closer.

As the chase car started to materialize, Bradley slowed and edged toward the side of the road to let it pass, but it stayed right behind him.

Stepping on the gas and shifting down, he jerked the Audi hard enough to throw him back against the seat. The gear wound out, and he shifted up to fourth, but the car behind kept closing, even when he tapped the brakes to flicker the taillights.

They were nearing an intersection, and he made up his mind quickly. At the last possible second, he jerked the wheel and ripped the Audi sideways through the tight turn. It was a dirt road, and he could see a rooster comb of dust in the glow of his taillights.

The pursuing driver was taken by surprise and missed the turn. Slamming on his brakes, Bradley jerked his car into reverse and flipped around, almost backing into a shallow ditch by the side of the dirt road. He was headed back toward the main road now as the other car completed a hurried K-turn and squealed back toward the intersection.

Bradley blew through the intersection and zipped past the driver. There was a short burst of gunfire as he blew by, leaving the other car headed the wrong way. Glancing in his rearview mirror, he saw the driver executing a second K-turn, and a second pair of headlights farther down the road.

He floored it now, trying to put as much distance as he could between him and his pursuer.

The car closed on him again, and he pushed his own vehicle to the limit. Already the Audi lurched from side to side on the turns, threatening to tear loose from the road and career off into the weeds and the barley fields beyond. In less than a minute the car was on his ass again, this time nudging him with its front bumper. He tried braking to slow it down, but the cars were melded together now, and the other driver kept his foot to the floor.

He felt himself losing control. Each turn was harder to negotiate as the speedometer needle climbed higher and higher. They were over fifty now, and still picking up speed. A particularly sharp turn was coming up, and Bradley saw himself skidding toward a wall of tall weeds and small shrubs.

The green wall rushed closer, and he hit the gas, hoping to break the connection long enough to negotiate the turn, but the other driver was one step ahead of him. He hit the brakes, felt the car slam into him and saw a wall loom large. The front wheels hit the stone head-on, sending the Audi up and into the hedge. His brakes were useless, and the car skidded through the barley and rolled over once.

He heard a car door slam behind him as the Audi went up on its side again and teetered. It banged down hard on its undercarriage as he tried to get free of the seat belt. There was a loud report, and the window on his door blew out. A steady hammering exploded as he hit the deck, cracking his head on the passenger door. He started to lose it. The hammering increased in intensity as a second car screeched to a halt back on the road.

Bradley's slippery grip on consciousness failed, and he drifted off, the hammering growing more and more distant until it faded completely away.

## CHAPTER SEVENTEEN

Willi Hauser pointed to the farmhouse. Bolan nodded that he understood. The two men with the German agent were carved from the same piece of granite. Blond hair spilled over their foreheads and down over their shoulders. They hadn't said a word on the long drive.

They reminded Bolan a little too much of the Aryan hulks from the Volvo, and the comparison made him a little uneasy. But Hauser swore by them, and he was almost out of allies. Bradley seemed to have fallen off the edge of the planet, and for the moment the remnants of Klaus Mann's team were all he had.

He pulled Hauser to one side. "You sure about this?"

The German nodded. "I am sure. We have turned over every rock in Bavaria, Herr Pollock. It has to be them."

"What if your Intel is wrong?"

Hauser shrugged. "Then we are—how do you say it—back to the first square?"

"Square one."

"Yes. That is where we will be. We will have to start all over again. There is so little time. I wish we could be more thorough, but without the time, we don't have any choice."

Bolan glanced toward the farmhouse far below. "How many men did you say?"

"Seven, eight. No more than that."

"All right, then. Let's do it. Make sure Gerd and Egon know what to do. There won't be time for a parley once we start down the mountain."

"They are well trained. I trained them myself. You can stop worrying about them. I can't think of two better men to have with us. Especially if this is as violent as I suspect it will be."

Bolan clapped him on the shoulder. They were nearly one mile from the farmhouse. Once they started down through the trees, it would be out of sight until they reached the sea of barley at the lower edge of the forest. From there, it was about three hundred yards to the house itself. All open, except for the grain.

Hauser stepped close to his men and said something Bolan didn't catch. Gerd, who was slightly taller than Egon, took the point. The Executioner fell in behind him, Hauser next and Egon bringing up the rear. The thin trees near the crest gave way to larger, older ones, and the undergrowth became denser, retarding their progress and forcing them to step carefully to avoid making too much noise.

According to Hauser's sources, the house was supposed to be guarded only by manpower. There were rotating shifts, with no more than two men on at any given time. There were no electronics to worry about.

The Aryan Bund was the German equivalent of the Aryan Brotherhood, and its members came from unsavory backgrounds. Many of them had done time in German prisons. At least two of its members had once been prominent in left-wing politics, rumored to have been affiliated with Baader-Meinhof. But the pressing realities of Europe's changing political face had driven them full circle. They were in love with violence, and the political stripe was just a pretty ribbon on the package.

According to Erika Mann, if they could find the Aryan Bund, they would be within a stone's throw of the answer, assuming they were asking the right question, but Bolan wasn't so sure about that.

Bolan knew Erika was at least as interested in getting revenge for her father's death as she was in helping him, but beggars couldn't be choosers.

They hit the barley and fanned out, forming a ragged line as they waded into the chest-high grain. The house seemed to float on a sea of waving stalks, its lower story half-hidden by the shifting surface. At the far edge of the field, they stopped. Hauser squirmed through the grain and halted off Bolan's left shoulder.

"Well, Herr Pollock, here we are. What shall we do now?"

"I'll get as close as I can and take a look around. If you hear gunfire don't wait for me, just come in. Otherwise, I'll get back and let you know what I find. Give me at least a half hour."

Bolan waited until Hauser told Gerd and Egon what was going to happen, then slipped through the last few yards of the grain and into a strip of tall grass. Two outbuildings stood beyond the farmhouse, one of which was a large barn and the other some sort of shed. No vehicles were in sight, and Bolan figured they must be using the barn as a garage to hide the vehicles from aerial surveillance.

A single light burned on the first floor of the house. The upper story was dark. Bolan sprinted through the tall grass, looking for some sign of the sentries. So far, nothing had moved. When he reached one end of the house, he made a wide circle. He was in shorter grass now, barely to his knees, and he dropped to his stomach and slithered through the thick green blades. He stopped every couple of yards, but nothing moved on that side, either. If sentries were posted, they weren't in plain sight. A small stand of trees jutted out from the forest beyond the farmhouse, like a thick tongue stabbing out of a dark face. He had more than a hundred yards to go before he could reach the relative safety of the trees, but he resisted the urge to get up and run for it.

He was almost to the trees when something caught the corner of his eye. He froze and peered into the shadows alongside the shed. Something had definitely moved, but there was no sign of it now. He waited for a repeat, for the shadow to show itself again, but the darkness remained motionless.

Bolan started to crawl again, knowing that as long as he stayed low, the shadows would protect him. Reaching the trees, he got to his feet, then leaned forward to get a better look.

The shed was a simple affair, not even head high, probably a chicken coop at one time. The barn was much larger, and he eased back through the stand of trees to circle in behind it. There was a small door in the back wall, but he couldn't see the main entrance even from the side. An old tractor stood behind the barn, its wheels all but swallowed by tall weeds.

Bolan swung far enough around to get the tractor between him and the barn. Ducking low, he charged through the grass, heading for the vehicle.

Then he saw it again. A solitary shadow. It ducked low and sprinted from the corner of the shed to the right-hand wall of the barn. Whoever it was, it wasn't a sentry. Bolan watched until the shadow slipped around the corner of the barn and disappeared.

The Executioner watched the building for five minutes, then made his move. He broke for the barn, stopping just behind the corner, and pressed his ear to the wall. Silence. Quickly he moved along the back wall until he reached the door in the center. He pulled the latchstring, and metal squeaked on metal on the other side.

The door wouldn't open, even with the latch raised.

The warrior sprinted to the far end of the barn, intent on finding another entrance, when headlights suddenly speared the sky far to his left. He watched as the vehicle rolled up and over the crest of a low hill, then started downhill, rocking over ruts in the dirt road.

It was still too distant for him to see the vehicle itself, and he cursed under his breath as he ducked back behind the corner of the barn. The lights were almost hidden by tall weeds on either side of the dirt road. Floating above the weeds was the blocky body of a dark-colored van.

The driver ground the gears, shifting up into second as he negotiated the narrow road. There was no doubt in Bolan's mind it was the van he'd encountered previously, and it proved there was a connection between the Aryan Bund and the team that had taken out Dolph Murray.

Bolan watched as the van approached the little compound, then he rolled out of the tall grass and toward the barn. He backed away from the corner when he lost sight of the vehicle. Starting back along the rear wall of the barn, he had almost reached the center door when it burst open in front of him.

A man fell through the opening and sprinted for the trees. A door slammed, and someone shouted. Bolan flattened himself against the wall, watching the shadow of the fleeing man stumble toward the trees. A moment later footsteps pounded toward the door from somewhere inside the barn.

Two more men broke through the open door, one of them leveling a submachine gun at the sprinting shadow. He stopped in his tracks and cut loose with a single short burst.

The first sharp retort, muffled by the walls of the barn, was followed by a second, louder explosion. The concussion punched the two gunners to the ground as Bolan turned to run. He was out in the open, and heard another shout behind him.

He turned to look over his shoulder in time to see both men scramble to their feet. They had seen him, and the SMG was swinging his way. Bolan hit the deck, just under a stream of .45-caliber slugs from the MAC-10.

He rolled around, leveling his AK-47 as the two men started toward him. The next blast took out the back wall of the barn, knocking both men flat again. In the brilliant glare of a blossoming fireball, Bolan could see one of the men on his back, his legs flailing as he tried to run while prostrate on the ground, his hands raised overhead to ward off the wall of the barn as it teetered toward him then fell with a deep-throated rumble.

The rush of air fanned by the falling wall swept over the Executioner as he got to his feet and raced for the trees. He heard a scream that was suddenly cut short as the monstrous weight of the wall slapped the earth and leveled everything beneath it.

## CHAPTER EIGHTEEN

Bolan hit the trees at a dead run. Behind him all hell broke loose. He flattened himself on the ground and looked back at the farmhouse. The whole area grew brighter as the remains of the barn, two walls of which were still standing, burst into flame and started to disintegrate. The old wood was brittle and burned rapidly.

As he watched, the entire front wall of the barn started to sag at one end, warping like a sheet of paper. It collapsed, sending up a shower of sparks that soared on the superheated air. Bolan could see several vehicles in the heart of the holocaust, already reduced to blackened hulks.

Breaking into a brisk trot, he moved along the edge of the forest, trying to work his way back toward Hauser and Gerd and Egon Schulz. They would have heard the gunfire, brief as it was, and he feared they might have started to move in.

The men in the farmhouse would mount a search for the arsonist. There was no way anyone could construe the explosions and fire as an accident. It was deliberate. Bolan knew that, and he had to assume the men of the Aryan Bund knew it, too.

A shout from the vicinity of the farmhouse drew the warrior's attention, but a quick glance over his shoulder failed to pick up anyone near the burning barn.

A moment later there was a tremendous explosion, and he saw the sudden ballooning of a fireball as the fuel tank of one of the trapped vehicles went up. Great plumes of flame, like huge orange feathers, sprouted in the heart of the blaze, as if a great peacock had just unfurled its tail. The tallest of the flames died down almost immediately as the gasoline was quickly consumed.

As he circled around the edge of the open space, Bolan could see the van now, its broad windshield reflecting the flames. Whatever doubt he might have had was obliterated. It was definitely the same van, which meant almost certainly that the two men who were no doubt little more than charred meat on blackened bones somewhere under the collapsed barn, had been the same two men who had left the mountain bunker two days before.

He hadn't gotten a clear look at them then, and he'd seen even less this time. But if it was the same van, it must be the same men. And tugging at the back of his consciousness was the shadowy figure he'd seen by the shed, then spring to the barn and burst out the rear door one step ahead of the sheriff and two ahead of the fires of hell. He'd been seen, but not before he'd managed to blow the barn to pieces, and virtually every vehicle on the farm along with it.

But who in hell was he? The man couldn't have been one of Klaus Mann's team. Erika was in charge, and she had sent Willi with him. The duplication would have been pointless at best and, at worst, dangerous to one or both. They might have blown each other away, neither realizing who the other was. No, that made no sense, and Erika Mann was not so much a novice that she would have made a mistake like that. Whoever it had been represented a second front, an assault from another angle, for another set of reasons.

He spotted Hauser then, one hand in the air, the other holding an Uzi. The raised hand came down, and the German broke into a trot. He burst out of the barley, flanked by the other two members of the team, who were armed with AK-47s.

Cupping his hands around his mouth, Bolan shouted for Hauser to wait, but the German didn't hear him. Egon Schulz was moving to the left, putting some distance between his brother and Hauser, both of whom continued their headlong charge. Bolan had no choice but to go after them.

Already the Aryan Bund gunners were fanning out in a convex arc, half encircling the blazing ruins. By quick count, Bolan tallied nine. They started to advance, their weapons held waist high. The irregular chatter of the rifles crackled like the burning timber behind them, both sounds almost drowned out by the roaring thunder of the blaze.

Hauser dropped to one knee as Gerd Schulz moved closer, one hand raised in the air in a smooth arc before disappearing. A black spot flew toward the barn but fell well short. It went off with a sharp bang as Gerd hit the deck. Hauser was already prostrate.

It must have been a fragmentation grenade. Slivers of red-hot metal scythed through the advancing arc, and two of the men went down. One struggled gamely to his feet and limped another couple of steps before going down again. This time he stayed down.

Bolan opened up with his AK-47, but at long range it was difficult to zero in on a target of choice. One of the soldiers on the left horn of the arc dropped to his knees, and the dull *whump* of a grenade launcher bellowed under the roar of gunfire. The grenade carried long and geysered grass and dirt in every direction, a cloud in the shape of a cone standing on its apex lingering in the air. The thick dust and smoke refracted the light from the burning barn for a moment and seemed to glow with an inner fire of its own.

Egon was on his feet now, fifty yards closer to the left end of the arc. It had been a smart move, but Egon was too impatient. If he had held his ground another minute, he would have been able to outflank the advancing line, gotten in behind it and forced the soldiers to divide their attention. But he had jumped too soon. And he was too close.

The two men on the end spun, their weapons firing in unison. Egon went down, and Bolan couldn't tell whether he'd been hit. There was no return fire, and it didn't look good. For any of them.

Charging ahead, the warrior tried to take the pressure off as the two men advanced toward Egon's position. Bolan squeezed off a burst from his AK, but the magazine ran dry before he'd scored a hit. He ripped out the empty clip and jammed a second one home.

Far to the left, Bolan heard the sharp crack of a high-powered rifle. He looked toward the trees but saw no one. He knew it was the same man he'd seen fleeing the barn, but there was no time to do anything about it now.

The line had stuttered to a halt. Three of the nine gunners were already down. Hauser was still flat on his belly, his Uzi ripping into the men at the right end of the line. Egon remained down, but the men were caught in the middle. Another rifle shot cracked, this time the gunman missing his target. But the second man after Egon must have gotten the point. He turned and started to run.

As if on cue, the others turned and raced back toward the farmhouse. Bolan had visions of a Western shoot-out, with the bad guys holed up in a line shack, and broke into a sprint, ripping short bursts from the AK as he charged across the open ground.

The men were in full flight now, and the warrior was gaining on them.

The Executioner sensed someone was on his left flank and looked over just long enough to see Egon limping after him. To the right, Hauser and Gerd Schulz were keeping pace. One of the Bund soldiers went down, this time under a withering fire from the Uzi, and Hauser raised a triumphant fist in the air as he stopped to ram home another clip of 9 mm ammo.

This wasn't working out the way Bolan and Hauser had hoped. They wanted to take some of the Bund members alive. They had to know who was giving them orders.

The first of the hardmen was already at the barn, and Bolan dropped to one knee. Firing from a stationary position, he was able to be more accurate. He took out the leader of the pack with a single burst, then walked his fire back until he climbed the legs of a second man, who staggered, then fell in a heap.

Three remained—as far as they could tell. They were still a hundred yards from the safety of the farmhouse when the middle man swerved toward the van, disappeared behind it, then reappeared on the far side, intent on getting out of there. The remaining two hardmen raced for the porch of the farmhouse.

Gerd Schulz put on a kick and sprinted ahead of Hauser, heading past the van and chasing toward the lane, his weapon held across his chest.

Bolan ripped a figure eight across the front porch of the farmhouse, stitched one man across the middle of his back and was looking for the second when the AK burped to a halt. He was reaching for another clip when the man's skull seemed to explode.

A moment later the distant crack of the hunting rifle drifted across the open field, then died away.

If the house was deserted, it belonged to Bolan now. If not, it was still his for the taking. He charged onto the porch, a fresh clip in his AK, and flattened himself beside the door. He glanced down at the bloody corpse lying across the threshold, then jammed the butt of the AK into the door panel and shoved it all the way open.

Egon Schulz pressed flat on the opposite side of the door, his eyes fixed on Bolan.

Bolan nodded, ducked into a crouch and burst into the farmhouse. He stepped to one side and waited for Egon, hampered by his bleeding leg, to come in after him.

"Room by room," Bolan said, taking point.

## CHAPTER NINETEEN

Bolan moved down the corridor, the AK at his hip. Three doors were set in the right-hand wall. The first one was closed. He stopped in front of it and cocked an ear. The shuffle of feet behind him whispered to a halt, and he leaned forward. The room beyond seemed deserted. With a jerk of his head, he positioned Egon Schulz on the far side, then planted a well-aimed kick dead center.

The door flew back and banged off the interior wall. There was no sudden burst of gunfire, only the sound of the banging door echoing in the high-ceilinged room. A small light burned on a desk in one corner. Bolan waited a beat, then charged in, sweeping the AK toward the left corner.

The room was empty, and he scanned it quickly. There was no closet and nowhere someone could hide. The room was plain, its walls decorated only with a huge swastika flag, the red muted somewhat by the dim light. A picture of Adolph Hitler, its frame off kilter, hung beside the flag.

The room was as empty and barren as the political thought to which it was a memorial. Bolan backed out of the room after checking under the desk.

The other two rooms were empty, as well.

Willi Hauser had stayed at the far end of the corridor to cover their tails. Bolan cocked an eyebrow, and Willi shrugged. "I don't know, Herr Pollock."

Bolan stared at the blank wall at the end of the hallway for a moment, then turned back toward the front of the farmhouse. He slipped past Willi and found himself in a large, rustic kitchen. Two doors were set in the opposite wall. He took the one on the right and found himself in a pantry, its shelves overburdened with cheap canned goods. An open box of instant rice lay on its side, and the rock-hard grains spilled on the floor crunched under his feet as the warrior moved into the pantry to the shelves at the back wall. Another dry hole.

The other door led out the back way into a closed-in porch. Crates of ammunition were stacked back against the wall, and two makeshift racks of raw wood held several assault rifles. A chain was looped through the trigger guards, a rusty padlock holding the chain closed.

Bolan went back into the house. There were too many blind alleys. Vermin seemed to be under every rock, but it was one dead end after another. He kept flashing back to the map, wondering where Bradley was, wondering what, if anything, he had been able to learn from the recovered papers.

"Let's take the second floor," the Executioner suggested. Willi nodded. Bolan sent Egon to watch the front, then led the way to a narrow staircase, which he started to climb.

The report was almost deafening as a bullet slammed into the wall just inches from his head.

Bolan swung around the AK, but the narrow stairwell and the banister along the top got in his way. He caught just a glimpse of someone darting through an open doorway. A steady hail of gunfire chewed at the rotten plaster of the stairwell as Bolan ducked.

"Two, at least," he shouted, starting back up the stairs.

A window broke on the floor above. They were trying to get out. Bolan shouted down the stairs to Hauser. "Tell Egon they're coming out. I'm going up."

The door was still open, and the Executioner pounded up the stairs. The men inside heard his footsteps, and two short bursts of autofire poured through the open doorway like angry hornets. A choking cloud of plaster dust swirled in the narrow hallway, obscuring Bolan's vision. He charged down the hall, stopping just short of the open doorway.

One more burst ripped at the doorframe, scattering chunks of wood and paint chips, which bounced off the wall and showered the stairwell. Bolan sprinted past the doorway, pinning himself against the wall on the opposite side. This time there was no gunfire.

He swung toward the door and set himself. Barging ahead, he saw a pair of legs, one still being pulled through the broken window. Bolan swung the AK-47 toward the window and squeezed off a short burst, hearing a scream of pain before a heavy body fell onto the fragile roof.

Gunfire erupted outside the window, but it wasn't aimed his way. He could see the muzzle-flashes spearing down off the roof, but the gunman was shielded by the wall of the house.

A second, more distant burst exploded, and the gunman ran across the small roof as Bolan charged toward the window. He hesitated before poking his head out, knowing Egon was below and might shoot at anything that moved.

He could see one man lying on the roof, curled in a ball with bloody hands locked over his shattered leg. An AR-15 lay beside him, but the man was unaware of Bolan and made no move to retrieve the weapon. Reaching through the window, the warrior snared the AR by its muzzle and dragged it toward him, then pulled it in through the window.

Another burst ripped at the roof, knocking the AR from his grasp. It lay half in and half out, its butt on the roof, its muzzle angled up against the window frame. Footsteps again, this time charging toward him.

Bolan backed away from the window and leveled his AK. He was expecting the gunman to get back inside, but the man raced past, then launched himself off the roof. The kick of his leap made the house shudder for a split second.

The Executioner went through the window, stopping just long enough to grab the abandoned AR and hurl it off the roof. Moving to the edge, he saw Egon Schulz lying on his back in the dirt below. A half-dozen red stains splotched the front of his shirt.

"Willi?" Bolan shouted. "You there?"

No answer.

Bolan lay flat on the roof and stared off into the darkness to the left of the barn. The gunman must have gone that way when he'd leaped off the roof. A second later the roof just behind him erupted. A hail of hellfire clawed at it from below. Hot lead ripped through the ancient boards and brittle shingles. Bolan rolled toward the house as the burst of fire tore along the front edge of the roof like a ripsaw.

Wood splinters and hunks of asphalt arced up and away, backlit by the flames from the blazing barn. Flush against the wall, Bolan knew it was only a matter of time before the slugs started cutting his way. He scrambled to his feet and dived through the window and back into the house. The gunfire clawed along the wall of the house and slammed into the body of the wounded man, putting him out of his agony. Bolan realized then that there were far more gunmen than he had thought.

Starting toward the open doorway, he heard footsteps on the floor below. Someone shouted in German, and the footsteps pounded toward the stairs. Bolan got to the door just as two heads appeared in the stairwell. He opened up with the AK, and one head exploded, spattering the wall with blood and brain tissue. The second man ducked out of the way and fell as the body of his companion slumped down the stairs. There was another door at the left end of the narrow hall, but to get to it Bolan would have to expose his back to fire from the stairwell. It was better to stay in the room, where he could see the window to the roof. If they got up from outside, he'd be trapped. He felt in his pocket for the remaining AK magazine.

It felt cold in his hand. It was the last one before he'd have to resort to handguns. He listened for the sound of feet on the stairs, but it was quiet. He heard creaking wood outside and moved toward the window, flicking off the light as he went past the switch.

The room was filled with an orange wash from the burning wreckage of the barn. The flames flickered, and the searing glow seemed to shimmer as if some live orange thing were oozing across the wall. The roof timbers creaked again, and he tensed, his finger on the trigger.

Heavy steps charged up the stairs, and he moved to the opposite wall, staring intently at the doorway. The roof outside suddenly echoed from a heavy tread. The timbers creaked softly as the weight moved closer to the wall of the house.

Bolan backed into a corner to the left of the window. He could hear whispers from the hallway. At least two men, maybe more, were getting ready to storm the tiny room. The timbers creaked again, and the warrior drew the Desert Eagle and held it in his left hand, the safety off. He held the AK in his right, his arm braced against the wall to keep it from climbing up and away from the target when he squeezed the trigger.

The footsteps charged. Bolan took a deep breath and squeezed off a round. The pointman dropped to the floor, writhing in pain, but he struggled to bring his rifle around. It was pinned beneath him, and Bolan fired once more, a single shot. The body arced, then lay still.

A second later there was a hard thump as an object hit the floor and rolled toward Bolan. He snatched at the dark sphere and flipped it back into the hall. He heard it hit, and someone rushed the room to get out of the grenade's deadly radius. Bolan cut him down with the last few rounds in the AK's magazine.

But he was out of position now, and he could see the man in the window, his long face draped in shadows as he raised the muzzle of his AR and leveled it on Bolan's midsection.

The Executioner raised his .44, but the man's midsection suddenly mushroomed, spattering Bolan with blood. The grenade exploded then, and the hallway ceiling came down.

Bolan wasted no time. The gunman on the roof was clawing at broken glass and thin air as he dropped his rifle and tried to hold himself up. The warrior barreled through the door and headed for the stairs.

He pounded down, two steps at a time, and burst into the lower floor. He didn't see the corpse until it was too late. He tripped over the outstretched legs and he fell, knocking the AK from his hands.

He reached for the weapon with one outstretched arm just as a dark boot landed on the muzzle.

"No way," said a strangely calm voice.

## CHAPTER TWENTY

The man was dressed in black, loose-fitting pants that were tucked into black boots with a dull mat finish. His face was coated with black combat cosmetics, and his eyes looked like patches of snow against the dark background.

Bolan looked up into the business end of a Holland & Holland .375, fitted with a Zeiss Diatal-C scope. The Executioner lay where he was, knowing the least sudden movement would draw a bullet.

"Can I get up?"

"Not yet. Leave your weapons on the floor. Remove the pistols carefully and make no sudden movement."

Bolan complied.

"Slide back away from the guns, please."

When he was far enough away for his captor's satisfaction, he lay still. The man with the rifle came forward and picked up both handguns, tucking them securely into his belt.

"What can you tell me about Michael Bradley?" he asked.

"Never heard of him."

"When did you see him last?" the stranger asked, ignoring Bolan's response.

"I told you, I don't know him."

"Come, come. I know very well that you know him. You went away with him after the attack on you outside his apartment building."

"So?"

"Did he put you in touch with Willi Hauser?"

"With Klaus Mann, actually."

"And now Klaus Mann is dead. Is that a coincidence?"

"You tell me, pal."

Again a vacant look swept over the man's face, and he shifted his eyes to the darkness beside the house for a moment. Bolan thought about making a move. The man must have realized it, because his eyes snapped back. A grin spread across his face.

The man backed off the porch. He took a couple of steps away from the wooden stairs, then waved the rifle. "Get up."

On his feet again, Bolan felt less vulnerable. "Why did you kill Willi Hauser?"

"I didn't."

Bolan believed him. There was no hesitation in the voice, and no attempt to sound hurt by the accusation. The voice was dead flat. It dealt in facts, not inflections. He wasn't lying about Hauser.

"Where's Gerd Schulz?"

The guy shook his head. There was a tinge of sadness in his face for a moment. He stepped to the left and gestured with the rifle again. Bolan didn't have to ask what he wanted.

Stepping off the porch, Bolan looked at his captor. "Which way?"

With a cocked head, the man in black indicated the direction. They moved toward the barn, Bolan five yards ahead of the Holland & Holland muzzle.

"Wait."

Bolan turned to look at his captor. The guy held a small radio transmitter in his hand. With the casual ease of someone changing TV channels, he waved the slim black box toward the house, which erupted in three separate explosions.

The man gestured with the rifle again. "Let's go quickly. I have something I want to show you."

"What is it?"

"You'll tell me when you see it."

They were moving down the lane between two fields full of chest-high grass. A hundred yards in, Bolan saw Gerd Schulz. Like Willi Hauser, he'd had his throat slit. The warrior stepped around the body, then turned. "Is that more of your handiwork?"

"I found him that way."

The lane curled to the left, and as they rounded the turn, Bolan saw an American 4×4 parked back among the trees. It had to have been a recent arrival, because the men in the van would have spotted it when they came past. Two men stood on the far side of the Bronco, their heads just visible over the engine compartment of the Ford.

Bolan turned to look at his captor, who betrayed no emotion. The man in black whistled shrilly, and both heads snapped toward the sound. When the men spotted Bolan, they came around the Bronco. Each was armed with an AK-47. Like Bolan's captor, they were dressed in black, their faces darkened.

One of them started to speak, but the man behind Bolan snapped, "Use English."

Indicating Bolan, the new man then asked, "Is this the one?"

"He is."

The new man shook his head. "I see."

He walked to the Bronco and opened the door, pushing the front seat-back down and climbing in. He slid across the rear seat, and the second new man gestured toward Bolan. "Get in."

The warrior climbed into the back and found himself staring at a Skorpion machine pistol. It rested easily in the commando's lap, but his finger was taut on the trigger. The apparent leader of the small band walked around to the far side and climbed into the passenger seat. The second new man obviously was the driver. He shoved the seat-back upright and climbed in.

Starting the engine, he looked at his boss, who nodded, and then threw the transmission into gear and started the Bronco forward.

Bolan turned to his captor. "Are you planning to tell me what this is all about?"

"All in good time, Mr. Pollock. All in good time."

# CHAPTER TWENTY-ONE

"How's he doing?"

"He's not that young. I suppose he's holding up as well as one would expect."

"As well as you would expect, James. Under the circumstances?"

"Under the circumstances, yes. But I've been giving it a lot of thought."

"I wouldn't expect anything less, James. You're the consummate professional."

"Don't try to flatter me. It won't work."

The man laughed. "I wouldn't waste my time trying to flatter you, James. Flattery eventually turns on the flatterer, comes back to haunt him. Besides, with what you are being paid, flattery shouldn't be necessary, even if it were useful or desirable."

"It's neither."

"Then what's on your mind?"

"I think we may be making a mistake."

The man leaned forward, resting the weight of his upper body on his knees with stiff arms. "What kind of mistake? All the information has panned out. I know that is due to Mr. Hisle's skill, your inquisitorial abilities and, of course and perhaps most of all, the drugs.''

"Mostly the drugs. Yes."

"And yet you have reservations?"

Harkness nodded. He was feeling a bit uncomfortable, even in the large room. He stood and walked to the window. With one hand on the heavy draperies, he looked out over the rolling countryside. The vineyards were clotted with thick green vines on trestles. Birds swooped low to pick off unsuspecting insects, then darted, true as arrows, straight up toward the clouds.

From his vantage point, the world was so beautiful, so peaceful. That might all come apart in a very short time. He knew that, and it had begun to bother him. He understood that his reservations about Marley's handling were much more than that, a tough but brittle veneer for much larger reservations. It was beginning to seem to Harkness that the elegant simplicity of the plan was more illusory, and far less desirable, than he once had thought. He was no longer certain of the wisdom of the course he had chosen, of the plan he had endorsed and was now busy implementing.

And there was no way in hell he could afford to let the man seated behind him get the faintest glimmer of those more profound reservations.

Harkness turned back, still keeping his hand on the draperies. "It might be worth a try to convince Jason of the rightness of our view."

# THE GOLD EAGLE TEAM IS ON THE MOVE AGAIN WITH FOUR NEW MINISERIES IN 1993 PROVIDING YOU WITH THE BEST IN ACTION ADVENTURE!

Omega Force is the last—and deadliest—option

PATRICK F. ROGERS

OMEGA

WAR MACHINE

The Peacekeepers are ready—
the toughest grunts on
the planet

WARKEEP 2030

KILLING FIELDS
Michael Kasner

Gold Eagle brings another fast-paced miniseries to the action adventure front—OMEGA—featuring a special antiterrorist strike force composed of the best commandos and equipment the military has to offer.

WAR MACHINE: Book #1 of this paramilitary miniseries will be available in February 1993. Look for Books #2 and #3 in June and October. (224 pages, $3.50 each)

Introducing the follow-up miniseries to the popular WARKEEP 2030 title published in November 1992.

This miniseries tracks the Peacekeepers, an elite military force that tries to impose peace in the troubled 21st century. Look for Book 1: KILLING FIELDS in March. Books #2 and #3 continue in July and November. (224 pages, $3.50 each)

"You mean we should make an ally of him? Enlist his service for our cause?"

"I wasn't thinking in terms so grand as that, but, yes, I guess that's what I do mean."

"Surely you can't be serious."

"Why not? The man's a patriot, always has been. Why not put it to him in those terms. It would spare his health, which is rather fragile at the moment."

"Do I detect remorse, James? Are you feeling badly about the way you have been treating Mr. Marley?"

"Not remorse, no. In the making of any kind of fruit juice, something has to get squeezed. I understand that, and I am comfortable with it as an operating principle."

"But . . . ?"

"But I am concerned about his health."

"Don't be. This will soon be over."

"What is that supposed to mean?"

"It means simply that his health will not be under siege for very much longer. We are close to getting everything we need from him."

"I understand that, but—"

"If it will make you feel better," the man said, cutting him off sharply but without any hint of rudeness, "talk to him. See just how amenable he might be to our revision of the future of the continent. Perhaps he is a man of considerably more vision than I have suspected."

"You don't object?"

The man shook his head. "Just don't tell him anything he doesn't need to know. You understand that if you do tell him and he doesn't agree, then you have placed his health in considerably more jeopardy than currently threatens him."

Harkness let that one pass. The meaning was plain. "Thank you."

"It's a grave responsibility you're assuming, James. I'm not sure I'd want to bear that burden myself."

"It's nothing compared to the burden you plan to assume if we are successful."

"That's very diplomatic of you, James. You're so much more complex a man than you try to appear. I hadn't realized that. I'm impressed."

"Don't be."

Harkness walked back to his chair and fell into it with no attempt to cushion the impact. He was exhausted, and he had been unable to sleep for several days. Ronny had been keeping him up, but he didn't like drugs and wished he could find a way to do without them.

Looking at the man across from him, he wondered how he had come to be sitting there. He knew the answer but he didn't want to face it. It was easier somehow to picture himself as a chip of wood, buffeted by winds and waves, forced this way and that by factors over which he had no control.

The fact was much simpler. He was ambitious and he harbored deep resentment. The resentment was probably unjustified, because his ambition was overweening. He had chosen to be in that particular chair at that precise moment. He knew that in every bone of his body but he didn't like it, even loathed himself a little.

But it was all spilled milk. He was in too deep to just turn and walk away. Maybe Jason could help him. The same Jason Marley he'd resented so much for so long. It was a slender hope but it was all he had. He shook his head slowly from side to side.

"You've decided something?" the man asked.

"Yes. It's a risk I'll take. I think he would be a valuable ally."

"If he can be persuaded."

"Yes. If he can be persuaded."

"You must understand, James, that he will agree to anything if he thinks it will buy him time or improve his conditions. I agree that it would be nice to have his assistance, especially if freely given. But…"

"I'm not a child. Of course I understand that. But I think we should try it. He's a brilliant man."

"Of course he is."

"Then what do we have to lose?"

"If you handle it properly, nothing at all. If you get careless, perhaps everything. I won't stand for that, James. I have come too far, risked everything to bring this endeavor to fruition. I will not tolerate failure. Even small failure is unacceptable. Don't make a mistake."

Harkness smiled. It was genuine, and he let it linger on his face long enough to provoke a response.

"You think I am joking?"

"I know you're not joking. You're not known as a man with a sense of humor. But I'm not, either. Joking is something I don't do well. And a man should not even attempt to do what he does not do well."

"Then we understand each other."

"Of course," Harkness said.

"Very well. Then I think we should talk about the next few days. You know the summit is moving ahead, right on schedule. Since his reelection, the chancellor is becoming more and more influential. He is pushing Germany farther and farther, faster and faster, in the wrong direction. We will never have a better time to stop that misguided momentum than on September 1."

"I know that."

"Then tell me, have you assembled the team?"

"I have. They are training right now. They don't know what for, but they will be told next week."

"These are men you can trust?"

"These are men who are professionals. They don't care about politics. They couldn't care less if we were going after the Pope and Mother Theresa."

"I'm afraid, James, that given the current state of the world, the President of the United States and the leader of a reunited Germany are far more influential than a dozen saints. It is a sad commentary, perhaps, but there it is.''

''You are the consummate cynic.''

''I am the quintessential realist. And reality commands our attention, James. We must seize the opportunity to prevent the corruption of German ideals. The chancellor is determined to turn his back on the very things that made Germany what it was, and what it should again be.''

''And you're determined to stop him. I can appreciate that. And you will. Leave the operational details to me.''

''I have, James. And I expect you to perform satisfactorily. But I must tell you that some of my colleagues are suspicious of a man who will do for money what should be done only from the heart. I know you disagree, but you are walking the edge of a very sharp sword, James. And there are those who would fill your pockets with stones.''

''A man who works for money knows he will get what he has worked for. A man who works from the heart may be bitterly disappointed. The history of the world is full of true believers who have turned on their colleagues. Stalin did in Trotsky, and probably Lenin, as well. How many of Castro's allies would shoot him for a plugged nickel? Even in your own country, it was a cabal of generals who turned on Hitler. I pose no such risk, because I don't give a damn what happens once that money's in the bank.''

''I think you did not always feel that way, James.''

"Of course I did."

The man nodded. "Very well." He stood. "I should like to see your plans for the assassination as soon as they are final."

"The day after tomorrow."

"I will be back."

"Don't forget me once you're cock of the walk."

"Never."

The meeting ended as it had begun, with words hanging in the air, swirling in a cloud of contradictory meanings. Harkness stayed where he was long after the door closed, staring into space.

## CHAPTER TWENTY-TWO

They were heading toward Munich. Bolan watched the countryside roll by. The land gradually flattened out, and the forests slowly gave way to farmland. With his head against the glass, he studied the faces of the three men with him in the Bronco.

There wasn't much to see, really. Under the smeared night cream, the immobile features had settled into three masks of broad planes. Slavic, Bolan thought. Eastern Europeans of some sort. But whose side were they on? There were enough right-wing groups in the remnants of the Eastern Bloc to fill Yankee Stadium for a convention. They were growing, and they were spoiling for the chance to even fifty-year-old scores. Like most fringe groups, they spent more time fighting among themselves for pride of place than they did their real enemies.

Bolan wondered whether he had stumbled into some sort of fringe war between extreme-right groups. God knew there was plenty of potential for that sort of thing. And whoever had minced Dolph Murray was definitely serious about his politics. Murray's elimination might have been a coincidence, or it could have been that someone had tumbled to his CIA connection and wanted him wasted for that reason, without regard to politics. One didn't have to be a Communist to use murder as an instrument of politics.

On the other hand, these guys could be hard-liners of a very deep shade of red. It was hard to find anybody who was entirely certain what was going on behind the veils of civility currently draped over Czechoslovakia and Romania, Hungary and Poland.

The deeper one dug under any rock, the more peculiar things slithered up and away from the shovel. It all boiled down to one simple fact. You couldn't tell the players without a scorecard.

When they entered the city limits, it was 4:00 a.m. Bolan was curious why they had made no attempt to hide him. He wasn't restrained, except for the presence of the machine pistol in the lap of the man called Joseph. Whether they thought that was sufficient, or were genuinely convinced that he would want to cooperate and were doing their best to win his confidence, he couldn't tell. But he was getting very curious indeed.

John, the man who'd led Bolan from the farmhouse, seemed to sense what he was thinking. "I think you should give me a chance to explain why we need you and, not coincidentally, why I think you need us."

He gestured to Joseph. "Put away the gun." Joseph obeyed without hesitation.

"You're pretty sure of yourself, aren't you?"

"No more than you, Mr. Pollock. I want you to understand that we could have killed you if we wanted to, or even stood by and let those animals do it. That would have been very easy and extremely cost-effective, to borrow a good financial term. But we don't want you dead. You are no good to us that way. All I ask is that you give me an hour to explain. I will answer all your questions to the best of my ability, except where you touch on matters sensitive to my government and, for that reason, out of bounds."

"And if I can't help you?"

"Then you walk away. No questions asked. No recriminations. I am not interested in coercing cooperation. I am interested in a conundrum of mutual concern, or at least, so I believe, and I think that once you are acquainted with the details, you will agree."

"Okay. As a gesture of good faith, how about returning my weapons."

"Very well."

The warrior accepted the Desert Eagle and the Beretta, checking to see that the magazines were loaded, then replaced each weapon in its holster.

They were rolling through a residential section now, and the houses on either side of the street were set well back from the road. Most were partially obscured by hedges and walls of flowering shrubs. This was where money lived when it was in Munich.

Bolan waited patiently for the Bronco to change direction, to speed up or brake to a halt. It continued to roll for another several blocks, then turned sharply into a steeply banked driveway. Cascades of flowers spilled down the banks on either side of the asphalt.

Up ahead, through a stand of silver birches, he could see a large house, its lower floor brightly lit, its upper windows dark.

The Bronco rolled past the side of the house, turned left and came to a halt alongside a carriage house that had been converted into a multiple-car garage.

John stepped out before James, the third commando, killed the engine. He waited for Bolan to step out behind the driver, then raised a hand. "Please come this way."

Bolan fell in behind him and started across the asphalt pad toward a steep flight of stairs. They ended on a wide patio, bordered on all three sides by flowering shrubs.

John didn't bother to knock. If he didn't live here, which Bolan doubted, then he was certainly a regular visitor. A big walnut door yielded to his hand and swung inward without a sound. The Executioner wondered about the apparent lack of security until he stepped inside.

Four men, all heavily armed, sat before an array of video monitors. John said nothing to them, and not one of them turned to see who had come in. They didn't have to; they already knew.

John led the way through a pair of sliding doors. Bolan could tell they were made of heavy glass, probably impact resistant, maybe even bulletproof.

Once inside the main part of the building, John took a right turn and descended a flight of stairs. At the bottom he punched a rapid sequence of numbers into an electronic lock. A heavy steel door slid into a recess in the wall. John stepped through, turned and waited for Bolan, then punched a large red button on the wall to close the door. He led the Executioner down the long, narrow passage. The last door on the left sported another electronic lock. John's fingers flew over the keys, the door whirred open, and John stepped inside. He waited for Bolan, punched the security close button and a light switch in the same motion. Cold light flooded the room.

John walked to the far side of a large oval table and sat. He invited Bolan to join him at a seat across the smooth, polished teak. When the Executioner was in his chair, John pressed a hidden catch, and a section of the table rolled back to reveal a control panel.

One click of a switch, and the panel raised three inches and tilted. John punched a button, and the lights dimmed. Bolan saw the man's eyes reflecting the small red-and-green diodes sprinkled over the panel. Another button, and a square of light, suddenly splashed on the wall at one end of the oval.

"Where are we?" he asked.

"We'll get to your questions later," John replied. "First I have a few things to show you...."

Bolan watched the wall. He knew there was a projector behind him. When John's fingers danced over the array of buttons, a soft whirring emanated from somewhere at the other end of the room, and a picture appeared on the wall. "Do you recognize this man?"

"Dolph Murray," Bolan answered, frowning.

"Deceased. How about this man?"

Murray's face disappeared, to be replaced by a long-range shot of a man in sailing attire. The edges of the photo were blurry. It had obviously been taken through a long lens, 500 mm at least. "Giovanni Badalamente," Bolan whispered.

"Deceased. What do these men have in common?"

"They attended a conference at a hunting lodge in the Bohmerwald. Kind of a right-wing gathering of the tribes, I suppose you might say."

"Anything else, other, obviously, than their recent demise?"

Bolan shook his head. "No." He knew Murray and Badalamente were both on the CIA payroll, but he wasn't going to say anything. Better to let John take the conversation where he wanted it to go.

"Then let me tell you something maybe you didn't know, but I think you may have suspected. They were agents of your Central Intelligence Agency."

"Are you sure about that?"

"Certain. Or shall I say...dead certain. How about this man?"

This one was a mystery. It was once again a long-range shot. It showed an older man sitting on a park bench. He had a newspaper in one hand and an alpine hat tilted back on his head.

"Don't know him."

"But you met him just a few nights ago."

"No. I never saw the man in my life."

"Mr. Pollock, if you are going to lie, there is little point in wasting my time or yours."

"I said that I never met that man in my life."

"But you were there when he died. I saw you...."

Bolan looked across the table. In the darkness he saw John's face outlined by the dim glow of the diodes. "Klaus Mann."

"So you admit knowing him."

"Not at all. I was going to meet him for the first time when the bomb took him out."

"I see. Let's continue, then. Like the others, he is deceased. They all have at least that much in common."

"What's the point?"

"I was hoping you would tell me. Perhaps we should all discuss this together."

"All?"

John pressed another button with more than a little theatricality. Then he leaned back in his chair and waited.

Moments later Joseph stepped into the room, waved a hand, then moved aside. A second man came through the door, his hands cuffed behind his back.

It was Mike Bradley.

## CHAPTER TWENTY-THREE

Bradley glared at Bolan. "You bastard!" he snarled. "You son of a bitch."

"You've got it wrong."

"The hell I do. You sold me down the river, you slimy fuck."

"Boys, boys, boys," John said, "settle down. You're both confused. Just be patient. It'll all become clear." John waved a hand, and Joseph stepped back out of the room. "Mr. Pollock, get the door, please," John said, moving toward Bradley.

Unlocking the handcuffs, he put a hand on the agent and said, "Please have a seat."

Bolan pushed the door button and walked back to the table. Bradley stood there, rubbing first one wrist then the other.

"I think we should continue," John said, lowering the lights.

Bradley interrupted. "Continue, my ass. Pollock, what's happening here? Who is this guy?"

Before Bolan could answer, John said, "All in good time, Mr. Bradley. Please, we have a great deal of information to explore and very little time. Actually I'm not even sure how much time, but we have to move quickly, nonetheless.''

John pushed a button, and another image appeared on the wall, this time a grainy shot. It didn't look like a photograph. ''Do you recognize this man?'' John asked.

''What is this,'' Bradley snapped, ''twenty questions?''

''Do you know who it is?''

Bradley snorted. ''That's Jason Marley. Of course I know who it is.''

Bolan leaned forward. ''Are you going to tell me that he's dead, too?''

John shook his head. ''What I'm going to tell you is that I don't know. I can also tell you that at this moment, there are only a handful of people on this planet who can answer that question.''

''Dead? Handful? Are you crazy?'' Bradley turned to the Executioner. ''Pollock, what's he talking about? You said 'too.' Who else?''

Bolan thought John would interrupt. When he didn't, Bolan said, ''I mean Dolph Murray and Giovanni Badalamente.''

''Hell, what's going on?''

''That's precisely what I'm trying to explain to you both, Mr. Bradley. Now, if you'll let me continue, please....''

Bradley slumped back in his chair. ''Sure, what the hell, don't let me stop you. I always like to get my news of the subterranean world from an imperfect stranger.''

In the dull light reflected from the image on the wall, Bolan could see John's lips curl into a quick smile.

''Let me show you something a little different.''

Another image appeared on-screen, this one some sort of official photograph. ''Grunhard Kloster.''

''Dead?'' Bolan asked.

''Yes.''

Another photo. ''Hans Dieter-Munger.''

Bradley was getting the picture. ''Deceased, right?''

''Right.''

Bolan knew already. ''Your men. Also working the right side of the street. Also attended the recent conference in Klingenbrunn. Murdered. Am I close?''

''You are exactly correct. Now, let me go back to Mr. Marley.'' He pushed a button to bring up the lights a bit, and a section of the wall rolled back, revealing a large TV monitor.

Bolan heard the whirring of a VCR, the snap of the tape as the play mechanism caught, and Jason Marley's face appeared on the screen. But it was a different Jason Marley. He had aged ten years. His face was slack, as if the flesh were melting and sliding down over the cheekbones. His eyes were ringed with dark circles. There was a thin strand of spittle dangling from one corner of his mouth.

His lips looked like those of a fish, and they flapped soundlessly for a moment, then a voice, as close to the sound of a voice from the grave as Bolan ever wanted to hear, croaked from somewhere deep inside the ancient-looking man on the screen. The words were difficult to understand.

It appeared that Marley was lying in bed. At first his words sounded like mindless rambling. They dribbled to a halt. Marley's neck grew suddenly taut, and he tried to raise his head. The effort was too much for him, and the look that crept into his glazed eyes was one of profound disappointment at the result of his effort.

"What is this?" Bradley snapped. "What have you done to him?"

"Nothing. We have done nothing. We don't even know where this video was taken. All we know is that it is very recent."

"How recent?" Bolan asked.

"Within the past three or four days."

"You sure?"

"The plane went down only five days ago."

"The plane? What plane?" Bradley demanded. Then he snapped his fingers. "The L1011! The DCI was on that plane!"

"'Was' is the key word, I think," John suggested.

"The bodies. They were looking for three bodies. Three missing passengers. But I didn't know who. They must have been killed in the plane crash, so this can't be that recent. It had to be before the plane crash."

"It was no crash, Mr. Bradley. We know that. And so do your people. The plane must have gone down after Mr. Marley was removed."

"Impossible!"

"Watch...." The video flickered into fast-forward. The sluggish motion of Marley's head became an obscene convulsion as the tape sped past. "There." The frame froze, then backed up a bit.

"There what?"

"Look at the newspaper, there on one corner of the cot. You can just see a piece of it."

"So? You can't see any date on it."

John reached down to the floor beside his chair. With consummate casualness, he placed the paper on the table and slid it across to his two captives. It was an edition of the *München Zeitung*. There was no doubt they were one and the same. The date of the issue was four days before. Bolan looked at John, waiting for the news he knew would come. "The day *after* the L1011 went down. Now, how could that be, unless Mr. Marley got off that plane before it crashed?"

"It couldn't be."

"Where did you get the tape?" Bolan asked.

"Just as you have been busy in the past few days, so have I. Our paths have nearly crossed on three occasions. Two of them you know about. The third is irrelevant. But two nights ago, we learned about some odd activity in one of the neo-Nazi groups we have been watching and, increasingly, worrying about. We broke into their storefront headquarters and found little of value, as if they knew we were coming. But we did find the tape."

"What else does the tape show?"

"It is primarily a record of an interrogation of Mr. Marley, by two men, one who asks questions and one who administers the drugs. We don't know where he is being held or who is holding him. No image of either of the interrogators appears on the tape. Voices do, but they are no help to us. But the questioner obviously has a considerable amount of inside information."

"And you want us to help you identify the interrogators?" Bolan asked.

"That is part of it."

"What's the rest?"

"We propose to help locate your director and to assist in extracting him from his current situation."

"Why?"

"I was coming to that. Watch the screen again, please."

The door concealing the monitor closed. The lights went down, and a map of the continent gradually materialized on the wall. It held several black X's.

Four of them leaped out at Bolan immediately. "You've marked the location of Dolph Murray's assassination, the murders of Giovanni Badalamente and Klaus Mann and the abortive attack on the Lufthansa plane at the Munich airport.''

"Yes. Also the crash site of the L1011, the murders of our two agents."

"That's eight, but there are more X's than that."

"True. Some of those are suspect and possibly related. We see a pattern beginning, though it's not yet quite coherent. We think something significant is underway. Something so secret that it was essential to eliminate any agents in the coalition of right-wing extremists who gathered at Klingenbrunn. We suspect that something more significant than systemized murder and random terror is close at hand, but we don't know what or when."

Bolan leaned back in his chair. "I think it's time you answered a few of our questions."

"Fair enough."

"For starters, who are you? It's obvious you're Russian."

John smiled again, a faint flicker that Bolan would have missed if he hadn't been waiting for it. "Captain Sergei Yenikidze. We have a lot to do. We'd better get started."

## CHAPTER TWENTY-FOUR

Jason Marley was alert for the first time in a week. He was still weak, too weak, in fact, to sit up. But he could see the world without its customary gauze wrapping. He could think clearly, and the sound of the morning came to him through the window high on the wall with unaccustomed clarity.

When the door opened, he rolled his head easily toward the opening. James Harkness, his usual tweed jacket looking a bit rumpled, stood in the doorway, his expression more hangdog than usual.

He seemed to hover at the threshold, as if waiting for permission to enter. Marley wouldn't give him the satisfaction of inviting him in. It dawned on Harkness only slowly that Marley was beating him at his own game. He had reduced the master of the waiting game to a nonentity, a mere obstruction in the doorway whose existence he wouldn't even bother to acknowledge.

Finally, when Harkness realized the degree to which he had ceased to matter to Marley, he said, "Good morning, Jason. You're looking better."

Marley rolled his head the other way on the cot. He noticed the fresh sheets, the stiffness of the new pillowcase, still smelling faintly of starch and the slightly scorched scent of the iron.

Harkness stepped gingerly into the room. "I think we should have a little talk, Jason. I have an interesting proposition for you."

Marley turned his penetrating blue eyes on his subordinate, but still said nothing. His face was relaxed, but it no longer felt as if his flesh were a thick coating of meat on bones to which it wasn't attached. He felt whole. The weakness was nothing. That would go away in time. But the feeling of dissolution, that had been horrible. He was determined that it wouldn't happen again.

"Would you like to hear my proposition?" Harkness asked. "Jason? Would you? Say something, damn it!"

Marley smiled. His mouth remained closed, the jaw set almost the way a spiteful child would do it. It seemed to jut forward with just a hint of defiance.

"Jason, it's very important. I really think we should talk about it."

"I have nothing I care to discuss with you, James. You used your drugs to suck every last word out of me. Now, when I can choose whether to speak or not, I choose not to. Go get your pharmacist if you want to have a conversation with me. Better yet, go talk to *him*. You have nothing to say which could be of the remotest interest to me."

"But that's where you're wrong, Jason. I think it's important, and I'm going to tell you whether you want to listen to me or not. Your life may depend on your response."

"I have no life, Harkness. You've seen to that. The moment you brought me here—sooner, the moment you murdered Harold in cold blood—you signed my death warrant. Even a dullard such as yourself should be able to see that, or has your ambition made you blind, as well as stupid?"

"Insult me all you want, Jason. I'm still going to have my say."

Marley chose not to respond.

"I suppose you're wondering why you were brought here. It's quite simple, really. You knew things we needed to know. You were the best witness, the horse's mouth, so to say."

"And you're at the other end of the horse, James. In fact, you *are* the other end of the horse."

"Cute. Very cute. But you can't deter me with sarcasm. Because this isn't about me or about my personal ambition. If I'm involved in any way, it's because my vision of the future, one I think you might actually share, is at stake. You see, Jason, Germany has always been our buffer against the former Soviet Union. You know that as well as I do. What you don't seem to understand is that it has to remain so, even though the Union has broken up. But the chancellor is an idiot. He thinks that the cold war is over. He thinks he can shape the future according to some idiotic notion of the brotherhood of Europe, the commonality of interest. But that's just so much misguided drivel.''

In spite of his determination not to become engaged, Marley found himself listening to Harkness very carefully. He wouldn't give Harkness the satisfaction of betraying that interest, but he listened. But he tried to keep his face impassive, hoping that Harkness wouldn't notice the strain.

''You don't trust the republics of the former Soviet Union any more than I do. But Kohl trusts them. He's playing right into their hands. Germany has to be stronger than that, more independent, more like the old Germany, the one that made Stalin tremble in his boots and catch his foul, garlicky breath every time he looked to the West. That's the kind of Germany we need. The chancellor doesn't understand that.''

Marley raised his head as best he could. The effort cost him some of his barely restored energy reserves, but he couldn't not do it. ''So you think you have all the answers.''

''Not me, no. But I know someone who does. You know him, too. He told me so. He told me you have known each other for a very long time.''

''And you believed him?''

''Of course. I checked it first, made sure it was true. It is, and I accept that at face value. But it's the future, not the past, that's important.''

"You propose to lead your own little cabal to make Germany's past its future, is that it?"

"In so many words, yes. That's exactly what I propose."

"So you sold your soul and stole mine in order to make this harebrained gobbledygook a reality, did you?"

"It will work. It can't fail to work. If Germany has a strong leader, it will stand between us and whoever rises from the rubble of what was once the Soviet Union. If Germany is strong and has a weak leader, the Russians win, can't you see? And we can't have that."

"So you've become a kingmaker now, in addition to all your other awesome responsibilities. You want to shoulder the burden of defining the future of Europe, and perhaps of the world? Just how do you propose to bring this bastard child of yours into the world, through the barrel of a gun? Will your Germany cling to a bullet and come kicking and screaming into the world through a rifled womb? That's not birth, James, that's an abortion. An abomination."

"You're wrong, Jason. You have to listen to me. You have to hear me out, then make your decision. Don't decide now. I can bring the man I'm talking about in to see you. He can convince you."

"James, not only are you a fool, but you're a madman. Do you seriously think the world is ready for a Fourth Reich? Do you think the world deserves such a horrible perversion? Does Germany deserve it, or does it deserve the chance to prove that Hitler was an aberration?''

''Don't be so weak-kneed, Jason. Face facts.''

''No, *you* face facts, James. You're dead wrong, so wrong, in fact, that if you succeed, you will be ignored by history but will still be the arch-villain of our century. You can't kick over a rock in this country without sending some dark, slimy memory of the past scurrying for new cover. Once and future Nazis are a dime a dozen. You won't convince me that one of their kind ought to decide the fate of Western Europe.''

''That's precisely what you must accept.''

Marley let his head loll to one side. ''Goodbye, James. Don't bother to wake me. Just put the bullet in my head. I would rather go out suddenly, sleeping.''

''But you—''

''No.''

''Jason, I—''

''I said no and I meant no.'' His voice sounded weary now, most of his feeble energy sapped by the enormity of Harkness's stupidity. ''Go away, James. You have pumped drugs into me and sucked out words and every shred of self-respect. I've given you the lives of good men, men with more courage than you can understand. And you have, or will soon, waste that courage the way every coward does it, by striking them without warning. For all I know, they

might already be dead. You have caused me to con-
demn them and they will never forgive me, nor
should they. Just as I will never forgive you, nor can
I. Now get out of my sight.''

''I won't give up that easily, Jason.''

''You don't have to give up, James. You're already defeated. The game is up and you have lost.
You lost the minute you sold your soul to this mad
scheme.''

''I can do it without you, you know.''

''I know. Just as they can do it without *you*. And
they most certainly will. It suddenly occurs to me
that this is an odd conversation, James. Two dead
men are talking to each other, but only one of them
knows it. But the other will learn it soon enough.''

Marley closed his eyes. He didn't look around
again until he heard the door close softly, then the
tapping of Harkness's heels on the concrete floor as
they moved away from the door.

For a long time he wondered whether he should
have agreed, just to buy himself some time. But he
knew better. He knew whoever it was who had seduced Harkness wouldn't be as foolish as his victim.
He would be shrewd, a hard-nosed man with no soul
and a vindictive passion for history repeating itself in
its most loathsome form.

Such a man wouldn't be as easily fooled as Harkness, who so desperately wanted his mistake to be
validated. But there was no validation possible for so
gross a misunderstanding of human history. Hark-

ness would learn that lesson the hard way. Marley's only regret was that he wouldn't be there to see it, wouldn't be there to say "I told you so."

He wanted to sleep. But he knew he would be unable to. Instead, he started sifting his past, trying to find the one man who could possibly be Harkness's candidate. It was such a long list. There were so many possibilities. It would take time, but he had nothing else to do.

He would discover the answer; he had to. He wouldn't be able to accept the certainty of his death unless he did know. But when he finally tracked it down, would the knowledge be of any real value? he wondered.

Then he knew for the first time that what Harkness really wanted wasn't to convert him, but to be converted. He had come with his best argument, hoping to be defeated, to be shown the error of his ways, to have an alternate reality offered to him on a silver platter.

But life wasn't that simple. And not understanding that simple fact, Harkness wasn't able to understand anything at all. He wanted certainty where there could be none. He wanted some kind of truth that made sense in a world where that kind of truth didn't exist. It was the fundamental misapprehension of seeing the world as a place where orderliness wasn't only desirable, but attainable.

Harkness couldn't stand to live with ambivalence. He preferred the cold, unyielding certainty of a Hitler clone to the fuzzy uncertainty of an ineffective chancellor.

And so he planned to orchestrate the assassination of the architect of a reunified Germany and hand the republic over to God only knew what kind of madman. That was the plan. It had to be. And there was nothing he could do about it.

## CHAPTER TWENTY-FIVE

Mack Bolan watched Yenikidze as the man spoke to someone on the phone, his face impassive as usual.

Yenikidze nodded twice during the call, asked one question, then hung up. Looking at Bolan and Bradley, he said, "We have a serious problem."

"What's happened?" the warrior asked.

"The small NATO arsenal at Rosenheim has just been attacked. The place has been destroyed."

"You think it's connected to what we're dealing with?" Bradley asked.

"Could be."

"Exactly what happened?"

Yenikidze shook his head. "No one knows. It is a small-arms depot, or rather I should say 'was,' and there was only a small detachment of British troops for security. There were no survivors. And no witnesses."

Bolan turned to Bradley. "Can you find out what progress has been made on the L1011 crash investigation?"

"I suppose so." He hesitated for a moment. "But I don't see what difference it—"

"If that plane went down without Jason Marley, we are dealing with a very sophisticated organization. They wanted him for some reason. I've got to believe it was to get information on your sources inside the right wing. If Marley was forced to give somebody up, it might explain what happened to Murray and Badalamente."

"You're trying to make a mountain of something less than an anthill."

Yenikidze interrupted. "I don't think so. When was the last time you lost agents in that kind of work in so short a period of time?"

"How the hell should I know?"

Yenikidze shrugged. "All right, let me suggest to you that it has probably been a long time. Add our two, Klaus Mann and the airport attack, and you have not only an obvious attempt to smoke out potential leaks, sources that might compromise an operation about to be undertaken, but the emergence of something much more aggressive."

"I still don't see how that could be connected to the plane wreck."

Bolan took over. "Look, Mike, if somebody inside the CIA is behind this, you've got a security problem of tremendous importance. It seems to me it would have taken some inside cooperation to pull off a stunt like getting Marley off that plane, then blowing the L1011 to cover the fact. With the wreck, you can't be sure about anything. Maybe the body is still out there. You keep looking, but you don't even consider the possibility that he *wasn't* on the plane. But we know better, and so far they don't know we know. We have to move while we still have that advantage."

"Unless they know we've seen the videotape...."

"Right."

"So why don't we try to find whoever made the tape? If they've got Marley, then they're about as deeply involved as you can be."

"Yenikidze and I will handle that. But neither one of us can get to the investigative data. That's something you've got to do. Get to Mitchell. Try to explain where you've been without telling him what you know. Dig up as much as you can. Look at the report drafts, check the raw data, talk to the investigators. Listen for scuttlebutt. Just find out what you can. And watch your back. Assume Mitchell may be involved."

"And what are you doing while I go poking around the garbage cans in my own shop?"

"We'll try to find the origin of that tape."

Bradley looked at Yenikidze, then at Bolan. "You and him?" he asked. "You believe that line of garbage? You trust this guy that much?"

"I don't have any choice. If he's right, we don't have much time. And if he's wrong, no harm done."

"Except he learns something about the crash investigation."

Yenikidze shook his head. "No. I don't care about that unless I am right. If Marley was taken off the plane, we have to know about it because it might tell us something we need to know. The information might be there, staring somebody in the face. But if they don't have the abduction as a working hypothesis, those details which tend to support it will mean nothing. You must be very cautious, because we must assume there is someone on the inside who may be involved."

"Your own outfit might also be compromised," Bolan pointed out. "After all, you said yourself that two of your agents have been terminated. I think we have to assume that both sides have been betrayed."

"I have thought about that. We will have to make certain that no one knows what we are doing. I personally will have no further contact with my superiors. Once we leave here, we cannot come back until we know exactly who is behind all of this."

Bolan looked at Bradley. "If you're in, you've got to say so right now. Once we start, there's no turning back."

"I'm in. I just think we might be jumping off the wrong end of the dock. And I mean, after all, there is such a thing as coincidence."

"In my line of work," Bolan said, "there's no room for coincidence."

"Okay. How do I get in touch with you?"

Yenikidze said, "Joseph will take you where you want to go. He will let you know how to establish contact."

"I was talking to Pollock."

The Executioner looked at Bradley. "Mike, there's no room for half measures here. This is too big for any one of us to handle. If we're going to turn this rock over, we're going to have to work together."

Bradley nodded. "I understand that, but—"

"Joseph will handle it," Yenikidze interrupted. "We have to hurry." He opened the door. "Joseph, Mr. Bradley will go with you. You know what to do."

Joseph nodded and turned on his heel. Bradley moved hesitantly toward the door. He sensed that Joseph wasn't waiting, and he broke into a trot.

"Be careful, Mr. Bradley," Yenikidze called after him. "All our lives may depend on you."

"Yeah, right."

Yenikidze closed the door on the retreating footsteps. "Now I think we should decide where *we* go from here."

"I'm curious," Bolan said. "What's in it for you?"

"In it?"

"What do you stand to gain here?"

Yenikidze offered a cold smile. "My father was killed at Stalingrad. We have rather vivid memories of another Germany. It is not pleasant to think about that time, but it is even less pleasant to consider the possibility that it might be repeated. That would seem to be the purpose of the men we are trying to find."

"You seem pretty sure of that."

"I am a logical man, Mr. Pollock. We know, you and I, that there are today in Europe many men who would wish to see the outcome of World War II reversed. Many of them are powerful men. Many of them have access to considerable amounts of money. Some of them are even the very same men who had responsibility for that war. No doubt we will be encountering some of these men in the next few days. Logic tells me that, and it also tells me that such men are far and away the most likely sponsors of this madness."

"There's logic and there's logic. There are, after all, other possibilities."

"I understand that. But we don't have the luxury of waiting to see what happens. We have to take the initiative. To me, that means that we start with the most probable and work our way back from there. Better a foolish alarmist than a complacent fool."

"That's fine if you have some place to start. Do you?"

"Not really."

"Let's look at the tape again."

"What good will that do?"

"We won't know unless we try it, will we?"

"Time, Mr. Pollock, we don't have much time."

"Unless we have something to go on, we have nothing *but* time."

"Fine. You watch the tape again. I have some things I have to do." He punched a combination of buttons on the control panel. The wall slid open and the monitor reappeared. It was already glowing a dull black.

Bolan took a seat at the table, examined the control panel and rewound the tape.

"Why did you do that?" Yenikidze seemed annoyed.

"If I'm going to watch, I might as well watch from the beginning. Any reason I shouldn't?"

"Of course not." But Yenikidze shook his head as if he couldn't imagine a greater waste of time. "I'll be back as soon as I can."

Bolan watched the door close behind Yenikidze, then waited for the tape to reach its beginning. The VCR clicked, and he pushed the Play button. The screen went fuzzy for a moment, then Marley's haggard face appeared. The picture flickered again, Marley vanished for a couple of moments, then slowly reemerged from the snowy flicker.

Bolan listened to the interrogation for a few minutes, then turned the sound off. He wanted to watch, try to get an impression without being distracted by the words. After fifteen minutes the image fluttered, seemed to bend over on its side, then reappeared. For a brief instant he thought he saw something in the fluttering picture. He rewound the tape and played it back.

There was something there, but it was too indistinct. Maybe, he thought, some sort of computer analysis might fasten on the image and enhance it, but that wasn't possible now. He sped through for a few minutes, watching the interrogation at high speed, thinking about the flutter, the image he thought he saw.

On a hunch he pushed fast-forward and let the machine run the tape all the way through to its end. Then, backing off a bit, he pushed Play again. Marley's head was motionless on a rumpled pillow. The picture flickered again, then there was another image, this time longer.

He understood then. The tape had been used before. The interrogation was recorded over whatever had been there before. But in those brief flickers between stopping and starting the second recording, a bit of tape passed the head without being erased or recorded over. It was simply a question of coordination, as if someone had taped the interrogation in pieces, watched it and reset for the next installment, but unintentionally letting a little bit of the old recording survive.

Here at the end, there was a little more. Not much, maybe a minute. But there was something there that might be useful. An ornate picture frame, overlaid with gold leaf and featuring very elaborate carving. A corner of the painting could also be seen. If they could find the place where that picture hung, they would have taken a giant step.

But how?

## CHAPTER TWENTY-SIX

Mike Bradley paced nervously. Mitchell was already nearly a half hour late. The park was deserted. The lights still burned, but there wasn't a soul around. He'd gotten there early to make sure they hadn't set a trap for him. Cruising around the Tiergarten on a bicycle, he'd explored every conceivable way in and out. The paths wound through thick trees and across open meadows, intertwined like a ball of snakes. As long as he got a head start, he should be okay.

Unless they decided to hit him from long range.

Once the sun went down, he'd hunkered in a stand of birches. He looked at his watch. It was nearly 2:00 a.m. He'd give Mitchell another five minutes. After that, he'd be smoke, lost in the wisps of fog drifting among the trees.

Near the edge of the park, he could see the light rack of a police car. It cruised slowly along the perimeter of the park just beyond the stone wall along the Tiergartenstrasse. The car passed a gate, and for a moment he could see in profile two officers in the front seat. There was someone in the rear, only one as far as he could tell, and all three faces were turned toward the opening in the wall. For a second his heart nearly stopped. It was a trap, he thought. Mitchell had turned over on him. But the cruiser passed by and a few seconds later, it was just a light bar again, glittering under a streetlight.

It started to rain, at first just a spattering of small drops hissing on the leaves. The breeze picked up, and the fog thickened a bit. He could still see fairly well, and the fog might actually be an ally in the event he had to cut and run.

It wasn't like Dan Mitchell to be late. In his head he tried to reconstruct the telephone conversation. He had spoken quickly to avoid being tracked. Maybe Mitchell had misunderstood. Maybe he had given his boss the wrong location. The Tiergarten was a big park. Maybe Mitchell was sitting on a bench somewhere, wondering where the hell Bradley was. It was possible, but he didn't think so. He had checked the map several times, marked the location carefully on his map, then written a terse but complete description. It wasn't a set of coordinates, but it came damn close.

Three minutes left, and then he would split. Maybe he could find a telephone and call Mitchell's home. But the man had a life, he had a family. If Mitchell was out, what would he say to Mrs. Mitchell? There was no innocent way to explain a phone call at two-thirty in the morning, even if you were calling an Intelligence officer. Wives were like that. They knew things, and suspected others. It would cause trouble, and he was already in enough trouble with Dan

Mitchell. In two minutes he would go back to the hotel. He could call Mitchell in the morning. If there was a morning.

The last ten seconds ticked off, and Bradley backed out of his nest in the birches. There was no sign of Mitchell, and not a hint that he might be on the way. He worried for a moment that it might be a trap, but then realized that if they wanted to snare him, they wouldn't have waited this long. They couldn't know how patient he was prepared to be, and would probably assume he was skittish and likely to bolt within a minute or two of the designated time.

Bradley stayed off the paths as he headed toward the gate. He saw someone across the Tiergarten-strasse, lingering in the shadows under a tall linden tree. The man seemed to be trying to avoid being seen from the park, but Bradley couldn't be sure.

The man in the shadows suddenly unfurled an umbrella as the rain started to beat down harder. He was big enough to be Dan Mitchell, his shoulders broader than normal for a man his size.

Bradley pulled his bicycle behind the trees, then pressed himself up against the rough bark of an elm. He could hear the man's footsteps on the damp pavement now, an occasional splash when he slapped a thick sole into a puddle.

Reaching into his jacket pocket, the CIA agent pulled his Browning 9 mm automatic and made sure the safety was off, then worked the slide to chamber a round. The man was beginning more and more to resemble Dan Mitchell, but he still couldn't see his face.

As he reached the shadows under the trees, the man slowed to a walk. He stopped for a moment and turned to look back the way he'd come, as if he was afraid of being followed. He leaned forward from the waist, trying to see through the rain falling beyond the protection of the trees, saw nothing and shrugged.

As he turned, Bradley got a look at his face. It was Dan Mitchell. Waiting until Mitchell was past him, he whistled sharply. "Dan!"

Mitchell stopped in his tracks and turned to look into the shadows. "That you, Bradley?"

"Over here, Dan."

"What the hell are you hiding from?"

"Get over here, quick. Don't let anyone see you."

"Let who see me, for Christ's sake? It's nearly two-thirty in the morning. Do you have any idea how ridiculous this is?"

"Wait until you hear what I'm going to tell you."

"It better be good." Mitchell stepped off the path and moved closer to the trees. "Gina is ready to cut my balls off and fry them up for breakfast."

"I'm sorry, but this couldn't wait, and there's no other way to do this."

"Do what? Why the hell couldn't you come into the office like I told you? Like you were supposed to a few days ago? What the hell is going on? Have you completely lost your marbles?"

"I hope so."

"What's that supposed to mean?"

"It's supposed to mean that I sure as hell hope I'm wrong. I'd rather be imagining things than have what I'm going to tell you turn out to be true."

"Well, get on with it. I should be home in bed."

Bradley paused for a deep breath. He trusted Mitchell, and hadn't realized until that moment just how much. "You have to promise me one thing."

"What?"

"This goes no farther than you. If you think I'm crazy, okay. But whether you do or not, you don't say a word to anybody."

"Mike, you know I can't do—"

"Yes or no, Dan. No bullshit."

"Christ almighty, Mike, I— Hell, all right."

"You break your word, you might get me killed. And yourself, too."

"All right. Spill it."

"You didn't find Marley's body yet, did you."

It wasn't a question, and Mitchell seemed confused at first. "How did you know we were—"

"You didn't, did you."

"No."

"Do you know why?"

"Oh, hell, it was a mess. You were out there, you saw it."

"I saw it, but that's not why. I'll tell you why. Because he wasn't on the plane when it went down."

"You're nuts. Mike, what's wrong with—"

"Dan. Read my lips. He wasn't on the plane."

Mitchell sighed. "Oh, and just how do you happen to know that? Have you been talking to him?"

"No, but I've seen a videotape of him. Somebody's holding him prisoner."

"That's ridiculous!"

"Dan, I saw it, okay? And there was a newspaper that came out after the plane went down. You could see it in the room where they were interrogating him."

"Interrogating...who? Who was interrogating him?"

"I don't know. They're not visible on the tape. You can hear their voices, but you can't see them. You said you were looking for three bodies. Who were the other two?"

"Why do you want to know that? So you can tell me you saw tape of them, too?"

"No. Because somebody on the inside is part of it."

"Part of what?"

"The plot."

"What plot?"

"I'm not sure, exactly. But I know there is one. Murray, Badalamente, the airport thing. Klaus Mann. All part of the plot."

"They're all dead. And how did you know about Mann?"

"Never mind how I knew. But it's all connected. I can't prove it, but I need your help if I'm going to get any closer."

"Mike . . ."

"Who was on the plane, Dan? Who's still missing?"

"I can't tell—"

"Dan." Bradley shook his head. "Look, I'll tell you as much as I can. But you have to help me out on this. I need to know. Whoever else is missing may still be alive, just like Marley is."

"But he isn't, Mike. He can't be."

"Then where's his body?"

"I don't know." Mitchell was struggling not to accept what he was being told, but he was wavering. Bradley could see it. He pushed a little harder. "Maybe we have it. We have some unidentifieds."

"Just suppose I'm right. Suppose for just a minute that somebody pulled it off somehow."

"How could you prove it?"

"I don't know. Maybe if I took a look at the raw files on the investigation. Maybe there's something

there you didn't notice because you weren't looking
for it, some glitch, some inconsistency."

"Mike, I—"

"Dan, please. What if I'm right?"

"Okay, okay. I'll see what I can do. Where can I
reach you?"

"No. We go now. There's no time for going
through channels. Besides, it's not safe."

"But I can't... Ah, shit! Let's go."

# CHAPTER TWENTY-SEVEN

Dan Mitchell's office was almost dark. A single light glowed in the corridor outside. The large plate-glass window let some of the light in, and Mike Bradley glanced over his shoulder nervously while he waited for Mitchell to turn on the overhead light.

"You sure there's no one here, Dan?" he asked. "I don't like the way it feels."

Mitchell laughed. "That's because you're crazy, and you're starting to realize it. It's the middle of the night. Why shouldn't it feel weird?"

"Laugh if you want to. When this is all over, you'll see who's crazy and who's not."

The lights flashed on, and Bradley winced as if he'd been hit. Mitchell noticed. "You really are spooked, aren't you, Mike?"

"You better believe it." He entered the office. "Let's get to it."

Bradley went to a large door in the center of one side wall. He inserted his magnetic clearance card. When the first lock acknowledged his clearance, he punched a long sequence of digits into the second security tier and pushed a button. "Hope I got it right,'' he said. ''I forget the numbers half the time. If I fuck up, security will be here in sixty seconds.''

A bank of green lights began to blink rapidly. ''That's part two,'' Mitchell said. ''One more to go.'' He punched in a second sequence, and was rewarded by a second row of blinking emeralds. Grabbing the large wheel mounted in the center of the door, he gave it a vigorous turn, then pulled back on a steel bar across the center. The door pulled outward, then slid to the left as he gave it a shove.

''Let's go, Mike,'' he said, stepping into the security file room and reaching for a light switch on the inside. A fluorescent bulb pinged once, flickered, then went on. Bradley stood in the doorway.

Mitchell looked at him. ''Come on, damn it! Look at all this garbage we have to go through. They've been piling shit in here for a week. How in hell you expect to find anything in one night is beyond me.''

''We don't have any choice, Dan. I don't even know if we will find anything. But we have to try.''

A long walnut table stood in the center of the room. Ordinarily it was clean and empty. But at the moment it was crammed with stacks of manila folders, binders, bundles of computer printouts held together with rubber bands and the assorted detritus that was the fallout of any anomalous event that occurred in a bureaucracy.

The chairs along either side of the table would be useless, because the paper mountain towered over the head of anyone sitting at the table. The far end offered the only clear space. Mitchell grabbed two of the chairs and arranged them across the end of the table. He sat, and Bradley couldn't see him until he got halfway down the table.

Mitchell patted the seat of the second chair. "Have a seat, Mike. The ball is now officially in your court. Tell me what we're looking for."

Bradley stood next to the chair, surveying the mass of documents. "Is there any order in this mess?"

"Not yet. And if you want to know whether there will be, I'm afraid I can't answer that. It's way too early. We don't even have all the papers. They are in such a tizzy back home that a lot of this is about as helpful as toilet paper. But every mother's son is cranking out paper to save his own ass. Some lucky son of a bitch will have the job of organizing it all. Someday. You're looking at the original haystack, son, and you tell me you don't even know for sure if there's a needle in it or what it looks like if there is one. Does that about sum it up?"

Bradley sank into his chair. "You got it."

"My wife will kill me for this one. I can feel it in my bones."

"Dan, I'm sorry. But you're the only one I can trust in the whole shop. And I'm not even sure about you." He watched Mitchell closely, not knowing what to expect.

What he got was a smile. "I guess I'd worry a little if you didn't. Tell me once more what we're trying to find."

Bradley set a legal-size pad on the table between them. He clicked a little extra lead out of his pencil point and drew two lines across the top of the first sheet. Bisecting the sheet, he moved back to the top. On one side he write Questions and on the other, Answers.

"Okay, basically what we have to figure out is whether, and how, they could have gotten Marley off that plane. We have to start at the beginning. Do we even know he was on it? I guess that's our first question. I'll bet everyone is working on the assumption that he was, but can we be sure?"

"All right, I'll take that one." Mitchell shrugged out of his jacket and draped it over the back of his chair. "It'll take a while."

"Hey, we've got all night."

"Yeah."

Mitchell got up and moved along the far side of the table. Starting at the opposite end, he began to work his way through the piles of material, using two chairs for the first stack as he examined the piles item by item.

Bradley walked down the other side and started doing the same. He wasn't sure what he was looking for, but needed to get some familiarity with the huge volume of material in front of him. Mitchell was a third of the way along his side when he pulled a file free and slapped it with the back of his hand. "This is a good place to start," he said, moving back to his chair.

Bradley continued sifting and sorting, trying to put together files that were related in some way. A huge computer inventory of recovered parts, bits and pieces, he put on the floor. It was nearly a foot thick, and putting it aside gave him a feeling of accomplishment, even though it barely made a dent in the mountain of data.

In the next stack he found a series of reports from the team of medical examiners. He grabbed them and brought them to his corner of the table and sat down. Opening the first one, he nearly lost it. Each of the thick folders was an autopsy report. The photographs attached to the left cover were more graphic than he could stomach.

Doing his best to ignore the photos, he read the first autopsy summary. It didn't tell him anything useful. The victim, who was unidentified, pending the receipt of dental records from the Air Force, had been burned beyond recognition, although the forensic pathologist had concluded the cause of death was massive head trauma and multiple skull fractures.

One by one Bradley worked through the reports. After eight summaries he had learned the names of seven of the victims. Positive IDs had been established on all but the first.

He was about to open the ninth folder when Mitchell said, "Okay, Mike, here's something. It doesn't help our argument much, though."

Bradley noted the pronoun and smiled to himself. Dan Mitchell's skepticism was shifting its focus. Instead of wondering about his subordinate's sanity, he was now an investigative partner. There was a puzzle, and he was looking for the solution instead of challenging the credibility of the man who had posed the question.

"What've you got?" he asked.

"Well, I got a passenger manifest. Marley's name is on it. So I guess he was on the plane."

"That doesn't prove anything. Those things are often drawn up in expectation of personnel, instead of actual records of who was really on the plane. We have to find something more concrete."

Mitchell nodded. "You're right. I guess I was just looking for a quick fix."

"Dan, it doesn't matter. But if we're going to prove he was taken off, we have to prove he got on it in the first place."

"You really believe they took him off, don't you?"

"I *know* they did."

Mitchell nodded and went back to the paperwork. Bradley opened the next medical report. He was inured to the gory details now and plowed through the summary report quickly. At the bottom something was underlined in red. The bright color on the bland black-and-white typewritten sheet caught his eye. He read it twice before it registered: "Cause of death—gunshot wound to the head."

Bradley stared at the words for a long time. He watched Mitchell poring through a manila folder. Mitchell seemed to sense something and glanced up. "Got something?"

"You bet your ass."

"Don't hold out on me. What is it?"

"One of the victims, identity unknown, pending receipt of further medical information, died of a gunshot wound to the head."

"What?"

"That's what it says here."

"Let me see that."

Bradley shoved the folder halfway across the table. He saw Mitchell's eyes wander involuntarily to the photographs. "Where is it? Wait, I see it."

He flipped through the pages. When he came to the section headed ballistics, he read to himself, his lips moving slightly and a soft whisper escaping them. "They recovered two .22-caliber slugs from the cranium," he said. "But they don't know who it is."

"Look, you don't have to know who it is to know that something happened on that fucking plane. If somebody got shot, what else happened? Who did the shooting? Why?"

"More questions for your pad...." Mitchell said, his voice trailing off.

"You got any plausible answers?"

"No, I don't."

"Then we better keep reading."

Mitchell put the folder on the floor, on top of the passenger manifest. Still shaking his head, he glanced at Bradley. "What the fuck is going on? Jesus!"

Bradley didn't have an answer. Not yet.

He picked up the next folder. This time the victim had a name. And this time the cause of death was the same. "Here's another one," he said. "Harold Carmichael. Shot in the head. Twice. With a .22."

"Harold? You're kidding!"

"I wish to hell I was, Dan. But it's all right here."

Mitchell leaned over to see for himself, then added the folder to the small stack on the floor.

Bradley checked the last medical report, but it contained nothing unexpected.

Mitchell continued plowing through a stack of loose papers. Bradley stood and walked back to the other end of the table. He was reaching for another folder when Mitchell snapped his fingers. "Here it is, Mike. Proof. Marley was patched through to the Secretary of State. From the plane." He held up a bluish piece of paper and waved it. "Onboard phone log. Communications on the ground made a record of everything. Marley talked to the Secretary of State while the plane was in the air."

"You believe me now?"

"Almost. You still got to show me how they got him off, and when. Parachutes aren't the answer, that much I know."

"Let's keep digging."

Bradley sat down with his next folder. Its first page was a summary of interviews of those present in the control tower at Tempelhof. It told him nothing he didn't already know. Starting on the individual interviews, he read carefully. It wasn't until the third page of the next-to-last interview he found anything that fit. "Listen to this," he shouted. "This is one of the traffic controllers talking."

Mitchell glanced up. "Go ahead. I'm listening."

"He says, 'I don't know, it was kind of weird. I don't know whether I should even mention it, but the plane, it was on the screen, then it wasn't. I went to get my boss, and the next thing I knew, it came back. It was off the screen maybe six, seven minutes. Maybe a little longer. I'm not sure. I didn't believe it at first, but it happened. I know that.'"

"You're shitting me!"

"It's right here, Dan. That goddamn plane landed, went back up and *then* somebody blew it out of the air. It had to happen that way."

"That's it, then. What do we do now?"

"We've got one more piece to find. We've got three unidentified bodies and three missing men. That's six possible names. We have to match them. The way I see it, we've got five candidates for the man or men who engineered this. Marley is one of the six. The other five names are the ones we want."

"Piece of cake. I've already got them right here." He held up a typewritten list. The only noise in the room was the click of his fingernail on the edge of the paper.

## CHAPTER TWENTY-EIGHT

Erika Mann entered the room, and Bolan felt as if someone had turned on an air conditioner. She crossed to the sofa and sat. She leaned behind the back of the couch, and the room was suddenly filled with the sound of a harpsichord. "Wanda Landowska," she said. "Bach always helps me think."

Bolan nodded but didn't say anything.

"I'm surprised you would dare to come back here," Erika went on. "You know how I feel."

"But you know you're wrong. You know Willi Hauser was telling you the truth."

"I know no such thing. I know Willi believed in you. And Willi is dead now. Please state your business. I'm afraid if I am in the same room with you for too long, I will lose my self-control."

"I want to introduce someone."

"I know who Sergei is. Don't bother to put a pleasant veneer on things, Mr. Pollock. It won't change anything. Not a thing."

Bolan nodded. "I told Willi that if I came across anything that might lead to the men who killed your father, I'd tell him. That's why I'm here."

"Why isn't Willi here to receive this news himself? That's a very interesting question, I think. Perhaps the most interesting thing about you. How your associates all seem to die sudden, violent deaths. Does Mr. Yenikidze know that about you? I'm sure he'd find it very interesting."

"If you're suggesting I killed Willi Hauser, you couldn't be more wrong."

"I'm not suggesting anything, Herr Pollock. Just making an observation. It is a curious thing, don't you think? Even if you are as innocent as you claim."

"I saw what happened to Willi Hauser," Yenikidze said.

Erika scowled. "I wasn't speaking to you, Sergei. I was talking to him." She stabbed a long, slender finger Bolan's way.

"But I was there. It was not his fault."

"But of course, you are here with him, which means you must also want something from me. Naturally, if you are in league with him, you would seek to exonerate him. Do you think I'm a fool, Sergei?"

"You know better than that. All three of us want the same thing. We want to get to the men who were responsible for Herr Mann's murder. It is just that our motives are different."

"And how is that, Sergei?"

Bolan fielded the question. "You want revenge. That's a plain, simple and understandable motive. I have no quarrel with it. I was once in the position to want the same thing.''

''And what did you do, Herr Pollock? Did you receive the logical suspect in your home and open your heart to him? Did you put your resources at his disposal? Is that what you did?''

Bolan shook his head. ''I killed him.''

''Go on,'' she prompted. ''Perhaps after all you are not what I think you are.''

''No one ever is. But Sergei and I have a more pressing and more complex problem. We have reason to believe the same men who murdered your father are also responsible for several other recent murders. We think they're planning something big. We've seen only the advancing tip of the iceberg. We have to know what lies below the surface.''

''And you expect me to help you, is that it?''

''We hope you will.''

Erika stared at Bolan for a long time. He didn't know whether she was thinking about his request or simply trying to find the words in which to express her refusal. Finally she heaved a long sigh. ''What do you want me to do?''

''Do you have video equipment?''

''Yes. Have you rented a movie, Herr Pollock?''

''Not exactly. There might be something you can tell us, something on the tape that could mean something to you but not to us. It's a slim hope, but it's one of the few we have.''

She stood immediately. Having decided she would assist them, she was suddenly all business. "Follow me, please."

She led them down a long corridor. At the far end an elaborately carved wooden door yielded to her touch, swung inward and revealed a flight of stairs. She started down, turning when she reached a small landing.

Bolan and Yenikidze followed her. When they were on the stairs, she pressed a button and the door swung closed. She pressed another button, and Bolan heard the snap of electronically controlled bolts.

At the bottom of the stairs, he found himself in a large, high-ceilinged room. Filing cabinets lined one wall. Three computers were angled in a nook in one corner, partially set off from the rest of the room by a chest-high partition.

In another corner a round table with eight chairs created a kind of wall-less conference room. An array of electronic equipment had been stacked with precision on steel shelving. Erika stopped on the far side of the table. "Give me the tape," she demanded, holding out a manicured hand.

Yenikidze reached into his shirt, removed the cassette and handed it over.

Turning her back, Erika threw a master switch and every diode on the wall began to glow. She shoved the tape into a VCR and pushed the Rewind button. The tape was at the beginning, the machine clicked, and she sat down.

She lowered the lights and pointed toward a screen for a projection TV. The first flicker was almost immediately replaced by the sickly visage of Jason Marley. With remote control in hand, she covered a button with one brilliantly polished nail and froze the image. "What am I looking for?" she asked.

"Anything that seems significant. Do you recognize that man?"

"Are you joking? Of course I do. He is the director of your Central Intelligence Agency. Is that what you wanted to know?"

"I wish it were. Let me give you some background."

"Please do."

"As far as the American government knows, Jason Marley was killed in a plane crash a few days ago. His body hasn't been recovered to date, but the official belief is that he was killed in the crash."

"And you don't believe it, is that it?"

"I know it isn't true. That tape was made after the crash. On the basis of internal evidence, it couldn't possibly have been made beforehand. What we have to find out is where he is. If we do that, and if we can locate the men who are holding him, I'm convinced we'll also have located the men who are responsible for your father's death."

"And what convinces you of that, reasonably or otherwise?"

"If Marley was taken off that plane somehow, then it had to have been done with inside help, CIA help. At the same time several CIA agents and—not coincidentally, Sergei and I believe—several members of Russian Intelligence have been murdered. All five of the men we know about were underground and had penetrated right-wing extremist groups both on the continent and elsewhere. It's our belief that these murders were engineered by the same men who abducted Marley. All as a prelude to something much larger, but again, we don't know what, only that such a conclusion is a logical extrapolation of what we do know."

"And what is the connection to my father? How does this help me?"

"I was going to meet with your father to seek his help. I think whoever killed him knew that, and knew what I was looking for. He might also have known, or believed, that your father knew something that would have helped me."

"And they killed him for that reason? Why not just kill you?"

"They have tried that, too. But I think they were afraid of your father, that his experience and his network would have given him access to their secret, perhaps only by accident, but they couldn't afford the risk."

"I see. And what am I to look for on the tape?"

"Anything that might be helpful. We don't know who the two interrogators are, for example. You might recognize their voices. Perhaps something in the questioning will give you an idea. Maybe something they ask will be based on something only a very few people could know. And at the end, there's some evidence that this tape was made by recording over a previously existing tape. There are some images that might contain something you could recognize. There is a painting, part of it. And a very unusual frame for the painting. Part of it can be seen in detail. Perhaps you will recognize the painting or the frame. Whatever you find of interest . . ."

"Very well." She lowered the lights the rest of the way. Releasing the tape, she sat back to watch.

Bolan found himself watching Erika Mann. Her extraordinary face looked pale in the wash of white light from the large screen. Her jaw was set like that of a stone sculpture, and her eyes remained fixed on the screen. From time to time she would lean forward to hear more clearly. The long fingers of her left hand drummed on the tabletop.

The tape was nearly two hours long. As it was drawing near its end, Erika Mann had still betrayed no sign of recognition. Once or twice she had glanced at Bolan, her mouth about to frame a question, but she had stopped with her finger poised over the Pause button then shaken her head and let the tape continue.

The screen fluttered then, and Erika leaned forward. For a moment the corner of the painting was visible. She backed the tape up and froze the image.

"Do you recognize something?" Bolan asked.

She didn't answer. Instead, she rewound the tape a bit, let it play, froze it, then let it move on. The camera panned away from the painting, then back, this time showing a little more detail of the frame and the canvas.

He watched her chew on her lower lip. Yenikidze, too, was leaning forward. "Well?" he asked.

"I'm not sure. It looks..." Again she shook her head. "I don't know."

"What about the interrogators?"

"Americans. Obviously trained in this sort of thing, so we can rule out simple terrorists. Those are agents. But I didn't recognize either voice. Their questions obviously tie them to the men who were murdered, and therefore to their murderers. But I don't see the connection with my father."

"Did you notice anything about the questions? Anything you wouldn't expect them to know unless they were connected to your father or had some ties to him?"

"Nothing."

She sat back in her chair, obviously drained by the experience. She had been hoping for something that wasn't there. Now, the high of that hope all but gone, she looked as if she hadn't slept for days. Her face betrayed the strain she was under.

"That frame," she said. "I just..."

She played that section of the tape once more. "I know I... I just can't be sure. But I think I've seen it."

"Where?" Bolan was on his feet.

"I don't know. A long time ago. I can barely remember. Let me think, let me sleep on it. It'll come to me, perhaps. Let me think."

"Isn't there anything you can tell us?"

"No. Unless, have you . . . Ernst Kreuger. Do you know who he is?"

Both men shook their heads.

"I'll get you the file." She got up and walked across the room slowly, looking as if she was about to collapse. Opening a combination lock on one of the heavy file cabinets, she pulled out a thick manila folder. Bolan met her halfway across the floor.

"Maybe this will help. I have to go and lie down."

## CHAPTER TWENTY-NINE

James Harkness sat outside the small room in which Jason Marley was being held. He found himself wondering what it must feel like to be confined not only in a thick-walled room, but also inside a body that refused to obey the simplest commands.

He had held Marley in secret contempt for years. It had seemed right to him. Like many men, he thought more highly of himself than his superiors did. And like most such men, he had allowed his frustration to push him toward resentment rather than dedication. Rather than work harder to earn the esteem he thought he deserved, he had chosen to channel his energies into sedition. If they wouldn't elevate him to their level, went his reasoning, then he'd bring them down to his.

He wondered now if Marley had realized that, and had held him in such low regard that he failed to consider Harkness a threat worthy of consideration. There was a peculiar kind of satisfaction in bringing down a man who looked through you instead of at you. But there was a cost, and Harkness had never stopped to consider whether he was willing to pay it.

The old man had surprised him, though. Paradoxically he respected the presently powerless Marley far more than the man who led the world's richest Intelligence agency. Harkness started to wonder whether it wasn't Marley he resented so much as the office he held. There was a danger, he knew, in getting too introspective. There was very little time for self-examination, and a man who thought too much was usually a man who was afraid to act.

Harkness had acted, and his gut was telling him he had done so hastily. He was getting frightened. Getting Marley to cooperate was a way of abdicating responsibility for that action. If Marley agreed to throw in, then he would, naturally, reassume his authority over Harkness. That would make him what he hadn't realized until that very moment he was happiest being—a follower.

Staring at the door, he tried to imagine what Marley would say. This was his last chance to cooperate. That had been made more than clear to Harkness. Marley had been adamant in their last discussion, and yet for some reason Harkness believed he still had a chance.

But this was it. The bottom of the ninth. The bases were loaded. So were the guns. If he made the right pitch, Marley was his. If not . . .

He reached for the doorknob. The metal felt extremely cold in his hand. When he turned it and pulled the door open, time would be up. He had to come away victorious now because he wouldn't have another chance. There had been no bones made about that.

He turned the knob.

The room was dimly lit. Huddled on one side of the cot, up against the wall with his back to the door, Jason Marley appeared to be sleeping. Harkness stepped inside and closed the door softly.

Leaving the light low, he pulled a chair alongside the cot and sat without making a sound. Staring at the back of Marley's head, he tried to envision what the old man was dreaming about. Or was he dreaming at all? Maybe, Harkness thought, he slept like a baby because he had nothing to fear.

Was that the product of a clear conscience? Harkness wondered. Could Marley have a clear conscience? The man had done things that would make Machiavelli blanch, but there was the distinct possibility that he believed implicitly in what he had done. That seemed to make all the difference. Harkness had always acted for an ulterior motive, trying to call attention to himself instead of trying to accomplish something for its own sake.

Maybe that was why no one seemed to give a damn whether he lived or died. Maybe they did give a damn, and he was so self-absorbed he couldn't see it. He hated thinking this way and wished that he could just reach out, touch the old man on the shoulder and have him roll over and say "You win...."

But it wasn't going to be that easy.

"Well, James, I suppose you've come back again. Still trying to peddle your nonsense, aren't you?" Marley didn't even bother to turn away from the wall. His voice sounded stronger than it had the past few days. Whether it was just being off the drugs or if he was drawing on some inner reserves of strength, Harkness couldn't tell.

"You make everything seem so trivial, Jason."

"Oh, that's not me, James. That's just the way things are. In your world. Trivial. You come to me like some spoiled child with your grand scheme. You think you're worthy of deciding the fate of Europe and, ultimately, of the world. I'd sooner have the beasts in charge."

"We tried that, Jason. The beasts are red. The beasts don't have a clue. But they don't give up. You know that. You spent your life knowing that."

"I spent my life the only way a reasonable man can, James. I watched and listened. I tried to learn from history and I tried to learn from events. I didn't try to impose my will on the world. I just wanted to ensure that history had a chance to unfold without any undue interference. Can you say that?"

"So far."

"And what about tomorrow or next week or next month? Will you still be able to say that? How will you feel when your dime-store Hitler starts uncurling the barbed wire and finding other ways to use the cattle cars? Can you contemplate that possibility with equanimity?"

"It won't be like that."

"Who is your hero, James?"

"I can't tell you, Jason. You know that. But you'll find out soon enough. I wish you could see it my way, I really do."

"Of course you do. You want me to validate your madness, as if that would make everything all right. But that isn't the way things work, James. Madness increases geometrically. You don't have the courage of your convictions. You want to borrow mine. But I don't share your convictions, and my courage, such as it is, serves my intelligence, such as *it* is. You've made your bed, James. And you'll have to lie in it, despite the fleas and the nails. You should have seen both, but you chose not to."

"You're such a smug bastard, Jason. Always were."

"And that's what this is all about, really. You have to exalt yourself at the expense of others, and if it brings half the continent down around our collective ears, so be it. Isn't that right?"

Marley turned to face his captor. He struggled to sit, but still didn't have the strength. Harkness watched him silently, then, for some reason he didn't understand, reached out and helped the old man.

Marley let his legs dangle over the edge of the bed. His head felt light, and it bobbed on his shoulders for a moment. He had to support himself with stiff arms. Harkness thought they looked fragile. The skin was pasty, and the muscles slack. Small pockets of loose flesh dangled from under his biceps. It looked almost as if he was wasting away. Marley reminded him of his grandfather.

The naked feet of the old man were splayed on the cold floor. Marley looked at them as if they belonged to someone else. He flexed his leg muscles, enjoying the resistance of the stone.

"You look very weak, Jason."

"I *am* very weak, James. But that changes absolutely nothing."

"It doesn't have to be this way."

"It can't be any other way. I am what I am, and you are what you have wanted to become. It's a pity, but there you have it."

"Don't be so condescending."

"I can't be anything else. You've lowered yourself. I won't come down to play in the mud with you. It's beneath my dignity just as it's beneath yours. I wish you could see that. I wish you could understand half as well as you think you do, James. It's probably too late for me. But you might not be beyond salvation."

"What do you mean?"

"I mean perhaps you can recover from this foolishness. You've helped to build the machine. You know where the cogs are. It's within your power to toss a careful monkey wrench into the machinery and bring it to a halt. So far, it isn't moving too fast. Once it starts to speed up, you won't be able to stop it. Why can't you see that the chancellor should have a chance to make his mistakes, just as Washington and Jefferson had a chance to make theirs?"

"How can you compare him to such men?"

"Because he, like they, is a product of his time. Men don't make history, James—they're made by it. They climb onto the tiger's back and ride to keep from being eaten. It's only the monsters, men like Stalin and Hitler, who are foolish enough to torture the beast they ride."

"Tell me something, Jason. What are you afraid of? You must understand that if you disagree with me, you have wasted your whole life."

"On the contrary. If I agree with you, I turn my back on everything I believe in."

"You're just too old to change. That's what it is."

"Maybe. It doesn't really matter, though, does it? There's nothing I can do to stop you or your puppet master from having your way, however misguided it might be."

"I resent that. You believe I can't think for myself. But I can."

"Then prove it, James. Stop it before it's too late. Walk away. Just go to the papers. The kind of vermin you're dealing with can't stand the light of day. They'll run for the dark, where they belong."

"It's history, Jason, not people. You can't change history."

"History is nothing more than the cumulation of men's decisions. It's as much what men choose not to do as it is what they do."

"You don't believe that. You're just trying to appeal to my vanity."

"I wouldn't try to compete for the attention of so voracious an animal as that, James."

"I wish it could be some other way, Jason."

"No, you don't. Because you hold the power to have it some other way. If you really believed that, you would *make* it some other way. But you won't."

"I have to go."

"Why, because I told you the truth? You can't stand to have responsibility, can you? It's too much for you."

Harkness stood and walked toward the door. With his hand on the knob, he stopped. "Goodbye, Jason."

"May you rot in hell, James."

Harkness pulled the door open and stepped into the hall. He looked back over his shoulder just as the door was swinging closed. He expected to see a defeated old man. Instead, what he saw was a man who refused to acknowledge defeat, as if the concept didn't apply to him.

Harkness was filled with envy.

## CHAPTER THIRTY

Mike Bradley looked up at the seedy tenement. "You sure this is where the kid lives?"

Mitchell checked the notes on his tiny coiled pad. "Yeah, 431 Spingarnstrasse, Apartment 4."

"Christ, I wouldn't live here if I was in the roach business."

"Look, one man's poverty is another man's lifestyle. Now, do you want to take a pass because the kid doesn't live someplace you'll see in *Better Homes and Gardens* or do you want to go talk to him?"

Bradley shrugged. It spoke volumes. He started up the stairs and heard Mitchell's feet on the worn stairs right behind him. It was still raining, and a stiff wind was slashing the tiny drops at a sharp angle, whipping the rain until it felt like hundreds of tiny needles poking at his cheeks.

The front door was open a couple of inches. Bradley stopped on the landing and looked back at the street, which was deserted. A couple of scraps of paper, too slick to soak up water, drifted on the breeze, scraping the pavement with a sound like crab claws in a bushel basket. He shook his head once and gave the door a push.

Inside, he moved over to make room for Mitchell, then reached into his pocket for a cigarette lighter. He flicked it, getting a flame that shivered in the breeze. He cupped his free hand around it and leaned toward the mailboxes.

Most of them had names taped in little slots below the greasy black doorbells. There was an intercom, but its speaker dangled from a hole in the wall by one wire. There was no point in trying to communicate with Friedrich Grunze, assuming the buzzer would even work, which he doubted.

The door to the inner hall was closed, but he tried the knob anyway. To his surprise it turned freely, and the door scraped open when he gave it a shove. Inside, it was even gloomier. He started down the hall, found the elevator and was already turning around when Mitchell bumped into him.

"We'll have to walk," he said. "The elevator's busted."

"Surprise, surprise."

"You take the point," Bradley said. Giving Mitchell a gentle shove, he turned his boss back in the other direction, then waited for him to start up the stairs.

Mitchell turned and said, "Fifty deutsche marks Grunze has a sick mother. Otherwise, I can't see him living here. I mean, a traffic controller's pay isn't Rockefeller's income, but it'll get you something a lot better than the bottom of the barrel."

Bradley rubbed his chin. "Maybe not. Maybe there's something more here than meets the eye."

"What, the kid's into dope or something, sticks his check up his nose—is that what you think?"

"I don't know what I think. I just don't get it. Not at all."

"So we'll ask him. If I can make it all the way up the goddamn stairs. I haven't been in a stairwell like this since I lived in the Bronx. Jesus. It stinks."

Bradley had noticed the smell himself. It reminded him of the passage under the subway tracks at Forty-second Street, where the winos used to piss.

He tried to breathe through his mouth, but there was no way to ward off the stench. On the second-floor landing, something moved in the dark, and he felt something slither across his foot. He didn't want to think about what it might be. He was just glad it wasn't hungry.

"Apartment 4 is at the top, I guess."

"We'll soon see, won't we, Mike?"

They were rounding the bend now, to start on the last flight. Bradley could hear music in the distance, like a small radio on very low volume. It seemed to be coming from the head of the stairs. He wondered if maybe Grunze was still up, despite the hour. Somehow he hoped so.

They reached the top floor, and Mitchell stopped. "You hear anything?"

"You mean the radio?"

"No, something else. I can't put my finger on it. Kind of low, almost like a moan."

Bradley listened, but he didn't hear anything. "Nope."

Light was spilling into the hall at the far end of the hallway. Mitchell was moving carefully now, as if some sixth sense had kicked in. Stopping halfway down the hall, he leaned close and whispered, "I don't like it. There's something funny going on here."

Mitchell reached under his raincoat and yanked a .44 Special Smith & Wesson Model 624 revolver out of his holster. He slid the safety off, checked the cylinder to make sure there was a round under the hammer and jerked his chin toward Bradley's hip. "You better get yours out, too."

"What for? We don't want to scare the poor guy to death."

"We don't want any kind of death here, do we, Mike? Especially not our own. Get your gun out."

Bradley pulled his Browning, worked the slide and nodded. "All right, Buffalo Bill, find the Indians."

Mitchell glared at him but started down the hall. As they drew closer, the soft music sounded no louder but became less tinny. It was coming from somewhere up ahead. There was only one light, and it was behind them. When they reached the last door at the end of the hall, Bradley could see that it was open a couple of inches.

"That's weird," he whispered. "This isn't the kind of neighborhood where you leave your door open all night."

"This isn't the kind of neighborhood where you settle for one door," Mitchell responded. He slid along the wall, darted past the cracked door and flattened himself against the wall. Bradley took a similar position on the near side.

"You first or me?" Mitchell asked.

Bradley mouthed the words "I'll go," got the go-ahead from his boss and swung around to use his left hand to push the door open. It swung back easily, opened two-thirds of the way, then bumped to a standstill. Groping along the inside wall, he found a light switch, waited for the nod, then clicked it on.

Bradley jerked his arm back, half expecting the sudden thunder of a shotgun blast, but nothing happened. The light on the floor got brighter, but nothing changed.

Mitchell shrugged. "I dunno," he mouthed.

Bradley backed up and cut toward the door at an angle. He was in and skidding across the floor before he knew what hit him. He landed hard on a moth-eaten armchair, doubled over its back. He looked back and saw the slick reddish smear on the floor.

Then he saw why the door wouldn't open all the way. She was on her stomach. Two dark holes, exit wounds, had blown out of her back. He'd slipped on the blood. "Dan? I think you better get in here."

Bradley straightened and moved toward a doorway on his left.

A dark, narrow hallway led to the rear of the apartment. The sound of the music, clearly discernible now, echoed in the passage. He flattened against one wall of the passage, groping for a light switch as he got close to the next door, which was half-open on a dark room beyond it.

He found no switch and paused at the end of the hall. The light was on the inside of the room. His fingers brushed it by accident. Friedrich Grunze was still in bed. But he was never getting up. Bradley started to back out of the room. He heard Mitchell behind him.

"Too late," he said.

Mitchell looked at him. "I guess if I had any doubts, now would be the time to cut them loose, wouldn't it?"

"Who's next on our list?"

"Hisle, Ronald. One of ours. He lives in a better part of town, thank God."

RONALD HISLE LIVED in a high rise off Wilhelmstrasse. It was a monstrous, accusing finger of beige and glass, jabbing up toward the constellations with a kind of belligerence usually reserved for war monuments.

Mitchell parked in a Visitors Only lot. Killing the engine, he started to open the door, then drew back. "You know, Mike, I got to admit, I thought you had lost a couple cards from your deck, which was never full to begin with. But this is spooky. I wonder whether we ought to go nationwide on this.''

Bradley shook his head. "We do, and we blow it. And maybe they blow us away. You saw that kid and his girlfriend. You want geeks coming after us for the same thing?"

"I'm dog-paddling, Mike. This is way over my head."

"That's where the cancer is, though, Dan. Higher up. We don't know who or where. We got to go this one alone. We got another team out there, but there's too much for either one of us to go it alone."

"Who else?"

"You don't want to know."

"The hell I don't."

"I'll tell you when we come down. Let's go see Hisle. If he's home."

"And if it's the grieving widow?"

"Hisle isn't married."

Mitchell led the way, barreling past the doorman, who looked too sleepy to care and was too frail to stop the big man in any case. They took the elevator up to the seventeenth floor. Ronald Hisle's apartment was the last one at the end of the hall, on the left.

The long hall was thickly carpeted. It was very quiet. Small bronze sconces, mounted high on either wall with low-wattage bulbs, offered the only light. They passed several doors without hearing a sound. They stopped in front of Hisle's door. Mitchell pushed the doorbell, heard a distant buzzer from somewhere inside.

After a minute, when there still had been no response, he leaned on the bell again, this time longer. Still no answer. Mitchell wondered aloud about getting the doorman, then changed his mind. Fumbling in his pocket, he pulled out a set of lock picks and worked the dead bolt. He wasn't a magician, but it didn't take long.

When the door swung open, Bradley was the first inside. The apartment was ordinary bachelor quarters. A stereo on a wall unit towered over everything in the living room. A few records were scattered around, including one on the turntable.

They drifted aimlessly from room to room. The place was so nondescript as almost to defy a determined search. It looked too ordinary, so determined to be uninteresting, as if to suggest nothing could be hidden on the premises.

They checked closets, drawers, under furniture, behind framed photographs, every conceivable place. They came up empty. Bradley plopped down on the sofa. Idly rubbing the tip of a finger on an end table, he kept thinking about the record, but he didn't know why. Mitchell was going through the kitchen again, searching cabinet shelves and in the cutlery and utensil drawers. He came back shaking his head.

"If this guy has a secret life, I think even *he* isn't aware of it."

Bradley laughed. He rubbed the dust off his fingertip and started to get up. Then it hit him. He rushed back to the stereo. "Come here, Dan, check this out."

Mitchell joined him, hands on hips, waiting for a big revelation, his face expectant. "What's up? You got something?"

"Check out the record."

Mitchell leaned forward. "Geez. I hate the Beach Boys. So, he's got lousy taste in music. So what?"

"Look at it, damn it."

"I did."

"Did you see any dust on it?"

The light clicked on instantly. "No. No, I didn't see any dust."

"But there's dust on everything else. Which can only mean somebody's been here recently to play that album. Hisle doesn't have family. If he doesn't have a lover, then he was here himself. And he's neither missing nor one of the unidentified bodies. I'd bet the farm."

"As long as you don't buy it...."

## CHAPTER THIRTY-ONE

"Where to now?" Bradley asked.

Mitchell checked his notebook. "I don't know if there's any point to all this, Mike. I think what we have is a situation where some of these people are lumps of charcoal in the morgue, and two or three of them are alive and kicking. Let's say Marley's one. Even if we figure out who the other two are, we can't do much with the information."

"I don't agree with that, Dan. If we know which two are still alive, and I think Ronny Hisle is one of them, we have a whole new approach. We can backtrack, see who they worked with, see where they've been, what they were working on."

"I agree Hisle's one of them. But I still say it's useless information. I vote we go home and get some sleep. You're running on empty, and so am I."

"One more. Let's just check one more."

"Who? Which one?"

"Any other nonmilitary on the list. I think that's our best bet."

"Two. Guy named Jennings. And James Harkness. Another heavyweight, he is. Supercilious prick. Jennings I don't know, but he's one of ours, too."

"You call it, Dan."

Mitchell shook his head in exasperation. "Aw, shit. All right. Harkness. If we're going to stick our head in a lion's mouth tonight, it might just as well be a big lion."

"Any family?"

"Sort of. An ex-wife. Different address, of course. In the States."

"Harkness it is. Can you pull their personnel records tomorrow to see if Harkness and Hisle, or Hisle and Jennings ever worked together?"

"What excuse do I give? You think the Company's full of termites? If you're right, I pull some files and send up a red flag."

"Use the plane crash as a cover. Hell, for all we know, those records are already in the file room with that mountain of garbage."

They reached the lobby. The doorman gave them a funny look and flinched when Mitchell moved toward him. In fluent German he inquired about Hisle—when he was last home, whether he had any recent visitors and, especially, if his pattern had changed recently.

The doorman answered in clipped monosyllables. Mitchell rephrased a couple of times, but got no more of a response. Mitchell shook his head in disgust and joined Bradley at the door.

"Son of a bitch was scared stiff. I don't know why, but he was, and he was lying through his teeth. Maybe we should stick around."

"No way Hisle's coming back here now. He shouldn't have come here in the first place. Maybe the doorman saw him and Hisle threatened him."

"Maybe somebody else scared him," Mitchell suggested. "But if Hisle did come back, he ran a big risk. When you're supposed to be dead and you aren't, it's pretty tough to explain why you're listening to the Beach Boys at home when everybody thinks you're a piece of toast on a marble slab."

"If you know anybody we can trust, maybe we can put a watch on the place. But I think it'll be a waste. What we need to do now is find out who else is still walking around."

JAMES HARKNESS LIVED in the Schoenberg district, not far from Tempelhof. The quickest route was back through the Tiergarten. Mitchell backed into the rainy street. The storm was pounding on the roof of the car; the rain was so heavy it ran down over the windshield in sheets, only temporarily disturbed by the wipers. It was hard to see out the front, and almost impossible to see through the rear window. Even with the heater on, the inside of the windows was glazed over with condensation.

Leaving the Wedding district, Mitchell hung a right onto Paulstrasse, heading for the heart of the Tiergarten. By the time he reached the stone bridge arcing over the Spree, the glass had almost cleared.

At the central plaza, Mitchell drifted into the gentle curve of one of the Tiergarten transverses. Bradley was looking out the window, his head against the glass. He was watching a pair of yellow lights in the passenger-side mirror.

It looked as if they were being followed by someone with his headlights off. Bradley leaned closer to the mirror. "You see that car behind us?"

"What car? I got all I can do to see the road."

"We got somebody on our tail. No headlights, just parking lights. Yellow, looks like a couple hundred yards back. See him?"

But the road curved, and the yellow lights disappeared around the bend.

"You sure, Mike? I didn't see anything."

"I'm telling you, Dan, somebody's on our tail. Bastard was probably watching Hisle's place. Hell, maybe he even followed us from Grunze's."

"Hang on." Mitchell jerked the wheel hard to the right and jumped the curb. His tires slipped on the slick grass as he jammed the transmission into reverse and backed in among a clump of shrubs. He killed the lights at the same moment but left the engine running.

Bradley counted the seconds. "Ten ... fifteen ... twenty... Should be along any second now." The words were no sooner out of his mouth than the yellow lights made the second half of the turn. It was a large American car, a Chrysler. It had German plates, but Bradley couldn't get the number.

"Gonna follow the sucker," Mitchell said. He waited for the car to put a little distance behind it, then stepped on the gas. The tires spun on the wet grass, and it took a moment to get any traction. By the time Mitchell managed to get back over the curb and onto the transverse, the Chrysler was out of sight.

Mitchell left his lights off and drove as fast as he dared. Rounding the next bend in the transverse, they caught a glimpse of taillights. The brake lights flashed on suddenly.

"Bastard knows we slipped him," Mitchell said. The car backed abruptly, threw its tail into a hard K-turn and came back toward them.

Mitchell threw on his lights and made his own K-turn, then stomped on the gas. The Chrysler was closing fast.

"Now that he knows we made him, he's not going to waste time on subtlety," Bradley said.

He reached into his jacket and pulled out his Browning. Slipping off the safety, he started to roll down his window. "We better make a run for it. Who knows what kind of artillery they've got."

"I got some of my own. Look under the seat."

Bradley groped under the seat and found cold steel. Even before he could see it, he recognized the feel of an Uzi. It had a suppressor screwed in place, and he hefted the subgun appreciatively. "I hope to Christ we don't need this little monster, but it's sure good knowing it's here."

The transverse skirted a small lake on the left. Through gaps in the foliage, Bradley could see its turbulent waters racked by the brisk winds glittering under the dim lights that ringed it. They were approaching a tight hairpin, and Mitchell had to brake to negotiate the sharp turn, almost reversing direction completely.

The Chrysler was gaining on them, and both men instinctively crouched in case their pursuers opened fire.

The first burst of fire pinged on the roof and trunk deck. One ricochet pierced the rear window and punched a hole the size of a fist in the windshield on its way out.

"Christ almighty, that was close," Mitchell shouted. He stomped on the gas, but the Chrysler had too many horses. "Hold on," he shouted.

The car lurched to the right, up over the curb and across the lawn. It was like an obstacle course. Mitchell jerked the wheel left, right and back again, trying to pick his way among the trees and ornamental rocks.

The Chrysler leaped the curb and roared after them. The heavier car had better traction than Mitchell's little Volkswagen. If he could find some open soil, he might get the Chrysler mired in the mud. Darting between a pair of small yews, he crushed a bed of flowers under his tires, then jerked the wheel hard to the left.

The driver of the Chrysler was good, and he anticipated the move, blowing by the yews on the left. The maneuver cost Mitchell some time, and the Chrysler was right behind them now.

"I think we got a better chance on foot, Mike. Could be time to bail out."

"Buy us some time, Dan. Try to open a little lead on him."

"What the hell do you think I'm trying to do?"

The Volkswagen was having trouble on the grass. Mitchell hung a sharp right and tried to angle across a slippery slope. To the left, the Neuer See loomed closer and closer. The lake was choppy, and its dark waters seemed to leap toward them as the Volkswagen broke loose and started to slide.

Mitchell wrestled with the wheel, but the car was out of control. The more he tried to use the gas, the faster the wheels spun. He jammed on the brakes in a panic, but they were moving too fast to stop.

Mitchell spun the wheel again, got the car under control, but too late. The slope steepened, and the Volkswagen nosed down into the water. The lake wasn't deep, but the car was hopelessly mired in the soft bottom.

Bradley and Mitchell flung open their doors as the Chrysler rolled to a stop at the top of the slope. Bradley had the Uzi and Mitchell had his S&W .44.

Floundering back toward the grass, Bradley slipped and fell. His head slammed into the rear fender of the VW, and he lost his grip on the subgun.

On the far side of the car, Mitchell heard him go down, heard the loud thud as head and fender made contact and then the splash as Bradley slipped back into the lake.

He raced around the car as the first burst of gunfire cut loose from the vicinity of the Chrysler. Mitchell dropped to his knee and emptied his pistol, sending the advancing gunmen flying.

But he was outmanned and outgunned. Reaching into his pocket for a Speedloader, he tried to take cover behind the VW. Recognizing their chance, the men uphill advanced toward him, opening up again.

Mitchell got to his feet and ran down alongside the car. He stooped to grab Bradley under the arms and try to haul him out of the water. Something ripped through the flap of his coat and walked up over his hip, blowing out chunks of bone and breaking two ribs.

He was already dead when he hit the water. Bradley, his head just above the surface, was pinned by the deadweight. The Chrysler's headlights flashed on, and in the sudden glare he could see the red water swirling around him. He tried to get out from under Mitchell's body, but as he hauled himself up onto the slippery bank, he was surrounded by a half-dozen legs.

He closed his eyes, knowing it was all over.

# CHAPTER THIRTY-TWO

Mack Bolan took up his position on the roof. He was protected from the street by a low stone wall that ran the full perimeter of the building. Crouched behind the barrier, he could watch the tenement across the street through a decorative loophole. If he had to use his weapon, he'd have to fire over the wall, but he'd cross that bridge when he came to it. Right now all he wanted was to watch.

Twenty-five feet away, looking through another loophole, was Sergei Yenikidze.

So far, he'd seen nothing to warrant any suspicion that Yenikidze was anything other than what he professed to be—an Intelligence agent from a foreign government who was no more enamored of the possibility of a fascist-leaning reunified Germany than any other man with half a brain in his head. But in the world in which Bolan moved, there were wheels within wheels. People did things that tended to seem rational for motives that might be anything but.

He'd have to keep one eye on Yenikidze, no matter what happened. He also was only too well aware of the possibility that the man might see him as a convenient tool, someone to use in part of a much larger scheme, someone who could be sloughed off once his usefulness was at an end.

Since he was still groping his way through the dark maze, the possibility remained that Yenikidze knew considerably more than he had been willing to share. If that was the case, there could be a dozen reasons for that reticence.

According to Erika Mann, Ernst Kreuger had a cell in the building they were watching. Her files contained convincing evidence that more than half of the men who were known to frequent the house where the tape had been found were also frequent visitors at the run-down tenement across the street. That in itself proved nothing, but it was highly suggestive. The puzzle was taking on shape slowly but surely.

To Bolan it was like sitting in front of a test tube watching a solid crystal materialize out of transparent fluid. It was a deliberate process, one that required patience and the intuitive understanding of the point at which it reached completion. One could sit in front of such a test tube forever and never see one more crystal form. There were limits, and knowing when they had been reached was where the expertise lay.

Yenikidze seemed confident that their information was correct. And there was no doubt that he carried himself like a man who believed he knew what was what. He hadn't betrayed a hint of uncertainty or self-doubt. But the line between confidence and arrogance was also a very fine one. Bolan wasn't about to let someone get him killed.

The Russian had diagramed the building, and Bolan felt he knew it inside and out. They were in a strip of ancient tenements in the poverty-ridden section of Berlin reserved for foreign workers. The majority of the foreign labor force were Turks, and the smell of Eastern spices drifted up on the cool evening breeze. Somewhere in the distance a window was open, either to let in the cool breeze or to let out the overpowering scents.

On the same breeze the steady thrum of an oud drifted up from a narrow alley, its bass strings echoing off the walls while the treble stabbed right for the clouds. The rhythm was insistent, throbbing and complex, accents falling in odd places for ears attuned to Western music. It would have been almost peaceful if they had been here for some less urgent, and less potentially lethal, reason.

Erika Mann's information was that Kreuger, widely believed to be the leader of a small group of Aryan Bund enforcers, was using the building in Guildstrasse as his headquarters. Kreuger was a man they wanted to talk to. If he hadn't been involved in the attack on Klaus Mann, he would know who was.

Since they were coming at a puzzle of unknown dimensions, they had to use whatever links came to hand. Kreuger was too brutally direct to have engineered the kidnapping of Jason Marley; that much was certain. If you wanted to ice a man, you called Kreuger. If you wanted anything else, anything that required the least little subtlety, you looked elsewhere.

But Kreuger was plugged in. If anything was taking shape in the contorted catacombs of the underground right, he would know about it. He also had a reputation for efficiency. It wasn't beyond the realm of possibility that he might have been hired to provide logistical support for the kidnapping.

Getting him to talk wouldn't be easy.

The dirty gutters below were full of garbage, the intermittent rain blocking the sewers with litter and sending huge puddles surging toward the center of the street. Even on the roof behind them, bags of trash, split open like overcooked sausages and spewing rotten food on the bubbled tar, filled the air with a heavy stench that felt like a greasy film on the skin.

Bolan knew they could be in for a long night.

The building across the street was a beehive of activity, but it was all taking place indoors, behind tattered shades and torn curtains. Viewed in fragments, it was difficult to interpret. Shadowy torsos attached to legs drifted past half-lowered shades, disappeared behind walls then reappeared fully fleshed but only dimly seen through filmy gauze undulating in the breeze.

Even through binoculars, the visibility was far from perfect. Faces in profile, little more than a collection of hazy features, darted past gaps in the window coverings. Erika had provided several perfect photos of Kreuger, but trying to match those clean images with the fragments drifting like fish in a muddy tank was frustrating.

Yenikidze squirmed along the wall until he was next to Bolan. "I wish we could just barge in and find out what we want to know."

"No way. If Kreuger knows anything, we can't take the chance of spooking him. If he's not there and we bust in, he'll get wind of it. If he goes underground, we won't have a chance in hell of finding him in time. It could take months. And if he is in there and they put up a fight, we might have to kill him. He's no use to us as a corpse."

"I understand, but I am getting impatient. I feel like I am watching a clock I don't know how to read."

"You are."

"How long do we waste time here? Even if Kreuger is involved, there's no guarantee he will come to this place."

"We give it the night. In the morning we talk to Erika Mann again. I think she knows something, or thinks she knows something, but isn't sure she wants to tell us. I think she recognized that painting in the videotape."

"We can force her to tell us."

"No, we can't. She's a very strong woman. And if we lean on her, we'll just make sure she stops cooperating. We can't afford that. She knows something but has to willingly hand it over."

"Her father was quite a man. No one was more hated in East Germany. And no one commanded more loyalty from those who worked for him than Klaus Mann. He was a very complex man, and he had his own way of doing things. We never completely trusted him. He was too independent. But I never heard of a single instance of his having compromised himself. He hated fascists and pursued them with the tenacity of the Furies. The only problem was that his passion distorted his intelligence. He was like your Senator McCarthy, but on the other end of the political spectrum and with a lot more power. And he was incorruptible. He could have been a great man if he hadn't been so obsessed."

Bolan had encountered men like that, and they were all cut from the same cloth. They viewed the world through selective spectacles and saw only two colors. Sometimes purity was more destructive than corruption. Klaus Mann might have been a textbook case.

They heard a car in the street below, and Bolan glanced through the loophole. The car moved slowly up the block, its front tires sending whitecaps across the surface of the puddles.

"What is it?"

"Not sure." Bolan watched the car cruise slowly toward him. It slowed even further as it passed the building across the street, then picked up speed again. It continued down the block and turned left at the corner. "Gone."

"Was it Kreuger?"

"Impossible to tell. I couldn't even see how many people were in the car."

Yenikidze cursed, then crawled back to his own loophole. He lay there on his stomach, the fingers of his left hand drumming impatiently on the soaking roof. The rain picked up, and both men were long since soaked through. The patter of the rain in the puddles behind them was a steady hiss, and small streams trickled past Bolan on their way to a drain spout in one corner.

The warrior pulled out the binoculars again, wiped the lenses dry as best he could and inserted them in the loophole, trying to keep the rain off. He didn't have much room to pivot, and the loophole allowed him to cover only half the building with the glasses. He heard a muttering off to his left again and raised his head above the low wall to look down into the street. Leaning forward as far as he dared, he spotted a car, too distant yet to tell whether it was the same one, plowing through the flooded street a block and a half away.

"Company coming."

Yenikidze scrambled to his knees, looked over the wall and said, "I think it's the same car."

"Looks like," Bolan answered. It entered their block, slowing as it passed beneath a streetlight. The Executioner could see two men in the front seat, but their faces were distorted by the rain cascading over the windshield. The car was dark blue, a Chrysler four-door sedan. It seemed less tentative now and rolled toward the curb in front of the tenement.

The front passenger door opened, and a big man in jeans and a ski jacket stepped into a muddy puddle as he got out. He cursed loudly, then ran a hand through his shoulder-length blond hair.

"That's Kreuger," Bolan announced. Yenikidze rolled toward him, keeping below the wall.

The driver's door swung wide and a man climbed out. He opened the rear door, then backed away a moment later, holding something heavy. Another step, and Bolan realized it was a pair of legs. The driver and the blond man were carrying someone out of the car.

Kreuger said something to the driver and the man nodded. They lowered the body to the sidewalk, then Kreuger descended a flight of steps to the basement, where he rapped on a heavy door. The door opened, and Kreuger stepped inside, leaving the driver with the body on the sidewalk. The body was limp. Its head lolled to one side, and Bolan trained the glasses on it. They moved toward the front of the car and started down the steps. For a brief instant the backwash of the headlights illuminated the lolling head.

"They've got Mike Bradley," Bolan growled.

"Is he dead?"

"I doubt it. They wouldn't have brought him here if he were. We have to get him out."

"The two of us?"

"You got it."

CHAPTER THIRTY-THREE

They went down the rear fire escape. Bolan hit the
ground first, Yenikidze right behind him, and moved
into an alley that stank of wine and rotten vegeta-
bles. The warrior darted forward, passing a row of
metal garbage cans and pressing himself flat against
the brick wall.

Ten feet from the mouth of the alley, he could see
just one corner of the tenement across the way. He
crept forward until he could see one glowing taillight of the Chrysler. Taking another couple of steps,
he could see that the driver's-side rear door was still
open.

The Executioner held up a hand, telling Yenikidze to stay where he was. He got into a crouch and
crept ahead until he was just behind the corner of the
brick wall.

Bolan could see the whole Chrysler now. No one
was inside. The dome light was still on, and the far-
side doors still gaped. He heard voices, as if someone was taking leave, but he couldn't hear the words
clearly enough to know what was being said. If he
could just get closer...

He was getting ready to risk it when Kreuger's blond mane bobbed into sight beyond the front fender of the car. Right behind him, the driver climbed the stairs out of the basement. Kreuger walked to the passenger side and got in, slamming the door. The driver shut the rear door on his side, climbed in behind the wheel and closed his own door.

Backing toward Yenikidze, Bolan said, "Kreuger just left."

"Left?"

Bolan nodded. "But we couldn't stop him without endangering Bradley."

Yenikidze nodded. "What do you want to do?"

"We've got to get inside. We've got to move fast, and we've got to know exactly where he is before we do. If it takes too long to find him, they'll kill him."

"You lead the way. I will do whatever you wish."

Bolan moved back to the mouth of the alley, where he had an unobstructed view of the front of the tenement. Crumbling steps led up to a small landing. One wrought-iron railing dangled precariously. The other was long gone.

But they had taken Bradley down. He had to be in the basement. "I'm going over," Bolan whispered. "When I get there, wait for my signal, then come across."

The Intelligence agent tapped him on the back. "Good luck."

Bolan sprinted across the street to the right corner of the building, noticing the basement had no windows on the front. He waved for Yenikidze to cross, and the Russian joined him. Both men ducked under a brick archway at the corner of the building, more to conceal themselves from a casual window watcher than to get out of the storm.

"Let's check out this building, see if we can get a look at the basement somehow," Bolan suggested. Behind him, a rotting wooden gate blocked off the alley. It was shoulder high, but it wasn't locked. The warrior gave it a shove and it swung back, its hinges creaking.

Beyond the gate a narrow passageway led into the darkness behind the building. The tenement on Bolan's right had several windows on its wall, but only on the second and higher floors.

The building to which they'd taken Bradley had a row of basement windows, all of which glowed with a dull orange light. The rest of the floors also had windows, resembling those on the front of the tenement. Most were lit, and none sported much in the way of adequate cover.

Moving into the alley, Bolan reached the first basement window and knelt to peer inside. The glass was filthy, and when he leaned close, he could smell the dirt.

There wasn't much to see beyond the glass. A torn curtain hung away from one corner, the cheap, dirty cloth bunched near the lower end of the dangling rod. Boxes and crates filled the room, but there were no markings to identify the contents. It was obvious that the room was used for storage only.

The next window was just as grimy, but this one looked in on an office. A desk and two chairs sat against one wall. Some filing cabinets occupied another wall. Like the previous room, it was deserted.

"Stay here and keep an eye on things, Sergei," Bolan instructed.

"Where are you going?"

"To check the others." Bolan didn't wait for an answer. He crept along the wall on hands and knees. The next window had thick curtains. They met imperfectly at the center, but there was very little to see through the irregular gap.

Bolan listened for a couple of minutes. He could hear voices, but they sounded as if they were coming from a long way off, maybe a room deeper within the basement. Twisting his body, he looked through the small gap from another angle. There was still nothing to see.

A low moan drew Bolan's attention. He stopped at the last window. This one, too, was covered, but there was a gap at one corner. He bent low to look into the basement room beyond. A pair of feet drifted into view. They were shod in combat boots, but it was all Bolan could see. He heard another moan. Then a voice, soft, almost soothing. "You like shocking things, Herr Bradley? Do you? Then I have just the thing for you."

Bolan heard a rasping noise he couldn't identify, then another moan.

The voice came again. "Shocking, yes?" The speaker laughed. Bolan heard the rasping noise again, and this time he knew what it was. They were using some sort of hand-cranked generator. He'd seen it used before, in Vietnam and in Brazil, where it was known as the Devil's Battery. And Mike Bradley was hooked up to the other end of the wires.

Bolan pushed past the window and groped along in the dark, feeling his way across the back wall of the building. He rapped his knuckles on a steel pipe, and as he felt along its dripping length, he realized it was a handrail.

Moving past it, he found another stairwell, twin to the one at the front of the building. He raced back to Yenikidze. "We've got to hurry."

The Russian grabbed him by the arm. "Mr. Pollock. We don't know how many men are inside. It would be suicide to try to break in before we know that."

"There's no time. He's being tortured."

"Let's go."

They turned the rear corner, and Bolan led the way to the stairwell. Yenikidze bounced down the stairs and felt the door with his hands. "One lock," he whispered. "Unless there's a bar inside, it should be easy. But the door opens out."

He reached into his coat, pulled a small beige wad wrapped in wax paper, and held it toward Bolan.

"Plastique." Working quickly, he dried the door as best he could, then secured the plastic explosive with a strip of tape, mashing it over the lock cylinder and forcing as much as he could into the lock itself.

The detonator was stabbed in, and he backed up the stairs. Pushing Bolan by the shoulder, he shoved him around the corner. When the next bolt of lightning ripped across the sky, he waited for the thunder to begin. Timing it almost perfectly, he sent the detonate signal at the same instant as the thunderclap exploded above them. The roar of the plastique was almost drowned out.

Bolan was already in motion. He swung around the corner into a cloud of swirling dust and headed down the steps. The door had blown inward, and light spilled through the opening where it used to be.

Three men charged toward him, but Bolan was in no mood for a protracted disagreement. He swept his AK-47 in a vicious semicircle, spewing 7.62 mm lead like a spitting cobra. The three men collapsed to the ground.

He charged toward the doorway through which the men had come. Yenikidze descended the stairs as another pair of men appeared on the threshold. Bolan fired again, but there was only one round left in the AK.

"Down!" Yenikidze shouted, and the warrior rolled to the left and hit the deck. He heard the Russian's AK hammering, its awesome clatter magnified by the small room. Getting to his feet, he leaped over the two bodies slumped in the doorway and turned left, slapping a new banana clip into the AK at the same time.

Bradley was in the next room, as near as he could tell. There was a wooden door, but it was half-open, and Bolan kicked it aside. A burst of autofire narrowly missed the Executioner's leg, and carved hunks out of the door and scattered slivers of wood in every direction.

Bolan was in a bind. He couldn't charge in, because he didn't know where Bradley was or how many men were in the room. Wild fire might take Bradley with it. But the tenement might be swarming with Kreuger's men. While he was debating what to do, he heard a crash from somewhere in the room, a cascade of glass, then a short burst of fire, followed by another, louder one.

He realized Yenikidze had kicked in the window. Dropping to the floor, he squirmed forward and poked the AK into the room. There was only the one man, his back toward Bolan, his Uzi clawing at the cellar window. Bolan opened up just as the man realized he was there.

The short burst was frugal but efficient. The torturer went down, and Bolan scrambled to his feet. He waved Yenikidze back to the stairwell, then turned his attention to Bradley.

The man was strapped in a chair, a thick wad of rag in his mouth. Bolan smelled the vomit as he cut Bradley loose from the chair and ripped the rag away. Bradley turned his head and spewed again as the warrior hoisted him to his shoulder.

He saw a shadow in the doorway as he turned and leveled the AK, but it was the Russian. He waved Bolan out and brought up the rear as the Executioner went through the ruined doorway and up into the rain.

Bolan set Bradley down, leaning him against a wall. "Get the car," he shouted, and saw Yenikidze dash for it.

"You okay, Bradley?" Bolan asked.

The CIA agent tried to nod, but he still didn't have control of his muscles. He tried to speak twice, and finally got it out the third time. "Feel like a two-amp fuse on a thirty-amp line."

## CHAPTER THIRTY-FOUR

The rain grew more intense as Bolan watched the alley across the street. It had been too easy. There was bound to be more trouble. The first burst of fire had to come ripping from the tenement at any moment.

He didn't have long to wait. He saw the headlights up the street as Yenikidze raced toward him with the car. At the same instant a shout echoed out of the narrow alley. He heard footsteps charging toward the street, echoing on the brick walls.

The Executioner unleathered his .44 Desert Eagle and pressed it into Mike Bradley's hands. "Use this," he said as the first gunner charged out through the brick arch and opened up. Conscious of the car and knowing that if they lost it, they were themselves as good as dead, Bolan headed away from the vehicle and drew the gunman's fire. Ducking into a shallow stairwell, he fired a burst from the AK-47.

The gunman lay flat on the ground at the curb. Another one darted out into the street and charged full bore. Bolan aimed carefully, squeezed and saw the man grab for his chest. A wild burst from an Uzi went high and took out a second-story window.

The car was coming closer as two more men barreled into the street. This time Bolan didn't wait. He squeezed off two quick shots and moved to his second target before the first hit the ground.

He fired a short burst, catching the fourth man in the pit of the stomach. He stopped and seemed to fold himself around the slug as if to ward it off. Too late—it had already ripped through and slammed into the stairs of the tenement.

Bolan scrambled to his feet as the car closed on him. He sprinted to Bradley's side, bending over the moaning agent as the car veered toward him, its passenger door swinging open. He struggled to get Bradley to his feet, then draped an arm over his shoulder and helped him toward the waiting Audi. He dumped Bradley in the front seat, ripped the rear door open and started to climb in when three shades went up on first-floor windows of the tenement.

He could see the outlines of three men through the dirty glass. A second later they opened up, and the glass was gone. Bolan swept the AK along the roof of the car until the clip was empty, driving the hardmen to cover.

Bolan tumbled into the back seat. "Go!" he shouted, slapping the seat-back and yanking his door closed. The gunners were already back in the windows as the car squealed on the slick pavement for a moment, then raced forward.

Yenikidze careered around the corner, wrestling the wheel to keep the car upright as he floored it and shot down the next block. There hadn't been a car in sight, and pursuit was unlikely, but the Russian was taking no chances. "Where to?" he asked without taking his eyes off the garbage-strewn street.

"Erika Mann's. We have to get some help for Mike. And if she's holding out on us, her time is up. I'm going to put a little pressure on her."

Yenikidze nodded. "Is Bradley all right?"

"He's weak as hell and he's got some tremors, but that'll take care of itself in an hour or so. I don't know whether he's up to anything tonight, though. If Erika knows anything, we might have to leave him behind."

"You trust her?"

"I don't know," Bolan admitted. "I have no reason to, but I have no reason not to, and I sure as hell don't have anybody else I trust. Not now. We have to find out what Mike learned, if anything. And what the hell happened to him."

He looked at the young agent, who had slumped against the passenger door. His limbs still twitched occasionally, and he seemed to be unconscious, but there didn't appear to be any permanent damage.

IT TOOK ALMOST AN HOUR to reach Erika Mann's place, but Bradley seemed to be doing better. He had stopped twitching. His breathing was still ragged and intermittent, but deeper than it had been.

When they pulled up to the heavy wrought-iron gate blocking the Mann driveway, Yenikidze rolled his window down as two men stepped out of the shrubbery. "We're here to see Erika Mann," he said, his German as smooth and accentless as his English.

The men shone flashlights into the car without opening the gate. "Who are you?" one of them asked.

When Yenikidze told him, both men stepped back out of sight. Bolan could hear a low conversation for a few moments. Both reappeared.

"Leave the car here," the spokesman said. "We will take care of it for you." With that, he waved a hand, and Bolan heard footsteps behind the car. He turned to see half a dozen men, all heavily armed, moving toward the vehicle. Their guns were leveled, and they were in no mood for an argument.

Yenikidze nodded. "We have an injured man. He can't walk."

"Don't worry. We will handle it."

Bolan and the Russian climbed out of the car. The six-man team moved into a semicircle around them. "Your weapons, please. Just a precaution."

Bolan didn't like it, but it was too late to have second thoughts. If they attempted to resist, they would be cut to ribbons. Reluctantly he handed over his AK and the Beretta while Yenikidze passed over his AK and a Makarov automatic.

The leader stepped forward and frisked Yeni-kidze, found the rest of the plastique in his coat and smiled. Tucking it into his own pocket, he patted Bolan down, found a clip for the Beretta and another for the Desert Eagle. They were useless without the guns themselves, and he left them where he found them. Looking at Bolan, he said, "Where is the .44?"

Bolan nodded toward Bradley. "In his coat."

When the gun had been retrieved, he ordered two men to carry the unconscious Bradley, and the gates swung open.

When they mounted the stairs and stopped on the broad front porch, Erika Mann opened the front door. "It's all right, Horst. They are okay." Then, seeing Bradley, she asked, "What happened to him?"

Before Bolan could answer, she stepped onto the porch and barked orders to the two men carrying the unconscious agent. She held the door open for them, then sent the others back to the gate. To Bolan she said, "Follow me." Without looking back she stepped into the house. The Executioner followed, holding the door for Yenikidze.

The men carrying Bradley were already out of sight, and Erika led them down the same long corridor to the basement door, opened it and stepped through. She didn't bother to wait for them.

When Bolan reached the floor, he glanced toward the TV screen. Erika walked toward the oval table and sat. Without preamble she said, "I have been looking at the picture over and over. I know I have seen it, and I think I know where."

Bolan didn't bother to take a seat. "Where?"

She shook her head. "In a moment. Tell me what happened to your friend."

"We don't know. We went to Kreuger's as you suggested. We were watching the place from the roof across the street when they brought Bradley in. Kreuger left, and we had to let him go, because we couldn't let them know we were there until we were ready."

"You're sure it was Ernst Kreuger?"

"No doubt in my mind."

"And he had many men with him?"

Bolan shrugged. "Only three when he drove up. But there were others in the building. I don't know how many."

"But you don't know how Mr. Bradley came to be there?"

"No. Why?"

"Because his supervisor was found dead tonight. Shot to death, on the edge of the Neuer See."

"Mitchell?"

Erika nodded.

"You don't think Bradley did it, do you?"

"I didn't say that. I only wondered what you knew. We shall have to wait until we can speak to Mr. Bradley. Then, if what he says is acceptable, I will tell you where I have seen the painting."

"You are making a big mistake, Fräulein Mann," Yenikidze told the woman. "You are making this a personal matter. The future of your country is hanging in the balance."

"You don't know that for certain."

"You don't know that it isn't, either "

"No, I don't. But I told you quite honestly that my first concern is the men who killed my father. I am now reasonably certain that neither of you had anything to do with it, but I am not completely convinced. And I want to know more about what happened to Daniel Mitchell. Specifically, what your friend Bradley knows about it."

"Can't that wait?"

"No."

"Why? If we get the men involved in the conspiracy, we will also get the men who killed your father. Isn't that enough?"

"No, it isn't."

"I don't understand."

"I plan to kill the man who killed my father. That is a condition of my assistance, and it is nonnegotiable. I want to look him in the eyes before I shoot him. And that is final. Don't even try to change my mind about it. If you want my assistance, and I have no doubt in my mind that you need it, that is how it must be."

# CHAPTER THIRTY-FIVE

Harkness was slumped in his chair  Ronny Hisle sat across from him, a beer bottle cocked casually in one hand. "They tossed my place," Hisle said.

'I told you they would. I told you it was stupid to go back there. Why the hell did you?"

'Hey  it's my place. I feel at home there. I can relax  Besides, I was careful. Nobody saw me. What are you worrying about? They took Mitchell out and they have Bradley  Where's the risk?"

"If he hears about it, you'll really be sorry

'Fuck him. ' Hisle raised a hand just over his head  "I've had it up to here with his Kraut bullshit  Sometimes I wish we never even started with that asshole."

"You sound like you want out '

Hisle shrugged. "Too late for that, Jimmy "

"You know I don't like to be called that."

"You're too damn uptight, Harkness. Loosen up. You want to live until you're sixty, you better learn to relax."

"I'll relax when this is over  Then I walk away from it all. That's when I'll relax. But until then, I have to worry for both of us, since you seem constitutionally unable to worry for yourself.''

"What's to worry about? Half the money's already in the bank. The other half'll be there in a few days. And even if it isn't, what's the difference? I can buy myself an island if I want to. Kiss off all these fire-breathing mothers. Let them play their little games, walk around with their cigars and speaking that damn language that sounds like somebody's puking. I'm sick of them all.''

"Don't let them hear you say anything like that.''

"Forget about it, Jimmy. I'm not stupid.''

"But you act like it sometimes.''

"All calculated. These bastards want to think they're smarter than I am. I let them think so. That way, I got a little in reserve in case I need it. You'd do well to do the same thing. You're always walking around telling everybody how much better than them you are. That's not too smart, especially not with this sour batch of Krauts. According to them, nobody's allowed to be smarter than them. If they think you are, they crank up the old ovens. That what you want?''

"You and Marley.''

"What about us?''

"He said something about the ovens, too, the other day. Do you really think these men are that bad?''

"I prefer not to think about it. I grew up a long time ago, Jimmy. Lost my ideological cherry in

Chile. Once that happens, you're never the same. You're kind of old to still have yours. Maybe it's about time you took a good political fucking. Make a man of you. That happens, you see the world through green-colored glasses.'' He rubbed his thumb and index finger together ''Money, money, money    that's what it's all about.'' He took a pull on the beer, then rubbed the cold glass against his forehead

''You're too cynical by half, Ronny''

''Hey, pal, you want to know what a cynic is? Do you?'

''No, but I know you're going to tell me anyway, so you might as well go ahead.''

''A cynic's a man who gets to bury all his friends. Some people think that's sad. Not me. Trot out all the flowers you want, as long as I get to smell every damn one of them. No way I'm going down the tubes for ideals, Jimmy  Ideals are the first thing to get sold out. And idealists are the first ones to go down in flames. Cynical pragmatism, that's the only way to go. You're the piper, you play any damn tune they want  Only you get paid up front and you don't take nothing but cash on the barrel head.''

''How is Marley holding up?''

''Talk about money make you uncomfortable?''

''No, of course not. I'm getting paid, just as you are. I just want to know how he's doing.''

''Change of heart about the old man, Jimmy?''

Harkness thought for a long time before he answered. Hisle had put his finger on it, but Harkness didn't want to acknowledge it. It seemed to him like a sign of weakness. But that's exactly what it was. He sighed. "I guess you could say that. I mean, he's a tough old bird, isn't he?"

"They're all tough old birds, Jimmy. You don't get to where Marley is if you're not tough. They look like butter wouldn't melt in their mouths, those guys. They have Ivy League educations and Wall Street trusts. They read poetry and collect paintings. But they have more than their share of blood on their hands, those old birds do. More like old vultures, they are, really. They create more than their share of corpses on the way up the ladder. As long as the blood stays below the rung they're on, then they keep on climbing. It just won't do to track blood on the white carpet. Then they get their asses in a sling."

"Even so. That doesn't mean they're not good men."

"Of course not. Blowing somebody's head off for money doesn't mean you're a bad man either, necessarily. It all depends on who you talk to. In my book Marley's all right. Colby was all right. Helms was all right. Hell, they're all all right. Just because they wouldn't have me to tea doesn't mean I think any the less of them. That's your problem, though, Jimmy. You *want* to have tea with them."

"Why do you see it as a class thing?"

"Because it is, old boy, because it is. And that was made clear to me very early on. It just wasn't *my* class. So I wasn't welcome at the palace. And you don't fool anybody with your English suits and your Percy Dovetonsils attitude, Jimmy. It isn't *your* class, either If you ask me, that's why you tried so hard. You wanted to belong. And when you did everything they asked and they still wouldn't let you marry one of their daughters, you turned on them."

"I'm not that vindictive."

"The hell you're not. And now you're going to get the chance to do what you always wanted to do. You're going to get to blow away the lord of the manor, and you're getting cold feet."

"What do you mean? Blow away the lord of the manor?"

"You know damn well, Jimmy boy. You don't really believe that crap you're feeding Marley, do you? There's no way on God's green earth Jason Marley is walking away from this. They will bury him deeper than Jimmy Hoffa. They have to. And they will. It wouldn't surprise me if they asked you to pull the trigger personally They understand you as well as I do. They know that for you this is as much about social climbing as it is money or politics. Maybe that's all it's about, actually You ever think about that?"

"Nonsense. They assured me Marley wouldn't be hurt. They assured me he would be more valuable to them if he were left in place."

"Oh, come on, Jimmy. How? How does he explain his little disappearing act? Fell on his head and wandered around in a daze? Get real. They've squeezed the lemon, the lemonade has been made. All that remains is to throw away the rind."

"But I promised him!"

"Of course you did. But that's all part of the game, isn't it? Marley knows. You can see it in his face. You can see it the way he stiffens his back every time we pay him a visit. He knows that one of these days, and it won't be long, we're taking him away and he isn't coming back."

"I won't have it."

"You will have it, whether you want it or not. You think I'm wrong, you ask the man the next time his royal herrness deigns to pay us a visit. Ask him! See if I'm wrong."

Hisle got up and drained the last of his beer. He flipped the bottle behind his back. It bounced off the wall and settled with a rattle into the wastebasket in the corner. "Need another beer. Bring you one back?"

"No, thank you."

"Sherry, then?" He grinned.

"Get out of here!"

Hisle laughed. "Touched a nerve, I guess." He walked out of the room and left the door open.

Harkness stayed slumped in his chair. He listened to Hisle's footsteps rapping on the hardwood floor. They faded away, then Harkness heard the slam of the refrigerator door Bottles clanked against one another from the impact, then Hisle tapped his way back. He stopped suddenly. Harkness still couldn't bring himself to move. He heard Hisle say, "We were just talking about you."

The newcomer stood in the doorway, his arms folded across his chest. "James."

Harkness tried to sit up, but he really didn't feel like moving. "Hello," he said.

"We have a few things to discuss." He looked at Hisle. "If you wouldn't mind, Mr. Hisle, Mr. Harkness and I have a few private matters we need to explore."

Hisle took a pull on his beer and said, "Sure thing." He pulled the door closed.

"What's on your mind?" Harkness finally said.

"A few things. To begin with, Mr. Hisle has been, shall we say, indiscreet."

"Youthful high spirits. Nothing more."

"There is no room for it, James. A little mistake like that can ruin everything. I'm not prepared to take that risk."

"Of course. I'll speak to him."

"No, that just won't do. That really won't do at all."

Harkness straightened now, leaning forward in his chair. "What are you suggesting?"

"I'm suggesting you address the problem I have just called to your attention."

"In what way? I said I'd speak to him. That should be sufficient."

"I've already told you it isn't. I don't want him chastised. I want him . . sanitized."

"You're joking!"

"I do not have a reputation as a man with a sense of humor, don't you remember?"

Harkness sighed. "All right. Tomorrow. What else?"

"Mr. Marley has served his purpose."

"We can't let him go yet."

"I don't mean that we shall. See to it."

The door closed softly, leaving Harkness staring at the dark expanse of polished wood. He shook his head from side to side. His hands rose to his temples, then clapped over his ears, as if the room had suddenly filled with some horrible noise. But it hadn't. There was nothing but one long, deadly silence.

It was deafening.

## CHAPTER THIRTY-SIX

Bolan and Yenikidze watched the doorway. Erika Mann leaned out into the hallway expectantly. Both men could hear footsteps approaching. It sounded as if Mike Bradley was moving reasonably well.

When Bradley entered the room, followed by Horst Halde, he looked drained but he moved without any apparent pain.

He flashed a grin at Bolan, who immediately relaxed.

"Sit down, Herr Bradley," Erika said briskly.

Bradley looked at Erika, then at Bolan and Yenikidze. The only place for him to sit was on the same sofa where Erika sat. He seemed uncomfortable with that, but shrugged and moved toward the opposite end and lowered himself carefully to the smooth leather cushions.

"I want to ask you a few questions, Herr Bradley. I want you to answer them completely and honestly. I already know some of what I need to know, and I will use that knowledge as a gauge to measure the rest of what you tell me. I tell you this because time is of the essence. I wish to cooperate with you and your friends, but only if that cooperation is mutual."

"Fair enough."

"Where were you earlier tonight?"

Fixing his gaze on Erika Mann, he said, "I arranged a meeting with my boss in the Tiergarten. We went to his office after I convinced him that Jason Marley was still alive. We started looking through reports on the crash of the plane on which Marley was flying."

Erika leaned forward. "Go on. Then where did you go?"

"Well, we found a few interesting leads in the mass of paperwork. We started to follow up on them Someone picked us up somewhere along the way. I'm still not sure where. Anyway, we were cutting through the Tiergarten again to get to the Schoenberg district. Somebody followed us. We tried to make a run for it, but..." He stopped. His face started to collapse. Chewing on his lower lip, he fought off the surge of emotion and choked back a sob. Starting again, he said, "They killed Dan. They took me prisoner I don't know where I was being held, but until these two showed up—" he jerked his chin toward Bolan and Yenikidze "—I figured I was going to die there."

"These leads you were following, what were they?"

Bradley told her It seemed almost as if he was glad to be talking about it, glad to tell someone who would believe him. When he was finished, he looked over at Bolan, then, glancing back at Erika Mann, said, "And that's God's honest truth. All of it. If you don't believe it, too bad."

Erika sat motionless for a long time. She seemed to be mulling something over in her head. Finally she broke the silence. "You did not look into Jennings?"

"We never got a chance to."

"And Harkness, either?"

"We were on the way there when we got bushwhacked."

"'Bushwhacked'?"

"Ambushed. They jumped us and shot the hell out of Dan. I guess they would have killed me, too, but they wanted something first and Pollock got there before they got what they wanted."

"And what did they want?"

"They wanted to know how much I knew about their little scheme and who else knew about it. I didn't tell them anything."

Erika seemed to mull that over. She was playing it close to her vest. Her face remained the immobile mask it had been. Her body language was under tight control. As Bolan watched her, he didn't have a clue which way she was leaning. He wanted to think she would help, put her resources at his disposal, but that was a long shot at best. So bent on revenge, she wasn't looking much past the end of her nose.

Bradley watched her as closely as Bolan. "I know what you want," he said. "I know there's only one thing in this world you really care about. And I can understand that. But our Russian friend here cares about the same thing, in a funny way. He told us his father was killed at Stalingrad. Fighting the same kind of monster that's planning to take over the government of Germany now. He wants revenge, too, or at least to make sure that his son doesn't grow up with the same need for that kind of revenge.''

''You don't know anything about me.'' Erika shrank from his urgency, backing herself into the corner of the sofa as if trying to get as far away from him as physically possible without getting up and running away.

''I know all I need to know.'' He glanced at Bolan, his face almost pleading for support.

Bolan didn't let him down. ''Fräulein Mann, you have to know now that we're after the same men. We have our own reasons, but our target is the same. If you know anything, anything at all that can help, you have to tell us.''

''All right,'' she said in a voice so low that Bolan scarcely heard it.

He leaned forward. ''You'll tell us?''

She nodded. ''It was a long time ago. My memory is not that clear. But I know I saw the frame from the video. You know that the Nazis raped every museum in the occupied territories. They confiscated art from private homes. Most of it ended up in the state treasury, or was supposed to. But it seems that even the SS had its Aryan imperfections. Toward the end of the war, much of the art that had been confiscated ended up in private stores, kept in vaults, hidden underground in mines, walled up in the basements of abandoned buildings. Anyplace one could hide something. They never believed that they would not win. They planned to come back for the paintings they couldn't send overseas."

"And the painting in the video is one of those?"

She nodded. "I think so, yes. It's a Matisse. I know who owned it and I know he didn't buy it. Reinhold Heintzelmann was one of Gehlen's lieutenants. He was something of an art connoisseur, or so he believed. I only knew this later, when I went to school. But as a little girl, I visited his home in the company of my father."

"Klaus Mann was one of Gehlen's men?" Bolan asked.

Erika shook her head. "No. He hated Gehlen. He hated everything Gehlen stood for. Gehlen was a dyed-in-the-wool Nazi, but he sold out his beliefs, as reprehensible as they were, to the highest bidder. There was no lack of eager customers in the West."

She paused to look at Yenikidze, almost apologetically. "Most Germans were afraid of the Russians. They would rather have the Nazis back than have Stalin's tanks crush them. Heintzelmann was like Gehlen. He had files on my father, because as a resident of Leipzig, he fell in Heintzelmann's sphere of concern. My father had to buy the files from him. And Heintzelmann kept upping the price. More information, more money. Always and always more."

"You're saying he blackmailed your father Where is he now?"

"Dead. Dead many years now."

"But—"

"Let me finish, please." She paused to wipe away a thin trickle of tears coursing over her cheeks. "My father killed him. As soon as he could. He knew Heintzelmann would bleed him to death and still sell him out as soon as the money was all gone. But Heintzelmann had the painting. This I know."

"But if he's dead, it doesn't help."

"But his son is alive. Siegfried Heintzelmann...."

Bradley sucked in his breath.

"My God!" Yenikidze muttered. "Him! Of course! I should have thought of that "

Bolan looked at the Russian Yenikidze ignored the stare for a moment Then, without looking at Bolan, he said, "The director of the Bundesnachrichtendienst The BND."

"Where can we find him?"

Erika stood and turned her back "He has a retreat, a hunting lodge, in the Bayerischerwald, east of Munich. It is near the village of Rohrstett, in the mountains."

"The perfect place to keep Marley out of the way," Bolan stated. "Did you ever visit the lodge?"

"Once. That's where I saw the Matisse."

"That tears it," Bradley said. "No way in hell we can take on the whole BND. No way."

Bolan disagreed. "I don't think we have to. There's no way the whole BND is in on this. It's probably just a cabal at the top, maybe just Heintzelmann himself. If we can get to him, and get Marley, then we have a chance."

"It explains one thing," Bradley said. "BND and the Company have worked together for years. Hell, it grew out of the Gehlen organization, with Company help. Heintzelmann would have had access to a hell of a lot. If he got to Jennings or Harkness, which he could easily have done, they could have given him the guided tour. With Marley on the block, they could have blown all our agents. It doesn't explain everything, but it explains a hell of a lot. It also explains why they would have wanted to kill Klaus Mann. Not only was he in a position to learn something they wanted kept under wraps, but it was also simple vengeance, to get even for Mann killing Heintzelmann's old man. Nice cover, too. Take out Mann, and it looks like it's just part of an underground war. The personal motive gets washed, and nobody gets wise."

"We still have one very big problem," Bolan said. "We know how it's worked so far, but we don't have a clue what the next step is, and that's the one that counts. Even if we take Heintzelmann, he won't tell us a thing. We have to get Marley, and we have to get the double in his shop, somebody who knows what the game plan is. Otherwise we're looking at a stone wall."

"First things first," Bradley said.

"No," Bolan contradicted. "Everything at once. It's the only way." He looked at Erika. "We'll need your help."

"Of course." The tears were gone. The stone mask was back. "I can offer you men and weapons. Not many of the former, but all you can use of the latter. But my condition still holds. I'm going with you. And Heintzelmann is mine."

Bolan shook his head. "No," he said. "It's too dangerous."

"Then I must refuse your request for assistance. I will do it my way."

"Don't you care about your country?"

"Father before fatherland, Herr Pollock."

"Okay," he said. "You can come along."

For the first time since he'd met her, Erika Mann smiled.

# CHAPTER THIRTY-SEVEN

James Harkness spent a restless night. When the sun rose, he was already awake. He slipped out of the lodge and stood on the wooden deck. Far below he could see the helipad and, beyond it, the crystal-clear waters of the lake. The trees had been cleared in a meandering swath down the mountainside. The grass was so perfect it looked as if the ground had been painted.

Harkness climbed down the wooden stairs and stood in the grass. He saw the dew on the blades and collecting on his shoes. Each drop seemed to spin on its own axle, the nearly perfect skin picking up the sunlight and breaking it into tiny rainbows.

The sun was reflected from the center of the lake, coloring the water a dark red. Off in the distance he heard a shotgun, someone hunting early A V of ducks suddenly burst over the canopy of trees and wheeled to the left, heading back the way it had come.

Looking back up at the lodge, he thought about Jason Marley, an old man lying on a cot in the fortified basement—bunker, really. Everything that had seemed so perfect, so logical, so damn right, now looked anything but. He felt as if his legs were getting sucked down into the ground, like a bad guy in a swamp in a B movie. Nothing was solid anymore. Events were slipping away from him, and he realized for the first time that he had never really had the control he had thought he had.

He continued to drift down the mountain. At the water's edge he sat on a rock. Reaching down for a fistful of pebbles, he tossed one into the water. It splattered the red skin of the lake. The ripples spread out farther and farther, almost lost to the eye before he tossed a second rock. It landed nearly at the center of the ripples, and he threw a third. This one landed a few inches to the left. The ripples interfered with one another, lapping into small peaks and then dying abruptly.

His life was like that now. Everything was off center. Nothing worked the way it was meant to, the way *he* meant it to. He saw himself in a new, and painful, light. He had been scammed royally. It was probably too late to do anything to set matters right. For a long time, his fist dangling by his side, still full of pebbles, he stared into the water, placid once more. But the sun made it impossible for him to look beneath the surface. He was blinded by the superficial light. There was an entire world under the surface, one he could not see, and the harder he looked, the more elusive it became.

He looked up at the sun itself, now beginning to lose its redness. Turning his attention to his hand, he uncurled the ingers and looked at the small stones. Sweeping his arm in a broad arc, more like an expression of disgust than a deliberate attempt to throw the stones, he let them fly out of his palm and curve out over the water, where they dropped with a series of soft plops and sank from view

Harkness turned his back on the lake and walked uphill, leaning forward to counter the pull of gravity. He went up far faster than he had come down. When he climbed the steps to the deck, Siegfried Heintzelmann was sitting at a small glass table, the umbrella above it furled and canted to one side.

"You are up early," Heintzelmann said. "Bad night, James?"

"I've had better."

"You are upset at Mr. Marley's fate."

"I don't know whether that's true."

"Oh, it very definitely is. But that is understandable. It always comes as a shock when the rug slips on the floor and we find ourselves in midair, wondering if we will survive the fall. The floor is so hard."

"You sound as if you speak from experience."

"I have had my share of ups and downs. But that is all behind me, or will be very soon. Tomorrow, in fact. Air Force One arrives at Tempelhof this morning. The chancellor and the President will be on their way to Hochburg within an hour after that. By tomorrow afternoon it will all be over. That should make you feel better."

"I suppose it will."

"You have planned well. I think you should know that."

"I do."

"But I wanted to tell you. It always means more, does it not, when someone else acknowledges what we already know to be true?"

Harkness turned away to look out over the lake. He was aware of Heintzelmann staring at his back. What was the man thinking? he wondered. Turning back, he saw Heintzelmann avert his eyes, as if trying to pretend he hadn't been staring. Harkness moved toward the sliding glass doors and stepped inside.

"About Mr. Hisle..."

"It will be tended to," Harkness replied.

Harkness walked toward the center of the lodge and opened the door leading down to the basement. The stairs were carpeted, and when he stepped onto the cold concrete floor at the bottom, his footsteps surprised him. Walking toward the far end of the corridor, he tried to soften the rapping of his feet, but each step slapped the concrete and echoed sharply from the high ceiling.

The door to Marley's chamber was open. As he stepped in, he was surprised to see the old man sitting in a chair. He was even more surprised to see Ronny Hisle standing against the wall, under the small window high above him. Hisle's face was wrapped in shadow as the early-morning light spilled over his head and shoulders

"Jimmy," Hisle said, "you're up early."

Harkness shrugged "Not so very."

"I think so. For a creature of such predictable habit, this is very odd behavior  Are you feeling okay?"

"Of course. Why shouldn't I be?"

"No reason, Jimmy. Just asking to be polite."

Harkness finally noticed the pistol in Hisle's hand. "What are you doing here, Ronny?"

Hisle shrugged. "Housekeeping," he said. He glanced at Marley "No big deal."

Harkness moved away from the doorway. The light coming in behind Hisle was bothering him. It made it hard to read the younger man. Not just the shadows, but the glare around him washed out those little tensions, the facial tics, the sudden shift of weight.

Harkness walked to a chair across the room from Marley and almost as far removed from Hisle, making a little triangle with one man at each apex  "You came here to kill Marley, didn't you?"

Hisle smiled. Distorted by the strange light, it looked more like a grimace. His head bobbed once, then again. It wasn't a nod, but it wasn't a denial, either  Harkness saw Hisle slide his tongue into one corner of his left cheek. "Maybe."

"No," Harkness snapped. "No maybe. You did. I know it. Heintzelmann sent you down here to do it, didn't he?"

"Hey, the man writes the checks. He calls the shots. So to speak." Hisle laughed at his own pun.

Marley remained quiet. He looked from Hisle to Harkness and back to Hisle, trying to remain calm. Harkness watched him from the corner of his eye. He had to admire the old man, who didn't seem nervous, let alone frightened.

Hisle was getting antsy. He wiped one palm across his lips. He moved away from the window, turning his head slightly as he did so. Harkness could see a thin line of sweat beads on Hisle's upper lip.

"You know, Ronny, it's not too late to call this whole thing off."

"Now why would I want to do that? Why would *you* want to do that?"

Harkness didn't answer. Hisle pressed his advantage. "Ask Jason. He understands this whole thing very well." Turning to Marley, he said, "Don't you, Jason?"

Marley shrugged. "I suppose I do."

"There, you see?" Hisle seemed pleased with himself, and with Marley for agreeing with him.

Harkness was aware of the weight of the Heckler & Koch .22 in his pocket. He tried not to think about it, but the weight kept calling attention to itself. He wondered if he would have a chance to pull the gun before Hisle ran out of things to say. He didn't think so.

"So," Marley said, "what's it going to be? Just the chancellor, or the President, as well?"

Hisle laughed. "Wise consumers always look for bargains, Jason. I don't expect you to understand that. You never had to worry about money much, did you? But I did. I think two for one isn't a bad sale."

"And you expect to get away with it?"

"Hey, when it's over, I don't give a damn. Heintzelmann will handle Germany. The Vice President will have his hands full just keeping a lid on back home. He'll be too busy to worry about anything else. And when the evidence points toward the former nasty boys of the KGB, everyone will leave the play satisfied. Once more, expectation is confirmed. The bad guys did it, and that's all she wrote. A rather neat scenario."

He looked at Harkness now, his smile even broader. "And little Jimmy is the playwright. Not a bad job, I think."

Marley shook his head. "Not bad at all. It seems I did you a disservice all these years, James."

Hisle laughed again. "That's what Jimmy always says. He's been one sour lemon ever since he realized his imported suits didn't cut any ice with the big boys. Of course, that wasn't the only reason. I think he really believes this is a necessary political step. Don't you, Jimmy?"

Harkness smiled now "I did, yes."

"But now you don't?"

"I didn't say that."

"But it's what you meant, Jimmy."

"No, it's—"

Hisle interrupted him. "I think it's time we cut out all the crap." He raised the pistol.

Harkness could see it clearly for the first time. It was a silenced Makarov PM 9 mm. The muzzle was point-blank. Even from across the room, it looked enormous, a black hole that would swallow everything. He could see more clearly now that Hisle was away from the window. He saw a slight flex of the shoulder under Hisle's cheap jacket. He pushed the chair sideways. He heard the gun go off, a very tame little spit, and felt something hot stab through his shoulder. He landed on the other shoulder and rolled sideways as Hisle followed his progress with the Makarov.

Harkness was reaching inside his jacket, thinking how the bullet had hit him before he heard the shot, and wondering why he hadn't felt the impact of the bullet before he heard the soft cough of the pistol.

His hand closed on the handle of the H&K, and he was swinging it around without thinking as a second shot ripped through his left arm. Hisle wasn't much of a marksman, he thought. The .22 was in his hand now, and he squeezed off three shots.

Hisle stood there, a look of profound surprise on his face, and a neat round hole just above his left eye.

The Makarov spit once more, but this time Ronny Hisle hadn't pulled the trigger intentionally.

Harkness crawled toward Hisle's collapsed body. He clawed at the Makarov and slid it toward Marley's slippered feet. Then he closed his eyes. It didn't hurt as much now, he thought.

## CHAPTER THIRTY-EIGHT

The helicopter put down six miles from the lodge. Erika Mann was the first one off the aircraft and into a waiting van. She'd brought Horst Halde and one other man with her

Yenikidze was silent as he climbed into the vehicle. Bradley moved sluggishly, but he had refused Bolan's suggestion that he wait behind. The Executioner got in last and pulled the doors closed. Moments later they were on their way.

They had nearly six miles to travel. Not wishing to alert Heintzelmann, they couldn't afford to bring the chopper any closer to Rohrstett. Bradley had argued for an airborne assault, but Bolan had vetoed it, insisting that they had to know what they were up against before they made their first move. If they were reckless, they would succeed only in alerting Heintzelmann and getting Jason Marley killed. Bradley was impetuous, but he wasn't a fool, and he had swallowed his argument with a shrug of resignation.

Minutes later, the van shifted direction suddenly, listing heavily for a moment, then coasted to a halt When the engine died, Bolan reached for the interior door handle, but his fingers closed over the back of Erika's hand. She twisted the handle open and gave the door a shove. She moved easily and dropped down from the van with one graceful hop. As she backed away from the open door, her dark uniform shifted like a kaleidoscope as blotches of sunlight played over the blue cloth.

Bolan climbed down next and looked up through the heavy foliage of a stand of elms. He could see the sun through gaps in the leaves. Patches of bright blue glowed almost white-hot around the sun and cooled down to a warm blue as he let his gaze wander to the east, where he knew Siegfried Heintzelmann's hunting lodge was located.

When the remaining four men had exited the van, Erika knelt on the ground with an unfolded map spread out in front of her. "Remember, here, just off the lake, Heintzelmann has his helipad. If he's here, and I hope he is, he will break for the helipad. If he makes it, he'll run for cover, and we'll never get him."

All six of them carried AK-47 assault rifles, back-to-back magazines already in place. Erika parceled out a dozen grenades and handed the other man, Peter Handke, an RPG-7 launcher of Russian manufacture and five rounds. "Peter," she said, "we'll come in halfway between the lake and the lodge. You take out the helicopter. You'll be on your own."

The youth nodded.

"Remember," Bolan told them, "we're here for two reasons—we want Siegfried Heintzelmann and we want Jason Marley Heintzelmann is to be taken alive if at all possible. Shoot to kill only to protect yourselves or Marley, otherwise take him alive. Is that clear?" He looked hard at Erika Mann, and she returned his stare without blinking or wavering. He wondered what was going through her head.

Bolan continued. "We don't know where Marley is being held, so think twice before using a grenade. Peter, if the chopper is taking off, make sure Marley isn't on it before you take it down. Understand?"

"Yes."

Bolan had studied the maps closely, and he took the point. They still had a klick to go. Taking the woods was the safest. Heintzelmann almost certainly had guards, and in all probability at least a modicum of electronic security. Coming in off the road was their best bet.

The woods were relatively cool. The shade was deep, and a slight breeze moving uphill off the lake kept the temperature down. It wouldn't be long now, Bolan thought. Not long at all.

JASON MARLEY LEANED OVER to reach for the Makarov His head was spinning, but he held on to the arm of the chair until his fingers closed over the butt. Harkness lay on the floor curled into a ball. He was still bleeding, but his shoulders rose and fell and his breathing was regular despite its shallowness.

The old man wondered about his subordinate. He couldn't understand what would have moved him to throw in with such a horrendous scheme. Could he have been that envious? Marley asked himself.

He lowered himself out of the chair and crawled on hands and knees across to Harkness. He felt for a pulse, which was steady but weak beneath his fingers. He rolled Harkness onto his back. Two wounds were apparent, one of which was serious and one relatively minor. The wound in the man's upper arm was bleeding more heavily than the chest wound, but posed no real threat if he could stop the flow of blood.

Marley was too feeble to handle Harkness easily. It took him a few minutes to maneuver the wounded man out of his jacket. Even then, he knew he would have difficulty with the shirtsleeve. Too weak to tear it loose, he tried to rip it vertically. At the cuff he opened the buttons and twisted the two strips around the wound and knotted them securely.

Marley was working on the chest wound when Harkness opened his eyes. He tried a smile, but it was just a feeble shadow that fell from his lips before it even curled them into recognizability.

"Stay still, James," Marley ordered.

"Just let me be, Jason. Let me die. I don't deserve any better."

"No, you don't, but the world does. You know what's going to happen. No one else does. You've got to hang on long enough for us to get out of here. You've got to do that, James, to atone.''

"Atone? Never There is no atonement.'' He uttered a strange sound that was either a sob or a gasp of pain, perhaps a bit of both.

"You have to hang on, James, do you hear me?''

"I want to die, Jason.''

Marley shook him. It felt ludicrous to him, a weak old man with barely the strength to move himself trying to shake some sense into a man who was unwillingly clinging to life by his very fingernails.

"Damn it, man, you've got to hang on!''

Harkness gave him another stillborn smile. "You're the boss.''

Marley jerked his head around when he heard a sharp crack somewhere in the distance. It sounded like a gunshot, but he couldn't be sure. He listened for a moment, thinking perhaps it was the beginning of an attempt to rescue him, but dismissed it out of hand. No one would know where to find him He knew about the plane wreck. If anything, they were still sifting the farmland looking for bits and pieces of his body, trying to puzzle him together from a stray arm and a charred hand, some knife-edged shards of blackened bone and a foot still wearing a shoe and sock. He'd seen that kind of carnage. He knew how long it took. And he knew that sometimes you gathered luggage and drew a wavering line through a name on a passenger manifest without having so much as a fingernail or strand of hair that belonged to the victim in question.

Harkness was a pro. It was actually a brilliant plan. Kidnapper and kidnapped both written off as casualties. No one would be looking for either breathing specimen. And it was that single fact that had convinced Marley they never meant to let him go. The presumed dead have to stay dead to make such a scheme work. But Harkness hadn't really seen that. So caught up in the logistics, he had missed the logic.

He heard a noise behind him in the corridor and started to move toward the door, still on hands and knees.

He heard gunshots again, louder this time, more of them. This was no hunting party. It was an assault. All he had to do was stay alive a little longer. And keep James Harkness breathing.

Siegfried Heintzelmann suddenly loomed in the doorway. The worried look on his face turned to a frown when he saw Marley kneeling in the middle of the floor.

His eyes flitted about the room, lingered on Hisle for a moment, then stopped at Harkness. "You stupid fool," he growled. "You could have ruined everything."

"I hope so," Marley replied, struggling to contain his surprise.

The gun appeared from nowhere. Heintzelmann pointed it at Marley, then at Harkness, then back at

Marley, as if uncertain which man posed the greater threat and therefore deserved to die first. Marley tried to back away, but the effort was too much for him.

The gun came back toward him. A sharp crack exploded behind him, and Heintzelmann dropped his gun, grabbing for his upper arm with the hand that had moments before held the pistol.

There was another crack, but this one went wide, chipping the woodwork of the doorframe. Marley realized he'd left the Makarov on the floor by Harkness and turned to reach for it. But Heintzelmann bolted.

Harkness lay still, the H&K .22 still in his hand. His eyes were closed, but he was still breathing.

Marley heard more gunshots and crawled toward the door. Heintzelmann wouldn't let them go if he could help it. The door closed easily, and Marley turned the lock. He was too weak to do much more than throw the steel bolt above the knob. He leaned against it, panting, listening to the sound of advancing gunfire.

"Did I get him?" Harkness mumbled.

Marley shook his head. Looking at Harkness, he realized the man's eyes were still closed. "Yes," he said, "but he got away."

"Too bad."

Marley crawled back and sat beside Harkness. "You've got to tell me, James," he said. "You've got to tell me everything.   "

## CHAPTER THIRTY-NINE

Bolan could see the lodge clearly The sporadic gun-fire that had broken out continued as his team spread out through the trees. Off to the left he saw Peter Handke lugging the RPG-7 grenade launcher and sprinting just inside the tree line heading toward the lake.

The Executioner had Yenikidze on his right and Erika Mann on his left. They were holding their fire to a minimum, not wanting to unleash the whole load without knowing what they were up against. As it was, they had been lucky to get as close to the lodge as they had before the two-man security team stumbled on them

More men were sprinting toward the trees across the broad swath of grass, angling down from the far corner of the lodge. Bolan eased out ahead, ducking low and racing toward the last line of elms. They were old trees, and their thick trunks gave him plenty of cover. If he could prevent the charging men from reaching the trees, he could force them back toward the lodge.

Two men flopped on the ground and opened up with automatic rifles. Their fire was heavy but undisciplined. The bullets hacked at the leaves behind him and tore hunks of bark off the elms as Bolan hit the deck. Yenikidze came up on his right as Bolan laid down covering fire.

Four more men raced across the open ground. Bolan took aim and dropped one with a short burst from his AK. Yenikidze took another. Bolan shifted his aim, but the two trailers had flattened on the ground a few yards to the right of their comrades. The grass wasn't tall, but with the undulations of the ground it was tall enough that it made the men hard to see.

He turned at a rustle in a clump of bushes to his right. It was Erika Mann, her AK poking through the leaves as she flattened on the ground beside him. Three more men swung around the corner of the lodge, but instead of charging straight for him, they darted across the bottom of the lodge and headed for the trees way uphill. If they made it to the woods, they'd be in a position to circle behind Bolan's team.

The Executioner barked a command, and Horst Halde and Mike Bradley charged forward. Erika pointed. Bradley spotted the three men, and he grabbed his younger companion by the shoulder and started uphill, keeping ten or twelve yards back to have some cover between him and the men on the grass.

An instant later a burst of gunfire erupted far down the hill. Bolan glanced toward the sound and saw four men on their knees firing into the trees. Behind them a helicopter flashed red and white lights as its rotor began to turn. Bolan recognized it as a West German MBB BO 105. It didn't appear to be that heavily armed, with only a single Rheinmetall 20 mm gun mounted on the right side. He shouted to Yenikidze and pointed.

"You stay here with Erika," Bolan ordered. "I'll go help Peter" No sooner were the words out of his mouth than a geyser of water erupted at the edge of the lake. Peter had cut loose with his first shot and missed the chopper. The RPG projectiles weren't heat seekers, and a hit required marksmanship that Peter might not have.

Bolan scrambled to his knees. Kneeling alongside Erika, he said, "If you get to Heintzelmann before I get back, don't kill him."

She glared at him for a moment, then shook her head slowly "All right."

Bolan got to his feet, tapped her on the shoulder and broke into a trot, keeping as low as he could as the soldiers in the grass opened up again.

Looking back toward the lodge, he saw a jeep career around the far corner and speed straight downhill. Two men, one in uniform and one in a business suit, were in the front seat. They were making a break for it, and he had to stop them from getting to the chopper

Erika had to have spotted the jeep at the same instant. Her AK chattered, and bullets sparked off the tail end of the speeding jeep.

Far below, another geyser of water erupted as Peter missed with his second round. The rifle fire from the four men protecting the chopper was still heavy, and Bolan dropped to one knee to try to cut down the odds a little. He loosed a short cluster toward the four gunners. Clods of dirt and grass jumped all around them. Adjusting, the warrior fired again, this time catching the man on the right, who went down hard, waving his rifle high over his head as he tried to keep his balance.

The jeep was already past Bolan now, and he focused his attention on it. Slicing the rest of his clip across the slope, he ripped up one tire, and the jeep started to list. The driver looked behind him at the blown tire, now spewing hunks of rubber, as he kept his foot to the floor.

The tire finally tore loose altogether, but the jeep kept on, swerving back and forth as the bare rim lost traction on the slippery grass. It was zigzagging toward the chopper now, moving more toward the center of the slope.

Peter broke from the trees, and Bolan saw him race toward the helicopter, the grenade launcher on his shoulder. It was a lunatic assault. Three men still guarded the aircraft, and they concentrated their fire on him as he closed the gap.

Peter's legs went out from under him just as the jeep went past. He seemed to know he wasn't going to get to the chopper, and he cut loose with his third round. It went wide and blew a column of mud and water up off the shoreline. Rolling to his right, he yanked the fourth round from his backpack and rammed it home.

The riflemen were charging him now, holding fire until they could get closer. Bolan sprinted ahead, opening up again and hosing 7.62 mm rounds above Peter's head. The charging gunners stopped in their tracks and started to fire at the Executioner. He dived to the ground and skidded several feet on the slippery grass, stopping as Peter tried to home in on the jeep He found his mark, and the jeep mushroomed into a ball of orange flame and black smoke.

The driver spiraled up and out of the fireball, then fell back to earth.

The helicopter was starting to lift off now, and the soldiers returned their attention to Peter. Bolan scrambled to his feet again as little gouts of sod spattered the German as he tried to roll away.

Someone leaned out of the chopper as the man in the suit raced toward it, his arms extended. Bolan could see bloodstains on the man's arms as he leaped toward the open door. He was grabbed by the coat and hauled aboard as the aircraft suddenly lifted off and wheeled to the left.

The Executioner turned his AK on the fleeing aircraft, emptying his clip as it disappeared behind the trees. He heard the engine coughing and sputtering, but he couldn't see the MBB behind the trees. Ramming a new clip home, he hosed the three men below, now racing along the lakeshore.

Spouts of water spumed up into the air as Bolan's deadly fire swept past, taking two men out. Both tumbled into the lake. One, hit in the head, lay facedown in the water. The other flailed his arms, trying to get away from the shoreline. The third man made it across the slope and into the trees on the far side.

Bolan raced to Peter's side, but he was beyond help. His shirt was soaked in blood, and the side of his head was a bloody pulp. His fingers were still curled around the RPG-7, stretched out ahead of him where it lay since his last futile attempt on the jeep.

Uphill the firestorm had subsided slightly. A small pocket of resistance had formed at the far corner of the lodge. Bolan ran for the trees, then threaded his way back uphill. By the time he caught a glimpse of Erika's blond hair in the trees up ahead, the battle was over.

Yenikidze broke into the open as the Executioner reached Erika's side. She was bleeding from a wound to her left arm, but it didn't look serious. Horst Halde followed the Russian into the open, and Mike Bradley had already reached the opposite corner of the lodge. Bolan glanced out over the lake where he saw dark smoke hovering off to the right. He wondered if the chopper was too damaged to fly but had no time to investigate. He had more urgent business to attend to.

Bolan climbed the wooden stairs to the deck, followed by Bradley. Yenikidze stayed at the foot of the ladder to make sure they didn't get trapped in the lodge.

"That was Heintzelmann, wasn't it?" Bradley asked as they stopped just inside the door

Bolan shook his head. "I don't know I didn't get a good look at him. But probably."

"How did Erika take it?"

The warrior shrugged. They heard the rotors of the helicopter, stuttering closer, and Bolan stepped back onto the deck. The MBB was hovering just past the edge of the lake, struggling back to the pad. Smoke was pouring from its open door and belching in black clouds from its exhaust tubes.

"Bullet must have caught an oil line," Bolan commented, heading for the stairs. Yenikidze was pointing toward the lake. On the way down the steps, Bolan saw Erika Mann racing across the open grass, just twenty yards from Peter Handke's body.

"Damn!" he shouted. He jumped from the stairs, knowing even before he hit the ground that it was too late. He saw Erika reach down for the RPG-7 She had the last round in her hand and rammed it home.

"Erika!"

She didn't hear or didn't care. The dull whoosh of the RPG drifted toward him He saw the thin trail of gray smoke, then the huge ball of fire as the chopper disintegrated. Debris was still raining down into the water when Erika turned to look up toward the lodge. She saw Bolan and raised a triumphant fist in the air.

Bradley grabbed Bolan by the arm, trying to keep him from charging down the slope. "Come on, Pollock. It's too late. What's the point? Now we have no choice but to find Marley, Jennings or Harkness."

Bolan nodded and started up the steps. The lodge seemed to be deserted. As he stepped inside, he saw the Matisse, high on the wall, up near a cathedral ceiling. He tapped Bradley on the shoulder and pointed.

"Jesus," Bradley whispered, "that's it. She was right!"

A search of the main floor turned up no one. It was as neat as a pin, and looked as if it hadn't been inhabited for a year. Even the kitchen was clean and neat. Not a drop of water sparkled on the smooth surface of the stainless-steel sink. Every dish was in place.

Bolan backed out of the kitchen and turned left, heading down a narrow hall. The door at the end was the last one on that floor. He reached for the knob, expecting it to be locked, but it turned easily. Keeping his AK ready, he jerked the door open and found himself staring down a flight of steps.

He went down first, Bradley close behind. The lower floor had a far different look and feel. Instead of the luxury of the upper floor, this one was utilitarian. The first room he found was empty, but he knew by looking at the walls that they were thick.

The next room was an office. It, too, was deserted, but it had been used recently The stub of a cigar still trailed a thin column of smoke toward the ceiling.

The next door wouldn't budge. Bolan listened, but heard nothing beyond it. He stepped back and fired a burst into the heavy wood, circled the lock, then planted a heavy foot in the center. The door started to cave in, but something held it. He kicked it again, and this time it gave way, springing back suddenly and slamming against the wall.

He felt Bradley pressing in behind him and found himself staring into the deep, dark mouth of a Makarov.

"Marley!" Bradley shouted.

The old man smiled distantly. "And who are you?"

## CHAPTER FORTY

Jason Marley held the pistol steady. "Who are you?" he repeated.

Bolan introduced himself and Bradley. Then he saw the bodies on the floor. Marley caught the motion of his eyes. "Ronny Hisle and James Harkness," he said. He let the Makarov sink to his lap and closed his eyes. Letting out a long sigh, he asked, "Siegfried got away?"

"We don't know."

"I was afraid he might. He was winged, but..."

"Brown suit? Wounded in the arm?"

Marley nodded.

"He's dead," Bolan said. "Unfortunately."

The director raised the pistol again. "Unfortunately? Why?"

"Because now we'll never know what he was planning. We might be unable to stop it from being pulled off, even though he's dead."

Marley smiled. "Oh, no, don't worry about that." Cocking a thumb over his shoulder at Harkness, he said, "James put it all together for him. I know all about it. Now, gentlemen, if you'll get me to a secure telephone, I have to make a rather urgent call."

Erika Mann suddenly appeared in the doorway. "This phone is secure," she said.

"Erika, you're as lovely as ever. How's your father?"

"Dead," she whispered. She let it all out then, starting with noiseless sobs and then weeping uncontrollably. Bolan reached out for her, and she stiffened for a moment, then allowed him to sweep her to his chest.

With his eyes he signaled Bradley to get Marley to the phone.

Stroking Erika's back, he got her gradually to calm down. As the sobbing started to subside, she turned her face up to his. The brilliant blue eyes were red rimmed but still startling. Her face seemed softer, almost as if the tears had started somehow to thaw the wintry cast of her features. She smiled gamely, but her heart wasn't really in it.

"I'm sorry," she said. "I must appear very foolish to you, Herr Pollock. I suppose we had better join the others."

Letting her hands linger on his chest, the palms flat, she stood on tiptoe and brushed her lips against his. She moved past him then, letting one hand stay in contact as long as she could. When it finally slipped from his shoulder, he felt for a moment as if he'd lost something he hadn't even known he had until the instant it was taken away. He turned to follow her out into the hall.

He walked along behind her, hearing Marley's voice somewhere up ahead. Erika turned into the next doorway, where the office was. Bolan followed, entering just as Marley hung up the telephone.

The old man sank down into a chair beside the desk. Clapping his hands, the brisk slap of palm on palm almost like a gunshot, he said, "Gentlemen and Fräulein, we should get busy. We have a bit of work before this foolishness is all over. Let's get to it, shall we?"

It took an hour for Marley to lay it all out. In the beginning he relayed what Harkness had told him before he died. He was still fatigued, and he had to stop frequently to rest his voice. Slowly the scope of Heintzelmann's scheme began to emerge. It was Marley's show, and he ran it with a firm hand, despite his fragile condition. It seemed almost as if there was some separation between mind and body, as if the clarity of the one was in no way affected by the debilitation of the other.

But as the discussion turned to the final phase, what was going to happen the following day, he turned more and more to Mack Bolan. The old man seemed to sense something in the big man, growing more animated as Bolan came front and center. He seemed to draw strength from Bolan's determination to write paid to the whole affair.

As the hour drew to a close, Marley leaned back in the chair. He looked at each of the faces arrayed in a semicircle around the desk. He closed his eyes for a moment, whether from exhaustion or simply to summon the energy for one final statement, none of them could tell. Finally, taking a deep breath, he nodded.

"I don't think I have to tell you what it would mean if this man Kreuger succeeds. We know where he is now, where he will be set up. But if he gets away, he'll go underground and he'll try again. We have to get to him, and we have to put him away. Whatever it takes, we have to do it. *You* have to do it."

"I don't like the way it's shaking out," Bradley said.

"It's the only way."

"You're using the chancellor for bait. It's not right."

Marley looked at him quietly for a long time. His head began to nod. "You're right. But it has to be done. The President is out of harm's way. We can handle the mechanics of that. But if we pass the word to the chancellor, the BND will be front and center. There is no way to avoid that. If Heintzelmann set this thing in motion as thoroughly as he did everything else, then the BND isn't to be trusted. There's no other way to protect the chancellor. We have to get the assassin ourselves. We have this one, single, murky window of opportunity. If we don't take advantage of it..."

He let his voice trail off. The silence seemed to swell. No one seemed willing to break it.

Finally, when it was apparent no one else would speak, Marley nodded his head again. "Mr. Bradley, I admire your moral concerns. But you must understand that there's no time to purge the BND of its poison. If we can get Ernst Kreuger, that will buy us, and the Germans, the time they'll need to clean house. As wrong as it may be to do it this way, *not* to do it this way is to expose the chancellor to an even greater threat. We can't know where or when Kreuger might try again. This is our one and only chance to be sure. Or as sure as men in our position can ever be."

Bolan watched Bradley closely. He sympathized with the kid, but there was no time to coddle him, to try to convince him that the world was a darker, nastier place than he wanted it to be. In time the death of Dan Mitchell would do that. And it would teach him that good men took risks for good ends. They had to be prepared to take great risks for great ends.

The Executioner knew, as the young agent didn't, that extremists won more often than they lost because they were willing to go to any lengths, use any tool, any terror, to get what they wanted. To have any chance at all to stop them, you sometimes had to meet them on their home field and play by house rules. It wasn't pleasant and, as Bradley so adamantly insisted, it wasn't right.

But it was necessary.

Leaning forward, Bolan finally broke the silence. "I think it's time we got started. We all know what we have to do, and we have less than twenty-four hours to get it done."

Marley nodded in agreement. "I wish I could offer you the assistance of my people. But—" he glanced at the wall, beyond which Harkness and Hisle lay, for a moment "—the poison isn't exclusively German. When this is all over, we shall all have to look long and hard at our mirrors. We won't like some of what we see. That's always the case. But we want to be able to say we did what had to be done, and we did it well."

Then, looking straight at Erika Mann, he said, "You know that we can't do this without your assistance, Erika. And you know that your father wouldn't have been reluctant to get involved. Someday, when this is all over, we shall have to have a long talk about Klaus. I can tell you some things that even you don't know. But there'll be time for that. At the moment all I can do is ask that you assist us in whatever way you can. Unfortunately I'm not as young as I once was, and will be able to do nothing but wait and pray."

Erika felt the pressure of five sets of eyes on her. But she didn't flinch. She looked at each man in turn. Her gaze found Bolan last, and lingered longest on the flinty features of the big American. It was almost as if she wanted him to tell her what to do. But this was a decision she would have to make for herself.

"I know that my father would have felt he had no choice. Therefore, I have no choice."

Marley nodded. "Then we're agreed. As Mr. Pollock suggested, he and Mr. Yenikidze will go after Kreuger. Erika, you will stay here and help with the communications. I'll have to be in frequent contact with the President once he advises the chancellor of the change in plans. In order to guarantee that communications link, we will need the defense of Mr. Bradley and Mr. Halde. Erika, Mr. Pollock will tell you what he needs. I hope it's something you can provide."

"We should get you to a hospital, Mr. Marley."

"We can't risk that, Mr. Bradley. If Kreuger hears of it, he'll know something has gone wrong. As it is, we can only cross our fingers and hope that he's unaware of what has gone on here this morning. I'll stay here until this is over. The minute you succeed, and I pray to God you will, contact us."

Bolan and Yenikidze stood. Marley allowed his eyes to flutter a moment, then fixed both men in his steady gaze. "God be with you, gentlemen. Now, I think I should rest."

They stepped into the hallway, and Erika followed them out. She reached up behind her neck and undid the clasp of a small gold necklace. She handed the necklace to Bolan and folded his fingers over it. "When you get back to the helicopter, show this to

Erich. Tell him 'The storks are nesting.' He will know what it means, and he will get you whatever you need.''

She looked at Yenikidze a long moment, then turned back to Bolan. ''Good luck, Herr Pollock.''

She turned then, and went back into the small office. Bolan watched until the door closed behind her.

## CHAPTER FORTY-ONE

Bolan stood atop a rocky precipice, looking down at the winding road. It passed through steep cliffs on either side, a slender white ribbon stretching off to the west where its serpentine tangles disappeared in the rocks a mile away. To the east, it snaked uphill, barely wide enough for two cars abreast.

On the opposite side, on a rocky point that sloped back away from the road far below, Sergei Yenikidze waved a hand, then disappeared among the shattered boulders.

The chancellor's limousine was due in three hours. Two hours before that, Ernst Kreuger and his team of assassins would be working their way up through the rocks on both sides of the road.

Bolan took the rifle off his shoulder and slipped it out of its goatskin bag. It was a beautiful piece of equipment. A Heckler & Koch G-3 SG/1, it was the latest sniper rifle for the West German police and army. It had a 20-round magazine and a folding bipod for stability. Semiautomatic, it fired single rounds of 7.62 mm ammunition and sported a 1.5 × 6 Zeiss telescopic sight.

The terrain was tailor-made for sniping. With so many boulders, crevices and crannies on both stone faces looming over the road, a man would have only fractions of a split second to nail his target. In an hour Ernst Kreuger and his men would be ants swarming among the rocks. Bolan would need the H&K and a considerable helping of luck to pull this off, and he knew it.

On the far side of the deep canyon, Yenikidze had his own G-3 SG/1. There were spots on either stone face where a man below, on the same side, couldn't be seen. Bolan and the Russian might be forced to make their shots at long range, covering those perches across the canyon's width.

The Executioner inserted the magazine and looped the rifle over his shoulder, then started working his way across the top of the canyon. He wanted to know the terrain as well as he could in the little time he had left. Once Kreuger arrived, there would be no time to wonder whether one route was better than another. He would have to think fast and shoot faster still.

He committed as much of the top to memory as he could, then started working his way down the steep paths that angled across the rocky face. Kreuger was going to want to be close. The rock walls were nearly a hundred feet high, too high for more than a couple of shots at a moving car.

Once the first round struck the limo, the driver would floor it, and the opportunity would be gone.

That meant Kreuger had to have made some provisions to slow the car, if not stop it altogether.

Harkness had left the last few details to the specialists, and Marley didn't know exactly what Kreuger had planned, only where and when. The matter was complicated by the fact that European politicians often didn't use bulletproof limos. They hadn't learned the painful lessons of Dallas, and many statesmen were fatalistic. They knew that a determined man could get to them, no matter what they might try to do to prevent it, so it was almost better to be alert than to be lulled by armor and technology into a false sense of security. Or so the logic, such as it was, went.

With forty-five minutes already gone, Bolan was no closer to deciding where Kreuger would position himself. It was a crap shoot. So many ideal shooting positions pocked the surface of the canyon walls that it just wasn't possible to predict which one Kreuger would use.

With a mental shrug of resignation, Bolan stood in the center of the road and looked up at the top of the wall. Even the target's eye view left a hundred options, any one of which would serve an assassin's purpose to perfection.

Despite his conviction that Kreuger was going to pick his spot somewhere down the wall, Bolan was reluctant to cede him the high ground. Better to be above and have to work his way down than to try to charge uphill into Kreuger's sights. He climbed back up, feeling the ache in his legs but unwilling to postpone the climb any longer.

He had to find cover, a point from which he could launch his assault with as little risk and as great a chance of success as he could manage.

Bolan found a notch between two boulders, one with a slight overhang, and he backed into the crevice, the G-3 across his knees. He watched the slope across the narrow pass. There was no sign of Yenikidze, which was as it should be.

Looking at his watch, he realized Kreuger was due. It was two o'clock. He could see some distance to the west, the direction from which Kohl's limo would be coming. There was no sign of it yet; it was far too early.

As the warrior stared intently at the road, he heard the sound of distant rotors. He had never considered an air assault. If Kreuger was going to launch an attack from the sky, the ball game was over. And there was nothing he could do but sit in the bleachers and watch it happen.

The chopper came closer, its rotor throbbing like a spastic heart. It was somewhere behind him now, about half a klick distant. The engine slowed, and he knew the aircraft was touching down.

He heard the engine idling now, the chopper on the ground. A moment later it roared, and the helicopter swept low, passing just twenty feet above his head, then swooped toward the opposite side of the pass and hovered just off the ground. He saw two men jump out of the aircraft, each carrying a rifle. Then the bird twisted and lifted off. Half a minute later the sound of its rotors was all but gone.

The two men scurried down the slope. Watching them, Bolan realized they knew exactly where they were going. He watched them closely, then heard something behind him, the sharp crack of one rock against another, then a muffled curse.

Again the sound of rocks, this time accompanied by footsteps. The sound drifted to his right—men were walking across the top of the cliff. Peering out from between the stones, he saw the unmistakable blond mane of Ernst Kreuger, an RPG-7 grenade launcher slung over one shoulder, an Iver Johnson Model 300 over the other. The second man carried an assault rifle, an AR-15, judging by the little Bolan could see of it.

The Executioner wanted to take them out, but he had to wait for them to stop moving. Stationary targets were essential. He was not armed to mount a headlong assault. He needed to call his shots and choose them carefully. Better to wait until Kreuger found his perch and came to roost.

The warrior spotted something moving in the distance. A vehicle was approaching, flying the German flag above the front fenders—the chancellor, and he was way too early.

Kreuger, too, spotted the limo and the lead car full of security, and started to run down the path. Bolan realized the chancellor must have changed his plans, decided to arrive at his secluded retreat early, since the President had changed his schedule.

The limo was closing fast. Kreuger waved a hand in the air, and Bolan saw the two men across the pass freeze in their tracks. They'd seen the wave. Kreuger pointed toward the road, then waved his hand in a circle, urging his team to hurry. There was still no sign of Yenikidze. Bolan crept out from cover and lay flat on the ground.

The limo was only five hundred yards from the mouth of the pass as Kreuger shrugged off the grenade launcher and tossed it to his companion.

The man with Kreuger crawled out onto a flat rock, then rolled on one hip and slipped a projectile into the launcher. Kreuger moved to the right a few yards and lay on the ground. He unfolded the stabilizing bipod on the Iver Johnson 300. Bolan was reluctant to start without Yenikidze. He tried once more to raise the Russian on the handset, but still got nothing but static in return.

Bolan had to move, and move fast.

The limo roared into the mouth of the pass. The man with the RPG-7 took aim. The Executioner stopped in midstride and dropped to one knee. He raised the G-3 to his shoulder and peered through the Zeiss. He found Kreuger, then the man with the launcher. Even as he squeezed the trigger, he knew he was too late. He saw the man spasm as the bullet hit him, but the missile streaked forward and the lead car disappeared in a cloud of smoke and flame. The chancellor's limo swerved to the left, narrowly avoiding the wreckage of the lead car, and jolted up and over a shattered fender that still flapped across the road like a bird with a broken wing.

At the same instant one of Kreuger's men across the road spotted the warrior and cut loose. Bolan had to duck even as he saw Kreuger raise the reloaded RPG-7. A second later another grenade smoked down to the pass. Bolan saw it hit a few yards in front of the limo, heard the squeal of brakes as the car swerved to avoid the explosion. The first crack of the G-3 had alerted Kreuger, who now rolled off his perch and dropped from sight.

Far below, the limo careered off the road and scattered sparks as its passenger side scraped against the rocks. The impact shattered the front right fender and blew a tire. Bolan saw the doors on the driver's side fly open.

A sharp report echoed across the pass, and Bolan glanced toward the steep slope across the road. The driver was out of the car now, an Uzi in his hands. He was looking up over the roof of the limo toward the slope and fell a split second before Bolan heard the crack of a rifle below him.

It was Kreuger's 300. Bolan sprinted to his right, trying to get a fix on the assassin. Two short bursts of automatic fire erupted from across the canyon, and the Executioner saw sparks scatter from the roof of the limo and its windshield dissolve into icy fragments.

Another man stumbled from the front seat, also armed with an Uzi. He took cover behind the rear of the car and stared up the slope. Another round erupted from the Iver Johnson 300, and Bolan raced downhill, heading toward the sound.

The bodyguard had been hit dead center and slid down the rear fender. Bolan could see a bright scarlet smear on the wheel and whitewall tire when the man fell and rolled away from the car.

He heard another shot from across the way, this one sounding different, possibly Yenikidze's gun. Bolan saw Kreuger then and drew a bead, dropping to one knee again. He got Kreuger in his sights, but the assassin must have sensed something. He scurried downhill as the Executioner tracked him and squeezed. The bullet slammed into a granite slab an inch from Kreuger's exposed shoulder. And the assassin was gone again.

A shot blew out the wide window of the chancellor's limo. Kreuger again. Bolan reached the dead man with the RPG, snatched up the AR-15 and sprinted to a cluster of large rocks a few yards distant.

No Kreuger. Another shot from the 300 punched a hole in the passenger door.

The Executioner spotted one of the assault team across the pass, looking back uphill and crouched behind a rock. Yenikidze was still alive, then. Sighting carefully through the Zeiss, he squeezed and blew the assassin away. That was two, at least. But the chancellor was down there, pinned in a car no safer than a cardboard box.

Racing downhill, Bolan saw Kreuger slither among the rocks for a moment, like some lethal iguana. The warrior climbed onto a canted slab of granite, then jumped from rock to rock for a short distance. Balanced precariously on the edge of a boulder, he saw Kreuger rise up on one knee. Bolan swung around the G-3 and got off a shot—just as the rock tipped. The bullet slammed into Kreuger's shoulder and he turned half-around, more in surprise than from the bullet's impact.

Kreuger was grinning. Ignoring the wound in his shoulder, he brought the IJ 300 to bear as Bolan grabbed for the Desert Eagle while trying to regain his balance.

The .44 opened up, and Kreuger straightened as two bullets slammed into his chest, driving him back and off the rock.

The Desert Eagle's massive stopping power was legendary. There was no need to confirm the kill.

Bolan climbed to his feet and looked toward the shattered limo. Beyond it he saw Yenikidze picking his way through the rocks, waving a fist in the air.

It was over.

**Gold Eagle brings another fast-paced miniseries to the action adventure front!**

### by PATRICK F. ROGERS

**Omega Force: the last—and deadliest—option**

With capabilities unmatched by any other paramilitary organization in the world, Omega Force is a special ready-reaction anti-terrorist strike force composed of the best commandos and equipment the military has to offer

In Book 1 **WAR MACHINE,** two dozen SCUDs have been smuggled into Libya by a secret Iraqi extremist group whose plan is to exact ruthless retribution in the Middle East. The President has no choice but to call in Omega Force—a swift and lethal way to avert World War III.

Follow the exploits of a crack direct-action unit in the thrilling new miniseries from Gold Eagle ...

## by DAN MATTHEWS

The President just unleashed the big guns in the toughest offensive of the war on drugs—SLAM, the ultrasecret three-man strike team whose mandate is to search-locate-annihilate the threat posed by multinational drug conspiracies.

In Book 1. **FORCE OPTION,** a dangerous Mexican-Colombian axis forged by two drug kingpins ranks priority one for the SLAM team—a team that extracts payment with hot lead.